The box

The box is full

The box is closed

The box is open

The box is empty

This novel is a work of fiction.

ISBN 0-9792622-1-6
ISBN13 978-0-9792622-1-0

For Library of Congress Cataloging-in-Publication Data
please contact publisher
slabypress@yahoo.com

Published by:

SLABYPRESS
W25952 State Road 95
Arcadia, WI 54612
U.S.A.

www.jsiwicki.com

Technical, Cover, and Book design by JBS

For information contact the publisher

'Nothing happens unless first a dream'
Carl Sandburg

ExPRESSION

John Siwicki

Creation is the ultimate expression

Chapter One

A midnight blue banged-up cab pulled over and stopped warping the lingering shadows painted on the pavement by the early morning sun. I cast my attention to the passenger side window, watched it sink down into the door, then poked my head into the car. I handed the driver a piece of paper. "Can you take me to this place?"

The driver looked at the paper for a moment with a contorted face deciphering the address, raising an eyebrow, tightening his lips, scratching his chin.

"*1120 West Dickens Avenue,*" he whispered in a low, taunting tone, then looked at me. "Sure, hop in!" he said, and motioned to the back of the cab grinning. "Want to put your bag in the trunk?"

"Okay," I said, suspicion tight in my voice. "Thanks."

I watched him pull a lever under the dash, then turned to see the trunk lid slowly creak open—and rise! A murky image of a lifeless body slowly developed in my mind.

I hesitated before putting my bag into the trunk-crypt, wondering . . . then warily peeked into the space. On the right side was a hole, *no corpse,* just an infinite black hole with a view of the street. "I guess it's okay," I mumbled, and tossed my bag on the opposite side. I noticed the loose silver **GTO** emblem dangling on the rear fender as I walked around the cab. That looks familiar, I thought, then jumped in the back seat. "Is Dickens Avenue far?"

"Don't know exactly," he said, "about thirty minutes," then added, "depends on traffic, but it's not far."

"Just wanted to mention," I paused, "well, you're probably aware of this," I cleared my throat, "but there's a hole in the bottom of your trunk." While waiting for him to say something, I thought, he must know.

"It's okay," he said without a second thought. "Anything that falls in—just ends up somewhere else." He grabbed a microphone and mumbled into it as we drove off, the car rattling and squeaking over the bumps in the road. I imagined the doors falling off, the hood flying up, the engine exploding, my obituary—*MAN DIES WHEN CAR FALLS APART ON HIGHWAY*—

Under my breath I said, *Will this old crate get me to the bed and breakfast where I'm staying?*

I saw the driver occasionally glancing at me in the rear view mirror. He was a middle aged guy, bald, big boned, big hands; a day's growth of whiskers, and smacked of a long night. I wonder how many people have ridden in this old heap. "You been a driver a long time?"

"Yeah, long time."

"This car looks like it's hauled a lot of passengers," I said. "Had it a long time?"

"Yeah, long time."

"Ever think about getting a new one?"

"Yeah, I think about it."

"Do you like driving?"

"Yeah, I do."

The *yes-no* man was not talkative, so I took out my laptop and tried to type as we left the tall buildings behind, careening around corners, zipping down streets like an orb in a pinball machine. The taxi was old, but still had some spit under the hood. I guess the old saying, *Can't judge a book by its cover*, is true.

"This old tank moves pretty well."

"Yeah, it really goes."

"Does it have a big engine?"

"Yeah, pretty big, hold on," he said in a sly tone.

He floored it; the momentum threw us back. "Wow!" I yelled with my arms braced against the doors.

"Yeah!" he bellowed, "Wow!" grinned, floored it again, and we flew down the street like a cannon ball.

The city was crowded with traffic, but we drove at a good clip; made it out of the concrete jungle and into a residential neighborhood. The driver slowed, then stopped.

"Here you are *somewhere else* that's the place over there," the driver said and pointed to the house with the white fence.

"Okay, just a second," I said, and put my computer away. "What do I owe you?"

"Sixty-six bucks."

I handed him a fifty and a twenty. "Here, keep the change."

He nodded, said, "Thanks." I watched him carefully tuck the money in his wallet like a mother caressing a baby.

I got out, grabbed my bag from the trunk and looked around, then up and down the street scanning the neighborhood as the taxi drove off. This is nice, I thought, better than I expected. I stood in front of the white picket fence that surrounded the house taking in the ambiance, then leaned over, grabbed a stick from the ground, and pulled it along the fence as I walked. The clatter sounded like a message being sent by Morse Code, dot-dot-dot—dash-dash-dash—dot-dot-dot, then I stopped at the gate for a moment watching the trees along the street wave in the wind as some kids rode by on bicycles. I heard the muffled barking of a dog as my eyes locked on the mammoth Victorian house. It looked like the picture I had in my bag. The windows reflected like a glint in someone's eye, alive, authentic, old, and stylish. The fence was a nice touch framing the whole picture, the wrap around porch with a swing, quaint, my imagination shook. I'll bet there are a lot of memories in this old place.

An elderly woman was cleaning on the porch, and I waited a moment until she saw me, then greeted her.

"Good morning."

She took out the cigarette that was tucked between her lips, rammed it in the dirt of an empty flower pot, and asked, "Can I help you?"

"Yes," I said, "I hope so. My name's John Bird Ray, then I opened the gate and walked toward the porch. "I made a reservation a few weeks ago."

"Well! Hello, nice to meet you," she said with a full-sized smile. "Okay, let's go in and get you registered."

She reminded me of a sinewy aunt of mine who had the same reddish tint in her hair, same gravely voice, and strong laugh. She lit another cigarette as soon as we got inside, while my eyes focused on the floral walls that were covered with what looked like family photographs. Walking through the place was an obstacle course of antique furniture. I took in all of the elaborate excess like a kid in a candy store under ceilings that were twelve feet high.

"Care for a cup of coffee?" she asked, then blew a cloud of smoke into the air. "It's fresh—just brewed it this morning, and you look like you need a cup."

"Sure, that would be nice, thanks," I said. "It's *just* what I need to wake up."

"Okay, let's go into the kitchen and get some."

"Looks like winter is on its last legs," I said as I followed her to the kitchen.

"Yes, it's nice during the day." She went to a desk in the corner, then said, "Could you fill out this form?"

"Sure. What's it for?"

"Just some personal information I need from guests when they check in."

"Oh—okay. Have you got a pen?"

"Here you go."

"Can I sit down and fill this out?"

"Sure—pull up a chair, and make yourself at home, my house is your house."

"Thanks," I said and sat down at the table. She placed a hot steamy cup of coffee in front of me. A black cup with a picture of the bed and breakfast on in it, and a silhouette of a person standing in front of the white picket fence looking at the house. "This is a nice coffee mug."

"You keep it," she said, "as a complimentary gift."

"Thanks," I said, then raised the cup to my mouth and took a sip. "Is this Vanilla Hazelnut?"

"That's right," she said in her gravely voice. "It's my favorite. Oh—do you use cream or sugar?"

"No, this is a great cup of coffee just the way it is."

"I'm glad you like it. Where are you from, John?" she asked as I filled in the form.

"Lacrosse, a small town on the Mississippi."

"Lacrosse, I think I've heard of it," she said. "So, what brings you to Chicago?"

"I'm taking some time off to write a book."

"You're a writer?" She turned, went to the counter and poured herself a cup of coffee.

"Well actually, it's my first book. I'm a photographer. I'm planning to stay at some bed & breakfasts in town for a couple of weeks, and hopefully leave with a draft or enough material I can compile into a book later."

"I see—that sounds like a good idea, but it doesn't seem possible to write a book in such a short time. How long did you say you were staying in Chicago?"

"I'm thinking about two or three days at each place," I said, and handed her the registration form. "I know I'm fighting the odds; just want to get a good start."

"Well, good luck to you. I've got you down for three nights, right?"

"Yes, that's right," I said trying not to inhale the second hand smoke that floated through the room and up to the ceiling. "I'm staying here at your place for three days, then heading downtown near Lincoln Park and Wrigley Field."

"This is the next place," I said, and took out some information I had downloaded from the internet. We both looked at a picture of an old three-story brick building.

"This is the room I reserved," I said and pointed to the basement with only the top part of the windows visible from the street. "Looks appealing, and captivating, doesn't it? What do you think?"

"Looks like a lonely place to me," she said.

"I thought staying there might help me write."

I shuffled through the other copies of places I had downloaded. "Here's another place downtown called Greystone. It's a renovated building from the Roaring Twenties. Al Capone owned it. Here in the article they say he hid millions somewhere in the building, and left clues to where it's hidden."

"You know that's just a bit to lure in visitors," she said. "There are all kinds of stories about Al Capone, but who knows, maybe you'll get lucky, and find something.

Stranger things have happened!" She took a puff, then crushed her cigarette in the ashtray. "Tell me if you do."

"You know we've been talking this whole time, and I don't even know your name."

"It's Tracy," she said.

"Tracy?" I repeated, and smiled because I was surprised, and said, "That's my aunt's name."

"Now, isn't that a coincidence," she said in her gravely voice, then cleared her throat.

I held up the next picture. "Let me show you this place. It was built by a famous architect. The story goes he fell in love with a client's wife after being hired to design and build a house for them. After the project was finished, the client's wife and architect ran away. They got married, then honeymooned in Europe."

"Sounds romantic, and sad at the same time, so bittersweet," she said. "What happened next?"

"It gets more perplexing," I said, and continued to tell Tracy the story. "She never went back to that house; instead returned to his architectural school, lived happily, and gave birth to twins—a boy and a girl." While Tracy lit another cigarette I paused and took a sip of coffee.

"Well, as the story goes, the architect was away on a business trip while the caretaker went on a killing spree at the school. His wife, children, and a few others were murdered, and the school was burned to the ground."

"That's some story," she said.

"I thought there might be some stimulation to write at that house, so I made a reservation. Ever hear that story before?" I asked.

"I think I've read something about it," she said.

"This is last place, and it's near a university. I'm not sure why, but when I saw this picture on the web it made me feel happy. I can't explain it; just want to go there."

"What do you think?" I asked, and showed her a picture of the rustic wooden house.

"It looks small, but that's a nice porch out front," she said. "Is that a cat sitting on the railing?"

"Yeah, it's watching something," I said. "When I first saw it, I thought it was looking at me."

"Yes," Tracy said. "It does! In fact it looks like it's staring right at me."

"Well, could I go to the room and unpack?" I asked as I put away the pictures.

"Oh, sure, I completely lost track of time, follow me," she said. "Remember, there's no smoking in the rooms."

"There's no smoking in the rooms, but you smoke."

"I own the place," she said. "I'm old, and don't give a rip what people think, or say about me anymore."

"Don't worry; I quit smoking a long time ago."

She looked at me and smiled as I followed her up the double wide staircase.

"I'd like to go for a walk later and get familiar with the neighborhood. Do you know any good places? Got any recommendations?"

"I think there's a festival this weekend," she said, "and the weather's supposed to be sunny. You might need a cab, or you could take the train, the station's about thirty minutes from here on foot."

"What kind of festival is it?"

"I'm not sure, but they have crafts for sale, some games to play, and some food. I think it's a local thing. We just had *St. Paddy's Day* you know. "

"Okay, I'll think about it," I said. "Thanks."

"Well, here's the room, and if you need anything let me know. Go right in."

The old floor squeaked under my feet; the flowery wall paper and knick knacks matched some oil paintings.

"Well, what do you think of the room?"

"It reminds me of my grandmother's house," I said as I looked out one of the windows overlooking the back yard. "I like it." I turned toward Tracy, who was standing silently looking at the wall, staring, memorized by the faded outline of where a picture once hung.

"You know this house has a bit of history attached to it, too," Tracy said, still looking at the empty space.

"Really, what's that?" I asked. "Tell me about it."

She turned toward me and said, "Well, I don't know if it's true, but the previous owner of this house told me about it when I bought the place years ago."

"What happened?" I was curious and had to know. "You've got to tell me now, Tracy. Come on—don't leave me hanging."

"Well," she said drawing it out, "years ago, way before this place was a bed and breakfast," she paused, "a man bought this house, but only lived here a short time."

I waited, curiosity running wild. "Okay, then what?" I asked. "What happened to him?"

"He vanished like melted ice."

"That's it?" I said a little disappointed.

"He went for a walk one day," she said, "then disappeared without a trace, and was never seen or heard from again."

"And no one knows what happened to him?"

"It's a mystery," she said. "One interesting item, he was a painter and writer like you. Maybe—writing his first book?" She shot me a smile. "Talk to you later, John Bird Ray," then she closed the door leaving me wondering about the guy who lived in the house. What happened to him, and why he vanished? I sat on the bed, fell back on the mattress, and closed my eyes. I bet he left a lot of memories behind, I thought, then felt compelled to start writing.

Chapter Two

*O*ne step forward, two steps back, a resolute dance that's been drilled into my head since I was a youngster to infer a mistake's been made, but now, I'm not sure. I wonder if this credo applies to aging, or any notion of time, memory, or dimension? Is forward actually backward? Is up really down? What's a reflection, a shadow, a rainbow? Do our senses create what we desire, imagine all things we see, hear, touch, taste, and smell, the thoughts that come to mind every second and every minute. Are these ideas daydreams that never end? What is everyone always thinking?

If I concentrate intensely, maybe

I can send my thoughts to another
person? Can I read other's thoughts?
Are the thoughts their own? Are messages
in the form of thoughts somehow sent
to the populace? Are we controlled by
an outside force? Telepathy, as a way
of communication has been investigated
and researched by governments, private
organizations, and groups using many
curious methods. Dreams, memory, NLP,
the ability to read minds all analyzed
to discover the unknown. Some
researchers believe plants possess the
ability to link to one another, and we
know animals display a keen sense that
may include telepathic communication.
For humans this ability would allow
the possessor both the knowledge and
power to control people or events,
and paint a picture one can only
imagine. Is it possible? Is it
bullshit?

I stopped typing for a moment and looked out the
window that faced the backyard, and thought, effortless, it
would be effortless to write a book if I could read minds.

The words of idle souls flowing
through my fingers like water tumbling
over rocks down a stream, out to oceans,
up to the atmosphere, transforming
part of my spirit into ideas that rain
down, and melt into someone's
imagination.

"I should get out of here for a while," I said as I looked around the room. Something was missing—people. "Go out to where people are," I mutter. I like this place; it has character, but I want to know what's out there. It's just the first day, I thought—and there's always tomorrow.

I'll go to the festival Tracy told me about and forget about writing for now, then maybe the inspiration will come. I'll start pounding keys early in the morning. I put on my coat and walked down stairs. It was quiet, not a peep, nothing but the lingering aroma of left over cigarette smoke.

"Leaving so soon?"

I jumped, "Tracy—you scared the dickens out of me," and caught my breath, then thought, you sneaky old dame.

"You're leaving?" she asked.

"I'm going to check out the festival you told me about."

"Just remember, you have to be back by midnight," she said, and pointed to the cuckoo clock on the wall.

"Will I turn into a pumpkin if I don't," I asked.

She smiled. "No, you won't turn into a pumpkin, but I lock the door, so you won't be able to get in."

"Okay, I'll be back, thanks," I said. "I need to enjoy this time here a little, have some fun, meet some people, and get some ideas for my book."

"Well, go have fun," she said, "but don't get lost like that other writer." She laughed, I laughed. What a strange lady, I thought, then walked out the door and headed down the street looking for inspiration. I wonder what hidden secrets are waiting for me out there?

A block from the bed and breakfast I noticed two kids, a boy and a girl around ten or twelve years old, playing in the street. As I walked by I said, "Hi, kids. Can you tell me which way the station is?"

"It's that way," the girl said.

"How long does it take to walk there from here?"

"Not long," the boy said. "Ten minutes."

"Thanks."

I heard the elevated train rattle and clank, then watched the moving heap of metal pass overhead and stop at the station. I climbed the stairs to the platform, bought a ticket and hopped on with no idea whatsoever where I was going. Then, for whatever reason, not sure why, got off at the first stop and ended up at a coffee shop. I bought a cup, and found a table in the corner to work.

My fingertips tingled while typing, while weaving the story, a microscopic needle buzzing in my brain stitching together words and thoughts, piecing together parts of a colossal puzzle. All the elements of a story floated in my head. How do I put it together? Who are the characters? Where are they going? What are they doing? What is this story about? What happened to the guy at the B&B? What secrets are hidden there? I read what I had typed.

Limbo—suspended maze of linked tunnels, a conduit carrying blood and bones, chasing shadows of the compass, disappearing into a myriad. Every day watching train doors release and lock as nameless crowds enter and exit the rolling compartment headed for nameless destinations. Coaches hitched together, offering individual freedom, limited space, like eggs in a carton or ice cubes in a tray, separate, but also part of a group. The city is ripe with excitement that overflows through these web-like tunnels, rolling, rising, and falling, above and below the surface. Commerce thrives for a chosen few and is a drubbing for the frail, but for a time the rolling wagons provide sanctuary from the elements of life that in the end consumes us all. Consumes us all? Yes, unless you know the secret that's kept from the masses. The elements of the orb, this earth that we rest on, and the welkin, hold the secrets of our humanity. Carved, written, and lost bits of the puzzle scattered hitherto, appearing piece by piece, collected information found and developed, line by line, signal by signal, unraveling a mystery, asking more questions than answers. The prime one being, what happened before the narration, before the song, before written history? Can anyone say with any certainty they know what the footprints mean? The secret of secrets, more powerful than any other knowledge since discovered.

I pulled my eyes from the computer screen and looked around the coffee shop. Who are all of these people? What do they want? What do I want? We're all sitting, sipping coffee, getting our daily fix of caffeine. Is that why we're here? I took a deep breath and let it out slowly. Only seventy-five thousand more words and I'll be done, I thought, then raised my cup and swallowed, forcing the last of the dark, bitter black liquid down my throat.

Chapter Three

Sitting in the coffee shop wasn't working, the words weren't flowing, I needed something more, so I left. As I stood on the street in front of the coffee shop I heard some clatter, voices, people laughing—it pinched my ears.

"Where's that coming from?" I asked a guy walking down the street.

"It's the spring festival," he said. "I think it's put on by the city."

"It sounds like someone's having a good time," I said. "Thanks."

Down one street a crowd moved with enormous energy; alive with excitement. I walked in that direction and found myself surrounded by artists selling crafts, street performers dressed in bright costumes, jugglers, a fire eater. A guy painted to look like a silver statue stayed in position, not moving a muscle, until without warning jumped forward and scared the hell out of a couple of girls. First they screamed, then laughed while tossing some money in a nearby can for him.

This was definitely what I needed, and joined in with the flow of the crowd. I glanced at my watch; it was 5:30 P.M. with a full evening sky above. I continued walking down the crowded boulevard making my way through a river of flesh that flowed in all directions. I marveled at the mass of humanity pushing, shoving, twisting through the streets. Watching heads bob up and down, people muscling their way along the sidewalks as vendors barked their spiels.

As I walked I had the notion about reading minds again. What if I could look at each person and know exactly what they were thinking at any moment? I looked deeply at the faces of everyone I met, hoping a thought would jump out at me, but nothing happened.

How about that guy over there stopping girls? I wonder what he's asking them. Wait a moment, I thought, I don't need to read minds to know that. What about that couple in layers of designer clothes and jewelry getting into that BMW, or those two police officers on the corner keeping a watchful eye on the ebb and flow of the crowd. What's on their mind as the day goes by?

I felt a tap on my shoulder, and turned. A guy stood there smiling, holding a hotdog. He held it up and said, *"Hey—hey—hey-You—you—you-Want—want—want-To—to—to-Buy---buy—buy-A—a—a-Hot—-hot—hot-Dog—-dog—dog-*! He slowly lowered the volume and slowed the pace of his voice to sound like an echo with a Morse Code inflection, and did so well, I bought one. I was enjoying this and kept on walking as more mouth-watering aromas from the restaurants along the street floated on the early evening air. I stopped a moment, and closed my eyes in a state of bliss peviously unknown to me, as the grinding clatter of the city flooded my ears overwhelming my capacity for clear reflection. It was a cacophony of the human condition, a din of words and sounds that filled the air with the soundtrack of the city. I opened my eyes and watched the people. My gaze darted from one scene to another within the urban landscape that stretched out before me. Although moving in constant motion and spontaneous, it appeared to be choreographed by some unseen hand becoming a moving mural, a living breathing rich-textured oil painting. How was this created? Was I the only one who could see the magnificence of this flowing painting of life?

I took a step forward and rejoined the parade of people sauntering along until I came upon some paintings displayed on makeshift stands. Some of the pictures were of street scenes not unlike the one I was on. Others were of thundering mountain streams, boats on canals, romantic impressionist works, flowers, and cats. There were so many pictures of cats; most of them brightly colored with unusually shaped bodies and long falcate ears. Cats are unusual animals, I thought, always observing—watching.

Soon, I found myself interested in the paintings. I can use one for the cover of my book, I thought. With so many choosing was a long process, so at first I couldn't make up my mind, but finally narrowed it down to two cat paintings. One was a bit cold with a dark grayish cat against a bluish splattered background, the other was painted a bright vibrant orange combined with vivid greens, and prevailing black lines. I'll buy the orange one, I thought, and nodded at a man sitting among the paintings whose look screamed artist. After he stood, I watched this six-foot-five maybe taller guy about fifty with short spiky silver hair, and piercing blue eyes, amble over in my direction. As he got closer, I noticed the paint on his hands and clothes, the patch of gray hair under his lower lip, a silver ring on his right ring finger, and a gold one on the left ring finger. The rings sparkled like fireflies as his hands moved. Now, face to face, he was wide eyed and flaunting a hearty smile when I noticed the reflection of my face on his gold tooth.

"Hi," I said. "Did you paint all of these?"

"I painted the flowers and the cats," he said with an accent I couldn't recognize. "This one here," then picked up a colorful flower painting to show me, "that one over there."

As I listened and watched; found him mysterious. How he raised his eyebrows when he spoke, how he used his hands, waving them around as he showed me the paintings. He pointed out several flower paintings that were so lifelike I could imagine their fragrance. In fact, they reminded me of my grandparents' garden.

"You do great work," I said. "I'm interested in this orange cat painting."

Turning the painting over, he showed me the price attached to the back.

"That's expensive! Too expensive for me," I said, nodding in disbelief as I staggered back astonished. "I can't afford it," then added, "could you go, lower?"

"Sure," he said with a smile. He'd obviously been through this routine many times before. "No problem. I can give you a thirty percent discount if you buy it right now."

"You're kidding, thirty percent? You don't leave much room for haggling," I hesitated. "I don't know?" thinking the price tag is all show. I moved my hand up to my chin, I toyed with my beard, and thought, I bet he'll go lower while I studied the cat painting.

He finally blurted impatiently, "Look!" I jumped back, and stood frozen for a moment, until he said with a wink and a carefully crafted smile. "I tell you what, for you, fifty percent. That's fair, isn't it? A good deal, and hard to turn down, yes?"

"Yes!" I said, returning his smile while reaching for my wallet, "I'll take it," pleased that I had cut the price in half.

He thanked me heartily while shaking my hand; giving advice on displaying the painting. "This painting can be put on the wall with or without a frame. The colors will go well with a white wall. Do you have a white wall?"

"Yeah, I've got a white wall."

He just continued talking, and in one breath said, "Do you know the golden ratio? Artists use it when creating a painting. It's the way we mimic how the world is designed. Everything in the cosmos uses this same formula even though it's a secret, and no one can really understand it. Who knows? Maybe there's a secret in the painting you've just bought."

Then, I jumped in. "A secret to help me write my book I hope, and thanks for the suggestions," I said still shaking his hand. "I'll make it work out somehow. I'll figure something out."

"So—you're a writer! Ah—an artist like me," he thundered while thumping his chest. "Why rush off? Have some tea." He grabbed a small teapot and two cups.

I watched him fill the cups. "Yes, that would be nice, thanks."

"Here you are," then raised his cup in a toast. "Salute!" spilling a small amount on the ground before drinking. "Some for the ancestors, Yes?" he said in a slow cool tone, then winked.

I raised my cup and followed suit, spilling a few drops on the ground, nodding in agreement. "Salute!"

We tipped our cups back, and swallowed. Almost

choking on it, I said, "This is some strange tasting brew."

We shook hands again, I thanked him for the tea, and complimented him once more on his paintings as I handed him the cup.

"Thank you again for buying my painting. I'm glad it's going to a place where it'll be appreciated. After all, what is life but a painting? I hope we meet again my friend," he said grinning, his gold tooth and rings flickering in the light.

"Thanks. See you," I said. "Yeah, who knows, maybe we will meet again." I nodded, and walked away, but turned one last time. He was still waving, so I snapped my hand to my brow like a soldier saluting. He returned the gesture, and down the street I went with the painting under my arm.

After walking a while I began to experience some buyer's remorse. Is this painting right for the cover of my book? Did I pay too much for it? I paused for a moment, took out the painting. I like it, I thought, nodding like a preacher who had just sanctioned a wedding. It should give me the inspiration I need. I put the painting back into the package while walking and watching the swirling, dancing patterns of neon lights that were slowly coming on. After about ten or fifteen minutes I found myself acutely aware of all the bustling activity around me. My heart was racing as I watched people moving back and forth—my thoughts sometimes a blur and confused, then clear headed. Out of breath one moment, then filled with energy the next, winning then losing. Is my mind playing some kind of game on me?

Chapter Four

I was back on a wide street and made for the nearest train station, cutting my way through the crowd, pushing and shoving with the others who were waiting there. The train arrived and we all filed on like cattle herded onto a stock car. My eyes fell closed on the crowded train, but opened when a sharp biting screech of steel on steel reverberated through the coach. As the train stopped at various stations one batch of riders got off and a new one took their place, during this time I sat down.

After one stop the seat across from mine was occupied by a beautiful young woman who smiled at me, then fumbled through her handbag finally pulling out a book. It had a photo on the cover of two people looking at each other, their mouths open like they were screaming. The title of the book was—*BULLSHIT*. She appeared interested in the book, but every so often looked up and glanced around the car. I smiled at the title of the book. It made me laugh and think about life—all of the bullshit I'd heard, read, and experienced. A moment later, I found myself typing about it on my laptop.

BULLSHIT - I'm on a train sitting across from an intriguing, sensuous looking woman with deep red shoulder length hair, skin tight blue jeans, and a black polo shirt under a dark green jacket, she was not hard to notice. The book she's reading has a title that sums up everything concisely, a word that expresses what's happening in the world—*BULLSHIT*.

There's celebrity gossip bullshit, how to lose weight bullshit, how to make money bullshit, how to make yourself happy and overcome your flaws bullshit, just useless, expensive how to bullshit. Recently, I saw a guy peddling bullshit in front of a crowd of cheering fans who were gleefully buying his crap. Is the entire world going out of its mind? Are people nuts? Have we all lost our marbles?

It reminds me of a movie about body snatcher aliens replacing real people with clones. In the end, the main character was the only real human left in town. All of his friends had been killed, and their bodies were shells being used by aliens. That's what must be happening now. Aliens are invading our bodies and changing us into blithering morons.

   {Alien Scene} – *In the Greenhouse of a neighbor.*
   "Those are nice plants you have," the last man on earth said.
   "Yes, they are," the alien in the human shell said.
   "What are they called?"
   "We call them—*Pods*."
   "Why are they called *Pods*?"
   "Because—they hold a living body."
   "Whose body?"
   "This one is yours," the alien who looked like his friend said as he pointed to the *Pod* that held his perfect double.
   After the momentary shock the last man on earth runs out, and escapes to woods where he lives today, looking for others who are fighting the aliens.

   She looked up from her book and smiled, then went on reading—I continued typing.

   There are reporters who travel around the world filming the worst situations, then use that footage as some kind of entertainment, so a network can raise its viewing numbers and charge sponsors even higher advertising rates. They peddle their bullshit products, so they can produce more bullshit to broadcast.

{News Report} – *Live from the studio.*

"Good evening, I'm Walter Crathers, and we're receiving a live report from our reporter, Mike Dragon, who is on the scene where a bank robbery is in progress. We can hear sirens in the background. Are you there, Mike?" the news anchor asked.

"Yes, I'm here, and on the scene, Walter."

"Great! Tell us what's happening, Mike."

"Yes, Walter, the police have arrived, and they are blocking access to the bank."

"Yes, okay, can you tell us anything about the bank robbers, Mike?"

"Yes, Walter, they are a group of citizens from a retirement home located nearby."

"And, what are their demands?"

"They are demanding medical care."

"What kind of medical care, Mike?"

"They want medical care for all people, Walter."

"Really!"

"Yes, Walter, they want medical care for everyone—even young people."

"What are they going to do if the demands are not met, Mike?"

"They say they'll strip, and walk naked in the street, Walter."

"Well, that might convince police to give in to the demands, Mike."

"Yes, I think so, Walter."

"Keep us updated on any changes, Mike."

"Will do, Walter! This is Mike Dragon on the scene."

"And, I'm Walter Crathers, and you're listening to, Inside, the inside of the news, outside. Good—night."

Someday, being born may be viewed as an illness, or a curable disease. In the future will people choose the characteristics for their children insuring there aren't any deficiencies. A brave new world order, a Utopia, where humans are engineered to be the best they can be. Strangely, that won't be anything new. The Spartans culled the defectives centuries ago, without any technology. They just threw the young defects over a cliff into a pit, and walked the old farts up a mountain leaving them there to die alone, then went back later to pickup the bones.

{Ordering a child} – *A couple ordering a child.*

"Well, I'm sure we can provide a child that will be compatible with your needs," the director, said.

"Great. We were hoping to have a son."

"No problem," the director said. "What features?"

"We'd like him to be tall, six-five, blond hair, blue eyes," the husband said.

"And some body hair on his chest when he grows up, I think that's sexy," the wife said, "and look like *Gatsby*."

"Athletic, lean, perfect vision, and smart," the husband said.

"I think we'll be able to give you everything you've asked for, and more," the director said.

"Have a look at this profile," the director said as he handed it to the couple.

"Yes, this is exactly what we want," the wife said.

"Will that be cash or charge today?"

I stopped typing for a moment, exchanging glances with the woman reading the *BULLSHIT* book again. To my surprised her focus was on me, and her alluring smile temping. I thought, This is it! She wants to meet. While feeling lightheaded I got back to writing again.

People aren't satisfied watching actors on TV anymore. They watch real people being tortured, arrested, stranded on a deserted island or winning some stupid contest. Who dreams up this reality TV crap? I can't fathom the appeal of watching people getting arrested on television. I'm as pleased as anyone that criminals are captured, but the only reason it's on TV is to make bags of money for everyone concerned, except for the poor schmuck being arrested in front of a camera.

{Reality Show} – *Writing a song contest.*

"Hello contestants," the host said.

"Hello," the contestants said.

"Let's lay down the ground rules for the show," the host said.

Contestants listen intently.

"First, a song must be written every week. It must reflect the theme for the week. This will continue for six months. The songs will be sung by other contestants who almost won on another singing show. The winner will receive the grand prize of one gazillion dollars."

Lots of cheering.

"Now, let's get on with it. The theme of the first song is"— **the host opens an envelope**— "Illegal activity."

More cheering.

"Good luck everyone, and we'll hear the songs next week."

Bullshit in italics is still Bullshit.

Long, long, ago were our ancestors as naive as today? Some propagate that we've evolved into civilized human beings from monkeys. However, if we evolved from monkeys over the millennia, what will we become in a million or a billion years? Will we still watch bullshit on TV? Will there still be television? Will we continue to consume vast amounts of bullshit as readily as now? Only time will provide the answers, and when the day comes, will the answers simply be more bullshit?

Before we stray too far into the future we should take a few steps back in time. Where are we from? How did we get here? Who started all that monkey stuff anyway? People like mystery, intrigue, and suspense, and it abounds in our history, another term for it—bullshit.

When I was a child I constantly looked for heroes. I desperately wanted a hero who would protect me, someone I could trust without doubt, and asked nothing in return. Then, one day a couple of guys came up with a great idea—the blue boyscout—Superman! Where is Superman from? He's from another solar system, a planet with a red sun, and before it exploded, Superman's father sent him off on a trip to Earth because he knew his son would be invincible as long as he stayed under a yellow sun If I met Superman, I'd ask, Who is your tailor, and where can I get one?

Are some people on earth from another planet in a distant solar system? If so, how did they get here? Could it be that life forms were sent to earth from a planet ready to self-destruct? Perhaps our alien ancestors were monkeys from another solar system, which would make us descendants of super alien monkeys.

When did humans first ponder the concept of planets, solar systems, stars, the sun, the moon, and all that astronomical jazz? When did humans first consider how all cosmic matter and energy developed from nothing into everything? How stellar subatomic particles condensed into stars, and over one-hundred chemical elements transpired from nothing. How planetary clouds of elements changed into our solar system? How organic spontaneous generation from rock and water spawned life, and how everything alive comes from one single cell organism? Micro varieties of traits expressed in compatible organisms. What does this mean? It's driving me crazy! The answer, no one knows anything about where humans came from, except those who believe in God.

I'm on a roll now, I thought, but stopped typing because I was struck by an image. When I was very young, I clearly remember my first grade teacher telling me, on the first day of class, to color inside the lines. Why color inside the lines? Why? Is that what art is? Is that what life is? I thought, Coloring inside the lines. I started typing again—

{Conversation, students and the first grade teacher}

"Good morning class," the teacher said. "My name is Mrs. Backspace."

"Good morning Mrs. Backspace," the children said in unison.

"Today is your first day of school. I want to tell you what you'll learn here."

"Yes, Mrs. Backspace," the children said in unison.

"First—remember, the most important rule of all, color inside the lines."

"Yes, Mrs. Backspace," the children said in unison.

"Second—always do your homework."

"Yes, Mrs. Backspace," the children said in unison.

"Third—no chewing gum in class."

Experts say left-handers use the right side of the brain; right-handers the left. What about ambidextrous people? We figure out how to make money, have fun, insult people, tell jokes, be creative, the list is endless, all done with our brain, which is a miracle of creation, and no one has any idea-whatsoever-how it works. The mind and imagination directs us to a better place, or down a path of ruin,

comes up with some unbelievable
bullshit along the way. So, coloring
inside the lines, well, if that's what
you like—more power to you.

Think about your childhood days.
Who told you about the planets? The
Tooth Fairy, Santa Claus, your parents,
a teacher? When did you learn how the
planets revolve around the sun? How
often do you look up at the night sky?
What's out there? Answer—No one knows!
This blows my mind! No one knows!

I took a break from my rant, and looked up at her
again. She looked at me again; I could feel her—emotion
transmitted through the air. I have to talk to her, I thought,
but was compelled to type again.

There are many theories how the mind
and body work together, but our very
existence is the biggest mystery of
all. Are we creatures of habit, gathering
wisdom on a journey through life that's
being interpreted by thought processes
that we slowly learn from our
environment? Is knowledge connected with
memory? Are both stored in DNA?

Take the tradition of greeting for
example. How people greet varies
according to culture. Most people in
Western societies shake hands when
they greet, but the type of handshake
varies. In France, they shake hands,
but sometimes kiss each other on both

cheeks, like some Middle Eastern cultures.

In many Asian countries bowing, sometimes with folded hands, or at a certain degree, depending upon who one is bowing to, is employed. Some greetings are exaggerated and have become a little absurd because they've been taught a certain way, done one way, and only that way—even today. I think a simple nod of the head is fine, but who am I to go against centuries of bowing, kissing, and handshaking. Tradition keeps us communicating, and it's in our DNA.

What about the wheel? It's been reinvented time and again. Maybe it will be again? Maybe, tomorrow? It's a simple and useful device for carrying goods, humans, and even monkeys. We couldn't live without it! Everything depends upon that simple and most ingenious invention. Who thought it up? Is there a patent on the wheel? Some say it was invented in Mesopotamia. Was it one, two, or a committee of Mesopotamians who conceived the wheel? Or perhaps, Mesopotamian alien monkeys?

{Inventor of the wheel}*The day it happened!*

"Look—I've invented the wheel!"
"What's a wheel?"

"A machine."

"What's a machine?"

"It's a device that does something."

"What's a device?"

"It's an apparatus that does something."

"Great! What does it do?"

"It rolls! Watch this!"

"Wow!"

"We can use the wheel to help us."

"How?"

"To move things."

"What things?"

"Monkeys!"

I think whoever invented the ball must have invented the wheel. A ball, the most basic solid shape is circular like the Earth itself. The circle is a never ending cycle going round and round, but where does it start, the beginning, middle, or end? Is the circle in the middle of another circle? Perhaps we're on an endless loop that floats in a vacuum of particles that attract and repel each other briefly, then continue on an endless journey. A great big humongous doughnut made of Adam, Eve, proton, neutron, alien monkey, Superman, Colonel Sander's secret recipe, me, you, and them!

Chapter Five

I went on and on, writing, typing, filling page after page with nonsensical free association; all because I saw the word bullshit on the cover of a book. As we made a number of stops she stayed on reading her book, looking around the train, and occasionally at me. A space opened up next to her, I thought, now's my chance. Why not?

I stood, the train stopped, she got up and left. I composed myself. Wasn't to be I guess, and sat back down watching the people around me, who were all busy reading or talking as we pulled into the next station. The doors opened, and a few passengers got on, then I saw the woman of my dreams walk toward me. I wiped my chin just in case I was drooling. My first thought, She's just walking through from another car on her way off the train.

However, she came over to me. I smiled, and she reciprocated with a radiant, glowing expression of charm.

While I collected my wits managed to mutter, "Hello."

"Mind if I sit here?" she asked in a soft, friendly voice.

I moved over clearing a spot for her. "Please. Sure!" I said. "You've just made my day."

"I've just made your day," she said. "Really? Why is that?"

"Because you're the most beautiful woman I've seen today, and you're sitting next to me."

She offered her hand and said, "Hi, I'm Veronica, Veronica Wrigley."

Veronica, I thought, that name sounds familiar. I felt energy transfer from her as our hands touched, then my fingertips tingled sending pulsations through my body. Maybe there's something to this greeting thing after all. Her eyes were beautiful, and sparkled as she brushed away her shoulder length dark brown hair. I watched her move like a ballet dancer. She was slim, round and feminine, but athletic. I found myself unable to find words; incapable to speak.

She shrugged, looked at me closely, and slowly asked, "And, what's your name?"

"Yeah—my name," I stammered, holding out my hand while staring into her dark brown mesmerizing eyes, "John—John Bird Ray."

Making a flying motion with her hands, she said cheerfully, "John Bird Ray, your name sounds free—and friendly."

The Lynyrd Skynyrd song "Freebird" floated through my head. I nodded, while thinking of a snappy comeback.

"Yeah, I get jokes about my name all the time," I said.

"Have we met before?" she asked.

"No, I don't think so, I'd remember you," I said. Entranced by her beauty, I groped my brain for something clever to say, but all I could manage was, "Do you ride this train a lot?"

"Yeah, I do," she said. "What about you?"

"I really don't know," I said.

She looked surprised. "What do you mean?" she asked. "Don't you know where you're going?"

My brain shifted into overdrive as warm beads of sweat grew on my forehead. What should I say? I'm such a bonehead, I thought, and searched the back files of my mind. I could make up a story or just tell her why I'm here. I wiped away the rills of sweat with the back of my hand.

She looked at me and said, "Well, John Bird Ray," paused, then asked, "Are you on a top secret mission?"

"Actually, I just got here yesterday, and—I don't know the train lines very well. I hoped being in the city would inspire me. I'm working on a book. The train just seems like a good place to write, so I got on for the ride."

She looked at me nodding.

"My mind opens up, and I get a lot of ideas from the people I watch on the train. That's why I'm riding the train."

She gave me a wide-eyed look while laughing, then asked, "Are you stoned?"

"Well, now that you mention it," I said. "I had some tea earlier, and have been feeling strange ever since drinking it. The guy who sold me this painting gave it to me, and now, I'm wondering if it was spiked with something."

I picked up my bag from the floor, took out the painting, and showed it to her. "What do you think?"

"It's an interesting painting, no doubt about that," she said. "It's unusual, and the cat has funny ears."

"I think I'm going to put it on the cover of my book."

"What does that cat in the picture have to do with the book you're writing?" she asked.

"They're mysterious?" I said, not really knowing why.

Nodding in agreement she said, "Oh, I see! You're writing about mystery?"

I shrugged, "This may sound silly, but I've been writing about bullshit."

We both burst out laughing so hard that all eyes on the train zoomed in on us, and that made us burst out in more raucous delight. We caught our breath, looked at each other somehow linked. What was she was thinking? Her facial expression spoke volumes and I couldn't turn away as I watched her gently bite her bottom lip.

Then she said, "Bullshit, okay, I've seen my share of that every day."

Pointing at the seat across from us, I said. "There was a girl sitting right there reading a book, and its title was Bullshit. For some reason after that, I felt compelled to write about bullshit. All the bullshit I've heard, watched, and read over the years. I can't explain why."

"I know exactly what you mean," she said. "I see the same thing every day, and it's never ending. You should be able to write more than one book on bullshit, one on government bullshit alone!"

She looked at my computer and said. "That's a nice computer. Is it new?"

"This? No, not new, I bought it from a second hand shop. A new one's too expensive. I used to write in notebooks and retyped it all later. I thought I could save time if I had a laptop, but they were all expensive, so I started checking pawnshops, second hand shops, and found this one."

"How much did you pay for it?"

"Three hundred dollars."

With a wide-eyed look of surprise said, "Really! That's seems like a good price. Do you know a lot about computers?"

I turned off the computer and put it into my bag. "I know they make writing a book easier," I said.

"You have one, don't you?"

"Yes, I do, but I have problems with it freezing up; sometimes it just crashes and won't turn back on, or my printer goes haywire." Then she asked, "Are you writing about anything else or is bullshit the main part of your book."

I put my bag on the floor, and laughed. "That's funny. No—not just bullshit. I'm working on a story I outlined a while ago, but I haven't connected all of the dots," I said. "I'm working on the characters, the relationships, what they look like, what they do, and who they know. The people in the story have to appear genuine to the reader. I've only written poetry up to now, so this is new territory for me." I looked at her and smiled. "I've got a lot of ideas, but weaving a story to get lost, and absorbed in when it's read is the trick. It has to be compelling, honest and enticing."

Veronica suddenly grabbed my arm and said, "Oh— this is my stop coming up. Talking about this is interesting, let's get together for lunch or something, okay? What do you say, John-Bird-Ray?"

Am I hearing things? Did she just ask me out?

Without thinking, still wondering if I had imagined it, I said, "Lunch sounds fantastic."

She got up and stood in front of the door waiting for it to open. "Let's meet where I got on the train," she said. "Tomorrow around one o' clock? You remember the stop, don't you?"

"No, what's the name of it?"

"Grand. It was Grand."

"Okay! Grand at one o' clock," I said, dripping joy.

Her eyebrows rose slightly as she turned toward me, I smiled. The doors opened and she stepped off the train waving. "Tomorrow—see you—" I watched her through the glass of the closed doors, but couldn't hear the rest of what she said, and only read her carmine lips as I waved goodbye. She turned one more time, then was gone, and out of sight. Did that really just happen? Am I dreaming?

I started working on my story again, occasionally looking around the train watching and thinking about how some people stand out. Sometimes it's their hair, clothes, or the way they move, while others capture no attention whatsoever. I started typing.

Chapter Six

*P*articles of attraction, that's what we are — magnetic particles full of electricity held together by a random DNA mixture. It decides our eye color, height, weight, intelligence. It spins around and around, and the best we can hope for is getting on, or off, at the right time. An endless cycle of planting, growth, harvest, and then it's dinner time.

I raised my head and was surprised, because the same woman who had been reading the book, *BULLSHIT*, was sitting across from me again, her piercing brown eyes soft as we exchanged glances. My mind conjured up images of a smoky jazz nightclub with a grand piano. I imagined music playing so clearly I hummed the melody, then as inconspicuously as possible measured her striking face and flawlessly proportioned body, shoulders back, bust full and firm. My eyes followed the line of her body down her thighs all the way to her toes, then back up to her lips. I had an image of her sitting on a bed. The images came to mind in single frames, one by one, pixilated, then vanished.

Our eyes met and fixed on each other for a moment. She took out a pen, wrote something, stood, walked over, and put a folded piece of paper in my hand. Before any words were exchanged, before any lingo rolled off my tongue, the train doors opened and she stepped off. We shared one last glance before she floated away as the doors slammed shut. I unfolded the paper. She had written a telephone number, and the name, *Samantha Loyde*. My mind flipped through various scenarios making up conversations, but no matter how they started—ended nowhere.

The train stopped again. People charged for open seats, desire for comfort pulling them in. This same contest went on every time the train pulled into a station. Then, at one stop a man wearing sunglasses, holding a white and red cane, stepped on the train and stood near the door. Had he been sightless from birth? Had an accident? Could he see anything at all? Curiosity had me, and I was fascinated when he slowly lifted his hand and moved his fingers in a strange pattern. A few moments later, he repeated the same process. It must be some sort of counting system, I thought, so he knows when the train reaches his stop. I made my way over to where he was standing.

"Excuse me," I said, but he just looked off in the distance, his head straight, and his chin up.

"Excuse me," I repeated.

"Yes," he said.

"Could I ask you a question?"

He turned not looking directly at me, "Hello, I'm afraid I don't recognize your voice. What's the matter? Is anything wrong?"

"Oh, nothing important," I said, "but do you mind if I ask a question?"

"No, I don't mind at all."

"Well, I . . . don't know how to say this . . . I—um—"

"Yes," he said, and stood silent waiting for me to speak.

He never really looked directly at me, so there was a long pause while I tried to move around to get face to face. "I saw you using some kind of counting system with your fingers. How does it work?"

"You're very observant my friend," he said as a smile crept across his face.

"You—have some kind of numbering system, right?"

"Why do you want to know?"

"I'm writing a book, and thought I could use it in my story. I'm looking for an interesting angle."

"Okay, but you must promise not tell anyone."

"It's a deal," I said. "I promise."

"Take my right hand." I grabbed his hand and held it.

"Now turn it over." I turned it over.

"Look at my fingertips," he said with a slight touch of merriment in his voice. "Do you see them?"

"Yes I see!" I said wide eyed and excited, swallowed, then asked, "What are those marks?" Then, slowly ran my fingers across the raised dots and dashes that were branded, or somehow attached to his fingertips.

"I don't really know," he said. "I was asked by a man some time ago if I wanted my vision restored, and of course I said, yes."

"But you can't see," I said looking at his face.

"No, not with my eyes," he said. "Take my hand, place

it to the side of your head, and close your eyes."

"Okay," I said, following his instructions, then waited with my eyes shut.

"Can you see?" he asked.

After a flash, I said, "Yes, I see something!" Then, found it difficult to breathe, choking, similar to the first time I went scuba diving, then said wildly. "I see! I can see!"

After he took away his hand I felt dizzy and drowsy, so I sat down. The train pulled into the next station, and stopped. I open my eyes, but he was gone. I felt like I had woken from a deep sleep. Did that just happen? Was it a dream, or from the tea the painter gave me? The delirium cleared up after a few minutes, but an image of the blind man's face remained in my mind. I took out my laptop and typed about numbers and patterns.

Morse Code, dots and dashes, signals, pulses of electricity, numbers, measurements, calculations, elements, theory, speculation, impending black holes consuming solar systems and spewing the residue out into another universe. Light years floating in space until the precise time as the hot dust of Andromeda and the gas blobs of the Milky Way collide into one center, one new universe, then vanishes into a black hole forever, and genesis. Numbers, patterns, sequence, coincidence, cycle, after cycle, after cycle, ice, water, steam. Patterns are inherent in many things, including the solar system. The Golden Number, DNA molecule, mathematical constants and irrational numbers that never end. Numbers are used to keep track of many things, from how tall we are, to the days in a year. Numbers can be used as a vehicle determining value. It's done every day, the more value we have, the more freedom we have according to some calculations. And gold has always had value, and was traditionally used in exchange for time and work. It's curious how wealth is concentrated in the hands of a few, then used for creating more wealth by lending it to others for their survival, or the dreamers who want to fly, and be free!

Humans are a fantastic creation of structure, have innumerable cells that function with reproductive capability, and as the father of medicine, Hippocrates, studied long ago, an innate instinct for survival. Since the microscope, cell study, their growth and repair intrigue us even more than ever today. Is it possible to catalog the billions of cells in the body? They all have specific functions that control everything we do, are, and will become.

I stopped typing, looked up and thought about how the train has a cradle effect that puts passengers to sleep. I was re-entering the dream world again before the train stopped and another horde rushed aboard. After the doors closed, a pungent odor brought tears welling up in my eyes. I turned and saw a man who hadn't bathed in some time repelling passengers like he wore a protective force field. He stood there alone, hair matted, clothes black and grimy, shoes falling apart, his eyes hollow dark-black-holes of space. The foul smell of body odor was overwhelming, so I stood by the door waiting until it opened, thinking, Come on door—open!

"Hey, Buddy, got a few bucks to spare," he said as he looked at me and smiled. He had old rotten-crooked-teeth ready to fall out. He poked me sharply in the back with his finger, then held up his hand trying to put it on the side of my head.

"Hey, Pal, got any spare change?" he repeated more aggressively. As his hand moved closer I saw the same branded symbols as the blind guy's scored in his fingertips.

I grabbed his arm at the wrist, slowly turned it over. "Here you go," I said and dropped some coins into his palm. The train doors opened allowing me to escape the fatal embedded touch, and rank assault on my nostrils. Walking away I felt edgy, then looked back at the train. He had vanished, leaving me wondering, what's the deal with the Morse Code on the fingertips? And, did that just happen?

With the lingering odor from the guy on the train in my nostrils I had my next topic, the sense of smell. I found a chair, sat down, and turned on my laptop.

Aroma and the sense of smell is possibly the first sense experienced after birth. Odors, aroma, and fragrance are powerful links with memories from our past. Marcel Proust wrote about aroma, how it links with memory, and how drops of essence bring back lost memories, powerful memories that create images with clear details about what's been said, and done many years before.

Scientists are intrigued by smells, and have discovered that humans have the ability to identify some 10,000 different odors. This is a mystery in itself, since there are only about 1,000 sensors in the nose. Apparently, nasal sensors are used in various combinations in the way the alphabet strings together thousands of words with only twenty-six letters. Altering a smell in the slightest degree changes the equation, and affects how we react. A specific odor can repel one person, but please another. Smell and taste work jointly, without smell the ability for taste is lost. Smell is used in sensing pheromones, and influences a wide variety of human emotions in social and sexual situations.

Of course, human beings have other senses that keep us in tune. We perceive everything through our senses while we do our best coping with what we call the real world. With one sense lost or deficient another will filter, and decode, providing information for our minds. It's astonishing that the decoding takes place in a fraction of a second. Our memories and senses are a riddle. What's the secret to how our senses calculate space, location, and time? Is it a mystery that will ever be found? Ever discovered? We live in a civilized world with rules, policies, and physics, but one smell can be a hidden world unto itself filled with pleasure or pain. Smell is one of the first senses awaken after birth, yet it's often overshadowed by sight, sound, and touch as we make our way through the maze of daily activities. Billions of nerves in our bodies generate ideas from everything we see, hear, taste, touch, and smell, and when we're missing crucial information our minds conjure up an answer to the missing piece of the puzzle based upon our past experience, sometimes with disastrous or wonderful results.

For instance, you hear a noise, see a familiar person, go to a place you know, and even though there is no noise, it's the first time you've seen the person, or been to the place, you're left with a feeling of déjà vu!

Chapter Seven

I headed for the platform looking for a train to take me back to the bed & breakfast. After a few minutes one screeched into the station. I got on, and it clinked and clunked down the track passing trains going in the opposite direction. Along with my reflection I could see passengers in the other train's windows. I glanced down the inside of the cabin as we slithered down the track. It felt like riding inside a huge mechanical snake. The rocking and rolling back and forth business was hypnotic, like some strange mechanical dance. Then, I shook my head and came out of the heavy-eyed stupor after hearing the train's horn blast. I sat, then turned to look out of the window as we navigated through a sea of concrete structures that rose and vanished into a sky filled with wonder and questions. Some of them were water-marked, crumbling, flaking paint, had cracked or broken windows. Piles of garbage decorated the lonely sidewalks and streets. The deeper we went into the city the more the high rises blocked out the last of the sunlight. We passed a gravel pit playground with children playing baseball under glowing park lights signaling that the day was about to surrender. This truly is a concrete jungle, I thought, as the buildings' shadows painted the city landscape in a mist of darkness. How do I write about this? A seat opened up, I sat down, took out my computer, and put my fingers on the keys.

```
    The fortunate have a powerful tool;
their wits. Imagine at any moment, on
any given day, a person can do whatever
comes to mind. Our shoes can take us on
a journey far and wide or keep us on
the same path day after day. We have
choice, freedom, liberty, independence.
Do unto others . . . take care of numero
uno.
```

I glanced down at the floor and noticed the shoes of the passengers, and thought, Why am I so interested in shoes? Then, wondered how people make a conscious decision to buy shoes. Anyone can buy any kind or color for any purpose: walking, running, hiking, climbing, and companies make billions selling shoes.

I slipped into a trance with a keen interest in the detail that went into making shoes. I reached out with my hand to touch my shoe. It vanished, then re-appeared building itself right in front of me, step by step, layers and pieces attached and assembled themselves in quick fashion—systematically. I was completely absorbed in watching this happen. All around me the invisible cobbler creating shoes for passengers of cordwain, wood, jute, rubber, plastic—

Then I heard a deep, mellow voice, "Nice evening, isn't it?" which broke the trance. I jumped, surprised. Looking up from my shoes I was greeted with a considerate, and serious smile from a tall guy in a well worn suit. The top button of his shirt was open, tie askew. He was chewing gum, and played with it between his teeth as he sat down beside me. You don't look like a businessman was my first thought. His hair was short and black; he looked tough, stocky like an athlete, maybe a football player or wrestler. His unshaven face and gruff baritone voice gave me the impression of a guy you wouldn't cross. I was startled, and he knew it. Then, as he opened his coat I saw a gun strapped on his belt. Our eyes met at that moment as he gave me a firm, no one's messing with me grin.

As I rubbed my eyes to get the cobwebs out, I said, "I'm sorry, what was that?"

"It's a nice night," he said once more, still playing with the gum between his teeth.

Nodding in agreement, "Yeah," I answered. "Sure is," then I looked around the train and at the passengers.

"You were dozing off there."

"Yeah, guess so, must be the rocking motion," I said. "It puts me to sleep, or in some kind of haze."

"Not everyone," he said. "I'm on the ball when I ride the train. In fact, I'm always watching what's going on around me. There are too many freaks—can't trust anyone. Never know you might get ripped off, or worse, if you fall asleep."

"On the train," I said, "with all of these people around? I've never heard of that happening to anyone I know. Of course, I just got here yesterday, but I've read about things like that in the newspaper, I guess." I wiped the sand out of my eyes once more, then pointed at his gun, and said, "You know, I couldn't help noticing you have a gun. Are you, police? Security Guard?"

"Detective," he said.

"What kind of gun is that?"

"It's a Colt .45."

"Really?" I said. "Looks big and heavy, especially to carry around all day."

"A little bit heavy, but it's partly psychological," he said. "Just the size of it scares the shit out of people." He grinned, leaned toward me, and in a muffled growling voice said, "Right?" then laughed. "Just kidding around."

I moved back and asked, "What do you investigate?"

"Homicides."

"I've never met a homicide detective only seen them on TV or in movies. I bet your job's a lot different and more intricate than that, huh?"

"Actually, it's not. We investigate a crime, gather all the evidence, then go to work trying to solve it just like the guys on TV. Sometimes it's easy, but now and then we come across crimes that will never be solved."

"How long have you been a homicide detective?"

"Almost ten years now."

"What about you?" he asked. "What line are you in?"

"I'm a writer and photographer," then changed what I had said, "I mean—photographer—slash writer."

"Okay," he replied and asked, "What do you write about?"

"Up to now, just poetry, but I'm working on a novel. I came to the city for inspiration. I'd like to finish my book, and get it published."

"What do you take pictures of?" he asked.

"Weddings mostly, portraits, pets," I said, "and I do some commercial work, and a bit of aerial photography."

"That's what I should do," he said. "Write a book about some of the cases I've worked on over the years. In fact, I'm working on a very interesting case right now."

"Yeah? What kind of case?" I asked.

"Sorry," he said grinning. "It's confidential."

"I see, but that's a great idea you have about writing a book since you're a detective, and know the inside story, and the background. I'd like to add an element of detective work into my story. I think you'd be perfect as the guy for my detective," I said. "You've got the look."

"You think so?" he said, nodded, and sat back posing.

"Yeah, you have the detective look. Mind sharing some ideas that might help me with my book?" I asked.

"Sure, I can help you out, but I'm getting off the train soon. Here, I'll give you my number, but don't use my real name in your book," then he took out a scrap of paper, "Sorry, I don't have a card," he said, and wrote down his number. "Give me a call sometime. If I'm busy or out you'll get my voice mail. It's best if you don't say anything about me or your detective character. Just leave your name and number. Don't talk about it to anyone, okay," he said and looked at me with a seriousness that made my skin shiver.

"Okay—" I said and nodded, thinking, Why the secrecy? "You can email or call me," and cautiously handed him my card, "I'm John Bird Ray."

"Well, nice talking to you, John Bird Ray," he said, "Good luck with the book. This is my stop coming up"

"What's your name again?" I asked.

We shook hands as he got up. "Nick Zinty," he said, and stepped off the train.

I gave him a nod, a wave and said, "See you," thinking, Never met a homicide detective before, as the doors closed and the train rolled on down the tracks.

Talking to Zinty got me thinking about criminals. Does the environment mold people into what they become, or is it destiny? We only know about the villains who are captured, the infamous criminals who have stories told about them, who've become part of history and legend. What about the ones we never hear about? The ones under the radar—hidden in the shadows—pulling the strings. Maybe I can work that idea into my book, I thought. I opened my laptop and started typing.

Sometimes a guy, somehow, gets caught up in a situation by chance. In the wrong place, at the wrong time. Tries helping someone out of a jam, and ends up with the wrong end of the stick. Basically he always gets the shaft.

Chapter Eight

I got off the train again for some fresh air, to stretch my legs, and look for some familiar landmarks. As I walked nothing was recognizable, so I continued down the street and hoped for the best. I studied the new and old buildings that stood vertical on both sides of the street. I could have been anywhere in the city. Now what? I marched on.

Then I saw the sign for Oak Street, and remembered the name; it was familiar. When I researched Chicago, I read that Oak Street was a popular shopping area, and home to some popular designer shops. I began to be more aware; completely absorbed in the elaborate and colorful high-end store window displays as I walked. There were so many, and they were interesting, too. I eventually found myself standing in front of them gazing wide eyed. It's the tea? I thought. Why else would I be interested in display windows. What do I care about designer stores?

The clothes in the stores looked expensive, first-rate, and I recognized some of the famous brands. As I watched customers go in and out of the shops, I wondered why they were so eager to buy brand name goods. I had read once that the word brand is mentioned in the epic poem, Beowulf. In the story brand means destroy by fire; and today it means expensive product. I walked by a small sitting area, sat down and typed.

I've seen cowboys rope and herd cattle into a corral during round-up, take a hot iron with a special design, and brand them to signify ownership. Companies do the same thing with products, creating social connections with customers, using logos, slogans, and jingles to associate brands to show ownership of customers. Now people wear the brand, and carry it around on bags. Will companies actually brand their customers like cattle in the future?

Businesses use the term DNA in advertising to show the unique profile, or blueprint of a brand. The public knows the product by the name; it's a living creature created from an idea. Corporations survey patterns of customers to define behavior and the brands they use.

The oldest form of advertising is evangelism marketing, or word of mouth, where satisfied customers tell their friends, and the word spreads. It works

```
pretty well for religion. That's what
I need for my book after it's finished,
I thought, a DNA blueprint.
```

Then, my computer died and there was no place to get a charge, so I put it away and started walking again. I came upon a second-hand shop called, *Alegre*. It was an old two-story building painted white, but under the peeling paint I saw old wood and brick. The place looked interesting, so I ventured in to see what I could find. I got my laptop at a pawn shop; maybe I would find something in this place.

The door had a clump of bells tied to the handle, so when I opened it they rang in a quaint jingly way, like entering a religious temple or shrine. Above the door was a wooden plaque that read: **WE LIKE EVERYONE - SOME WHEN THEY COME AND SOME WHEN THEY GO** — Interesting, I thought. The shop was well organized, jewelry on one side in a display case, guns under lock and key behind the counter, and some old books in the back that looked fascinating, so I strolled in that direction. I walked by some old musical instruments on the left, then nodded to the man standing behind the counter who was talking on the phone. He returned my greeting with a smile. He was an older gentleman in good shape with chiseled features, dark eyes, short white hair and beard, probably speaking Spanish, sounded like Spanish anyway. I didn't see anyone else in the shop, so I thought, I must be the only customer here. There was a nice old winding-wooden-staircase in the back, and to one side some paintings that looked familiar, just like the one I had bought, so I walked over for a closer look. Sure enough, they were like mine only painted in different colors, but the same cat with the falcate shaped head.

I headed over to the counter when the man stopped talking on the phone.

"Hello," he said, a big hearty grin on his face.

"I like those pictures over there. Do you know who the painter is, his name, or where he lives?"

"Yes, I do. He comes in once in a while to drop some off. I've been selling them for years now."

"You wouldn't happen to know how I could find, or contact him."

"No, not really. He just stops in with paintings, and I sell them. People like his work. What about you, like it?"

"Yes, I do." I took out my painting. "I bought this one from him," and showed it to the clerk. "He was selling them on a street downtown."

"It's nice! Looks just like his other paintings. He likes cats. Why do you want to find him?"

"Well, it's a long story," I said, "but I'm a writer and bought this painting from him earlier," I showed it to the clerk again, "to use on the cover of my book, but didn't ask his permission. I want to ask him if it's okay."

"Oh, I see. Well, if you give me your name I can pass on the message."

"That's fantastic! Here's my card."

"Okay," he said. "I'll give it to him when he comes in. That's the best I can do."

"Thanks, by the way, my name's John."

"Nice to meet you, John. I'm Hector, this is my shop."

"You have a nice store, Hector, I'll come back and look around before I leave town. Thanks for your help."

"Okay, see you again," he said, "bye."

I walked out of the shop and headed down the street, thinking, I want to see the painter and ask him about the painting, and the tea I drank. Exactly what was in it, and why he gave it to me?

Chapter Nine

I walked by a café and was struck by how the buildings got older and more interesting. Either my photographic eye was kicking in, or I was going through a time warp. There was a row of three-story brick apartments, shops with teal-colored shutters, tall windows that reached from the second floor to the top floor, and one window on the third floor that had a big green eye painted in the middle.

On the first floor was an exotic looking Japanese restaurant with pictures of food in the window, a salon, and a cigar shop next door. Into the alley I walked through a brick archway, and ended up standing in front of a travel agency. *Pomona Travel* was written in gold above the shop window on a sign with a black silhouette of a tall sailing ship. In the corner of the sign was a small skull with crossed cutlasses. A pirate travel agency, I thought, that's an interesting idea. Maybe they have a treasure hunt vacation.

My eyes drifted to a display with photographs of some exotic places. Thoughts about going to a more interesting place instead of coming to the city, especially after seeing the pictorials in the window, came to mind. What's wrong with me? I should go to some tropical paradise, mountain retreat, an exotic get away—that's where inspiration is!

The one about Bora Bora grabbed me.

Palm trees, sandy beaches dotted with red hibiscus, white gardenia and yellow plumeria blossoms.

I had never heard of plumeria blossoms before, but they sure were beautiful in the pictures.

Beaches surrounded by turquoise water under a sun-drenched cobalt sky.

Just reading about it gave the impression of being in a mythical place.

Bora Bora, a dazzling treasure, a gift from God, a barrier reef with an array of tropical fish, sea life, and off in the distance, towering wind-swept peaks climbing out of the sea.

I closed my eyes to create a mental picture of myself standing on the beach in the picture of the advertisement. I blocked out all noise, traffic, people, felt the sand between my toes, and the sun on my shoulders. A cool breeze blew lightly in my face and through my hair. In my mind I was there, standing on a sandy beach, the smell of the sea and the sound of the waves crashing to the shore on a sun-drenched afternoon. I was holding a Rum and Coke under a cloudless sky, watching the spry palm trees being gently massaged by a tropical breeze. Behind me a rustic hotel almost hidden by the surrounding trees, emerging bungalows that were framed like a painting with color from the tall plants, wild and vivid flowers dancing in the garden along with the breeze. My eyes fixed on the horizon, which was a blur of sea and sky. I walked along the beach, stood there silent, my eyes closed, soaking up the moment.

Back to reality I shook my head thinking—the tea, it's the tea. When I opened my eyes there was clamor from the traffic, gas fumes, noise from people passing by, and a woman standing on the other side of the window in the travel agency looking at me. She was smiling and adjusting pamphlets in the display. I returned her smile, raised my hand and waved, then she motioned for me to come into the office. First I looked around to see if she was looking at someone else, then pointed to myself. *You want to talk to me?* I said, but sure she could only see me mouthed the words. She nodded and gestured for me to come in, and I did—to satisfy my curiosity.

I walked up to the carved arched wooden doors that rose above my head at the entrance. I felt the cold carry to my hand as I grabbed the gold polished handle, opened the door, and stepped on the marble floor that lay in front of me, each square embossed with an Aztec design. The person who owns this place has expensive taste, I thought.

I walked up to the girl standing by the window.

"Hi," I said. "Did you want to speak to me?"

"Yes," she said with an alluring and tantalizing smile.

Her lips were full, and I lost my breath as I motioned back and forth with my hand pointing to her, then to myself.

"Do we know each other? You look familiar."

"No, I don't think so. I just couldn't help noticing that you were looking at the brochures."

Then it came to me, and said, "Wait a minute, you're the girl from the train." I snapped my fingers and pointed at her. "You were reading the *BULLSHIT* book—and you handed me your telephone number."

"Do you still have it?" she asked.

"Yes, I do." I burrowed deep into my pockets. "It's somewhere. Let's see—" then I remembered putting it in my wallet. "Here it is," I said and unfolded a familiar piece of paper. "Your name's Samantha?"

"It's great that you remember me," then extended her hand, "I have a big favor to ask."

As I let go asked, "What do you mean—big favor?"

She looked at me, smiled sensuously, and asked in a sultry voice, "Ever been to Bora Bora?"

"Just in my dreams," I said. "A moment ago I was day dreaming about it after reading the advertisement in your window."

"Bora Bora looks beautiful, doesn't it?"

"I just got to Chicago, and have no plans to go anywhere until I finish writing my book. I was thinking that I made a mistake after seeing the brochures. Maybe I should have picked somewhere more interesting or exotic."

"You're a writer?" she asked. "What do you write?"

"A bit of poetry, and I'm working on a book. I've been writing all day."

"Going to an exotic place could help you write," she said, then handed me a brochure

I took the brochure from her and opened it.

She leaned over and whispered in my ear. "Looks wonderful, doesn't it?" then walked around me.

"Yes, it does," I said as my eyes followed her, "but I'd be too busy having fun and not get any writing done. You know what Oscar Wilde said, *'I can resist everything, but temptation.'* Writing takes a lot of focus, concentration, an enormous amount time, and besides, I don't have the money. Are you planning a trip?"

"I want to go somewhere, but not sure where. Have you got any suggestions?" she asked, then smiled. Her hair had fallen down across her face, and she brushed it away gently with her hand. Now, I was interested in what she was going to do next and couldn't take my eyes from her.

"I guess it depends on how much money and time you have," I said. "Traveling can be expensive."

She moved closer, brushed against me and said, "Money's no problem, and I have lot's lots of time."

"So, you're rich?" I asked. My head was moving back and forth, first left, then right, trying to keep up with her steady movements.

"I guess I don't really know."

I gave her a puzzled stare and said, "You don't know if you're rich! How could you not know that?"

"Well, if I need money, I just ask my father."

"You just ask for money and he gives it to you," then added, "wish I could do that. You know, I'd like to meet your father. Does he give out grants?"

"I guess he's rich," she said.

"Well—what's on your mind?" I asked with a hard stare, waiting for an answer.

"Actually, when I saw you on the train I wanted to say hi, but you were talking to someone."

"Who was I talking to?"

"A man," she said as we circled each other like lions preparing to pounce and attack.

"There were lots of people on the train. Can you give me hint? Maybe—tell me—what he looked liked?"

"He was tall, a big guy, rough looking, like a football player. Do you remember him?"

"Oh, you mean the detective."

"Is he a detective?" she asked, still circling.

"Hey, that's what he told me. In the homicide department for ten years. Do you need a detective?" I asked. "Are you in some kind of trouble?"

"I think he's been hired to follow me."

"You're kidding!" I said, "What for?"

"No, I'm not," then she added. "He's been following me for a while now. He pops up everywhere. I was just wondering what you talked about." Her face became warm, and she blushed. "Did he ask about me?"

"Not a word that I can remember. I did notice a gun under his coat, and asked about it, then we talked about writing, and how I wanted a character in my story to be a detective. He wrote down his number and gave it to me, and I gave him my card."

"So, he has your phone number?"

"Yeah! I was thinking about giving him a call."

"Oh, I wouldn't!" she said with a worried look as her voice elevated. "I'm almost certain he's been hired to follow me."

"Come on! Follow you? Why?"

"Okay, he's being paid to watch me, report what I do, and where I go."

"Why would anyone want to know what you're doing?"

"I don't know. I just have a funny feeling about him."

"Why?" I repeated.

"I don't know why," her anger came out, then she turned, looked at me with soft-sad-begging eyes while pursing her sensual lips. "Help me, please?" she moaned.

"Okay, what do you want me to do? I wouldn't be standing here talking to you if you hadn't signaled for me to come in here. What do you want?"

"We've been standing here in this office for some time Do you know why no one has asked if we need any help?"

"I give up. Why isn't anyone helping us?"

"Because this is my business, and my travel agency," she said.

"This is your travel agency?"

"Yes!"

"These people work for you?"

"Yes, they do."

I looked around the office at everyone staring at us, while trying not to, nodded and smiled back at them.

"See!" she said with a simper.

"Okay, so this is your office, and they work for you." I said yielding to her, then asked. "What do you want from me?"

"Can you to help me get away from the detective."

"How am I supposed to do that? And, won't he just find you again? He is a detective," I said. "Can't you ask one of your employees for help?"

"I could, but I'm not sure I can trust them," she said. "We don't know each other, so I have faith in you."

"But—can I trust you," I said. "I don't know what you're involved in," then added, "what can I do?"

"I need some time to myself—I have to be alone," she said. "You're a man, aren't men good at that sort of thing. Didn't you play cops and robbers, want to be James Bond, or Jessie James when you were a kid?"

"You're a fruitcake," I said shaking my head. As I looked at her melancholy face I saw a beautiful desperate girl who needed a knight in shining armor.

"Will you help me?" she begged, then handed me an envelope. "This is a return ticket for a trip to Bora Bora, flight and hotel for two weeks. All you have to do is show up at the airport, get on the plane, and help me lose the detective."

"Can I leave anytime?"

"Yes, it's an open ticket. You can leave and return whenever you want."

"Is it only for one?" I asked.

"Yes, only for one. Well . . . are you going to help me—or not?" she barked.

I opened the envelope and looked at the ticket. Sure enough, there was a first class round trip ticket, and a two-week stay at a hotel in Bora Bora. I noticed N-e-c-k-e-r written on the outside of the envelope. "Who's or what's Necker?" I asked.

"Oh, I don't know," she said and waved her hand in an unconcerned manner. "Just a name of an old customer."

"The name of a customer? You're trying to save money by using old envelopes. I thought you were rich."

"Well, being rich doesn't mean we waste resources," she said. "How do you think people become rich?"

After a short silent moment I said, "Okay, I'll help you." I can't say no, I thought, it's why I came here, excitement, intrigued, and to get ideas for my book. "Is the guy somewhere around here now?"

"Yes, he's over at the coffee shop across the street."

"That place with the red tables and chairs?"

"Yes," she said.

"Let's go take a look," We walked over to the window. I stood behind her as we looked out the window together; my head buried in her soft curls. "By the way, your hair smells great."

"Yeah, it smells great," she said exasperated. "Pay attention—please! Look over at the window on the left. Do you see him?"

"Yeah, I see him. It's the same guy I talked to on the train."

"Now, do you believe me?"

"Yes, I believe you."

"Should I go over and talk to him?"

"No—don't do that!"

"Do you think he knows you're here?"

"Well, he followed me here."

"Does he know about this business that you have?"

"No, I don't think so," she said. "He probably thinks I came in here to plan a trip."

"He won't if you stay here, too long," I said. "He's got to see you walk out of the travel agency, and follow you somewhere crowded. We have to think of a place, somewhere busy, a big store, a hotel or something."

We stood there in the travel agency looking out the window watching the café across the street trying to think of where we could lose Zinty. We picked up some brochures, and pretended to look at them, pointing to the pictures, acting like customers as we watched the café. This woman had a secret of some kind. She was not telling me everything. What was it? I thought. I watched her play with the brochures and smile, leading me on, leading to oblivion. Am I being shanghaied? I thought.

"We could walk down the street until we get to a big store that's crowded," she said. "Wouldn't that work?"

"Walking is too slow, and he'd be too close, I don't think we can get rid of him if we walk," then I had an idea. "Let's call a taxi," I said. "No—we'll call two cabs, and tell one driver to drop you off at a big hotel, and I'll take the other taxi. You check into the hotel, and I'll meet you in the room. We'll wait him out, or maybe we can sneak out unnoticed. Okay?"

She looked at me. "Do you think that'll work?"

I saw hope in her eyes, "Sometimes it does," I said, "in the movies." Do I know what I'm doing? I thought. "Okay, here's the plan. Ask one of your employees to call two taxis. Have one come to the front and the other one stop at the next block, or in the back alley. I'll get into the second one, okay?"

"Right," she said nodding.

"Tell the driver to take you to a busy hotel," I said. "Do you know any busy places?"

"The White House Hotel is pretty big," she said, "and busy, too."

"Okay, I'll meet you there. We'll check in, wait for a while, then we'll drive to your place after we're sure we've lost Zinty."

"Who?" she asked.

"Zinty!" I said. "You know the detective guy, that's his name, right?"

"I don't know his name," she said. "Only that I think he's following me." She walked over to the counter. "James, could you call two taxis? Have one stop in the front of the agency, and the other one come around back."

"Sure, Samantha," James said, then picked up the phone and called for a taxi. After a few moments he walked over. "They should be here in a few minutes."

"Okay, Zinty's still at the café," I said. "I'll keep an eye on him after you get into the cab to see what he does, then follow you."

"After you get to the hotel, check in and get a room. Tell the desk clerk your husband is parking the car and will be asking for the room number. What name will you use when you check in?"

"I don't know," she said.

"Don't use your real name. Use another name. How about my name, Ray? Then, I can show my driver's license if they ask me," I said.

"Your name's Ray?" she asked. "What's your last name?"

"It's Ray. My first name is John."

Nodding, she said, "Okay, I'll use Ray—John," then giggled in a silly, and strange way.

"Yeah, that's funny," I said and looked out the window. "Here's your cab pulling up. See you soon. Just act nonchalant when you walk out and get into the cab."

I watched her get into the cab, and it drive away. She looked at me from the rear window of the taxi, then toward the café where Zinty was sitting. My focus turned to the café as Zinty came running out like a gazelle. He jumped into a black Mustang, and chased after Samantha's cab. I hurried toward the back of the travel agency. "Bye, James," I said, he smiled. "And, thanks for the calling the cab." As fast as you can say, Woodrow Wilson, I was out the back door and into the waiting taxi. "Hi," I said to the driver.

He nodded. "Where to?"

"Take me to the White House Hotel," I said, then thought, I must be nuts getting involved in this. I've just met this woman. What am I doing?

Chapter Ten

As we drove I caught a glimpse of Zinty, but had lost sight of Samantha. "I'm in no hurry," I told the driver, so not to draw any attention on the way to the hotel. "Take your time."

After about twenty minutes of driving through heavy traffic, the driver said, "There's the hotel just ahead on the right. You want to be dropped out in front?"

"Sure, that's perfect," I said. The driver pulled up and stopped as I took out my wallet. "How much?"

"Sixty-six bucks."

After I paid him I stood stunned for a moment. "Whoa!" I said with my breath taken away. This is some place, I thought, as I glared at my reflection in the gold plated doors at the entrance. Then I stepped inside, the exterior was unbelievable, the interior—incredible, with more gold, exotic carpets, and huge mirrors everywhere.

I took my time going through the lobby because I thought Zinty might recognize me. Then, I spotted him, and feigned looking in a display window of a store. In the reflection I saw him ride up the escalator scanning the place.

I stepped into another section of the lobby and was stunned by more magnificence. "I've never seen a hotel like this," I muttered. In the middle of the room sat a huge golden grandfather clock; my guess worth a small fortune. I wonder what it costs to stay in this hotel. She must have checked in by now, I thought, so I walked to the front desk.

"Hello, may I help you?" the clerk asked.

"Yes, my wife checked in a few minutes ago while I was parking our car, and I'd like the key to my room."

"The name, sir?"

"It's Ray, R-a-y," I said.

"May I see some identification please?"

"Sure," I said, and handed the clerk my driver's license.

"Thank you, Mr. Ray. Just one moment. Ah—yes, here it is room 6101."

He handed me the key for the room. "Thanks."

Walking to the elevator I thought, I'm crazy for doing this, but maybe I can use the experience in my book. As the doors closed I felt jumpy. On the sixth floor I found our private chamber. I put the key in the door, opened it, and said, "Knock—knock. Hello honey—I'm home." Samantha was sitting on the king size bed rubbing her feet.

"Sore feet?" I asked.

"Yes, how about a foot massage?"

"I'd love to have a massage, thanks."

And whispered under my breath, *Not what happen in Room 101.*

"You know what I mean," she said still rubbing her feet. "You give me the massage."

I walked to the window; took a look outside, and when I turned around, Samantha was lying on the bed, her feet dangling over the edge. I walked over to the door, checked the lock, then went back to the bed.

Her eyes widened as she sat up, looked at me, and asked, "Is he in the hotel?"

"Yeah, saw him in the lobby."

"What are we going to do now?"

"Well—we just wait him out. I'll go for another walk around the hotel in a while."

"Should I go with you?"

"No," I said firmly. "You stay in the room. Don't worry; every problem has a solution. I'll come up with something. We have some time to kill, Samantha, let me give you that foot massage." I thought I might get her to tell me more about what was happening if she was relaxed. I sat on the edge of the bed and put her feet on my lap.

"What are you doing?" she said in a surprised voice.

"Something I saw on TV. I watched a guy give massages on a beach in Thailand. He pulled his client's toes until they cracked. You know the same sound when you crack your fingers."

Samantha's toe cracked."That feels strange," she said.

"Doesn't it feel good?" I asked.

"Yeah, I guess so," she said, but a little weird.

"There, I've cracked all of your toes," then asked, "Ready for the massage?"

"Okay," she said, and held her breath.

"Here we go."

"I can't take . . . it tickles," she said laughing, kicking, and moving around.

"Try to hold out as long as possible without moving," I said."Hold still." Gently, I caressed the soles of her feet, then slowly moved my hand up to her knee. Her eyes were closed, she was breathing deeply, stirring, twisting, aroused. I watched her squirm as my fingers walked over her knee, up her thigh, then her body flinched as they slipped to her toes.

Probing for a tid-bit of helpful information, I looked at her and said, "Tell me more about the detective?"

Her eyes opened. "Let's not think about it for a while," she said. "Let's just imagine we're on our honeymoon," then added. "We did check in as husband and wife."

"Husband and wife! You're moving a little fast for me."

"We're just pretending," she said.

"Let's pretend we're on our first date and get acquainted first, then come up with a plan to get out of here," I said.

"I don't know much about him, only that he's been following me for a while now."

"He's been following you for a while. How long is that?" I asked as she turned away. I put my hand under her chin and pulled her face toward me, "You said—he knows you see him when he's following you, right? Maybe he's just some kind of weirdo who wants to go out with you, and doesn't know how to ask for a date."

"I don't know," she said and turned away. We've made eye contact a few times. I'm sure he knows."

I adjusted the pillows on the bed and sat back. "I just don't get it, Samantha. Why would Zinty follow you? He's not a private detective; he's a cop. You're not into something illegal, are you?" She got up and walked into the bathroom. Then, in a raised voice, I said, "Maybe someone wants to get to your father, and Zinty was hired to follow you—to get to him. Can you think of anyone?"

She yelled back, "I don't have anything, or know any reason, and can't think of anyone."

"You said you were rich. Your father is rich, right? Maybe someone just wants money." I stood and stretched.

"I think it's time for a walk down to the lobby, and see if I can spot him. Stay here! Don't go anywhere!"

On the way to the elevator, I thought, just get out, leave. Why am I here? What am I doing? Don't be a fool!

I got out of the elevator on the second floor where I had a clear view. It was another chance for me to actually take in the splendor of the hotel while trying to spot Zinty. As I looked around I saw some nice comfortable chairs and sofas in the middle of the lobby, a huge carpet with a bright swirling pattern, and more gold trim. I waited a moment—watching, then spotted Zinty sitting on a chair in the lobby reading a newspaper. He knows we're here. He knows we're here . . . echoed in my mind.

I went back to the room and announced, "Zinty's still here," and tried to pry any information, I thought she might be holding back.

"I saw him reading a newspaper in the lobby. He looked relaxed, like he was on vacation. Are you sure you can't think of any reason why he's following you?"

She became evasive, so I finally said, "What do you really want from me?" in a forceful tone. "What do you want from me?" I asked again softly. "What's this all about? Tell me something."

"I thought you could help me get rid of him, that's all," she said.

"How am I supposed to do that?" I said. "He's a cop!"

"Scare him away," she said.

"Scare him away. I'm not that scary, and he has a gun. How—"

She cut me off before I finished my sentence. "I don't know," she said and was about to cry. "Let's stay here tonight and think of a way. Okay? Please?"

This was becoming quite the adventure. I wanted to stay and go. Finally I said, "Fine, I'll stay."

I walked over to the window stared out at the city lights for a minute, then picked up the remote, and turned on the TV. "Well, let's see what's on," I said and looked at Samantha. "Get comfortable we're going to be here for a while," then sat on the bed and flipped through the channels not paying attention to what was on TV.

"Actually, I feel a bit grimy, I think I'll take a shower," Samantha said. She got up and sashayed into the bathroom humming, "Some Where Over the Rainbow" then the bathroom door closed. Listening to the water run made me restless, and it was hard to get comfortable. I moved the pillows around, fluffing them, finally leaning back on the headboard, and glared at the TV.

What have I gotten myself into? I thought, then fell back on the bed rubbing my face, looking toward the window watching the city lights begin to glow. What'll we do if Zinty's still here tomorrow?

Chapter Eleven

*S*amantha came out of the shower wearing only a towel, while drying her hair with another. I couldn't take my eyes off of her and said, "This hotel has nice towels," but I was really thinking about what was under it.

Then, she caught me by surprise, "Your turn," and threw the towel she was using to dry her hair at me.

"Go take a shower, Johnny," she said, adding a playful smile. "You'll feel better."

"Okay," I said. "Sure why not?"

I stood and walked toward her; our eyes locked as we brushed against each other. Samantha's clean, fresh fragrance filled the room, she was sensuous. We stared wildly at each other, absorbed, then kissed and embraced. The passion erupted into a sudden flow of burning energy like Mount Vesuvius laying waste to Pompeii. As we held each other I drew in Samantha's essence like a bloodhound.

I studied her face, she caressed mine. Again we looked deeply into each other's eyes, her hands moved in stages slowly down the front of my legs, around, and up my back. This was getting serious. I held her tightly and caressed her. My hands stirred around her waist. We kissed again and again. Then abruptly, I lifted my hands in the air and pulled back—

"Whew! I'll take that shower now," I said as I took a deep breath and swallowed, "then we'll talk more about how to get out of here without Zinty seeing us."

She beamed a mischievous smile at me. I grinned back, and walked into the bathroom whistling the theme song from *Mission Impossible*. She's not shy, I thought, and what a body. I smiled looking back at her, and in my best German accent said, "I'll be right back—don't go away."

The bathroom was moist and steamy, and the lingering tang of her fragrance floated in the air from the wet towels that were piled on the floor. I closed the bathroom door, turned toward the mirror, and noticed a word written there. What does that say? I looked closely at the steamed up glass, S-h-i-l-o? What does that mean? I thought. Right underneath was [. . . - - - . . .] Who wrote that on the mirror? Samantha? I stood there looking at my reflection having second thoughts again about getting involved in this mess, and feeling uneasy. I came to this city to write a book. I should leave right now, but I promised to help her. Over and over I tried to justify staying, and thought about flipping a coin—leaving it to chance.

Then, I turned quickly after hearing a noise from behind, and noticed the door had opened slightly. I was about to close it when Samantha paraded across the room. She stopped, then stood gracefully next to the bed. I'm sure she knew I was watching her because her timing was impeccable. The towel covering her strikingly gorgeous body fell slowly to the floor revealing her lean, tan shapely outline, and soft-silky-skin. My eyes followed the curves of her body from the nape of her neck down to the floor, and back up again. I was paralyzed and couldn't shut the door. She stood there silent, frozen, next to the bed unclad just her head in motion. A moment later she switched on the radio that was on the table next to the bed, slowly raised her arms and moved with the slow bluesy beat that filled the room. A lead guitar with long sustaining notes looped up and down the musical scale. First high notes, then low gritty ones. You're divinely sensual, I thought, as I watched from the bathroom, studying her, and listening to the tranquil beat of the music. This was a moment when the clock didn't exist. Eternity is the only word I can think of to describe this glint of time, eternity in a moment of two people who met by chance, shooting stars crossing the midnight sky. When the music ended she sat on the bed. After a moment she slowly rubbed lotion on her body, first on her arms, then over her stomach, gradually, gently caressing . . . glowing. I stood frozen, taking sudden deep breaths in awe of the beauty in front of me. *Go to her*, a voice in my head whispered.

She turned, looked at me, and said in a sultry voice, "Hurry up and take that shower. I'll be here for you."

I closed the bathroom door dazzled with wonder, and the memory of her dancing naked burned in my brain.

After about twenty minutes I got out of the shower, grabbed one of the towels from the floor and dried off. The shower was refreshing and I felt like a new man. I could hear the TV through the door, and thinking she was there, I walked out of the bathroom sporting a big smile. "Well, what do you think? I'm all cleaned up. Samantha?" There was no answer. "Samantha!" I said as my voice elevated with alarm. She was gone, and so were her things. Only her fragrance brought back the moment at the travel agency, when I stood behind her looking out the window with her silky hair in my face. The last indelible image of her dancing left branded in my memory. Why would she leave?

All I thought was what I had told her, *Stay in the room,* and repeated it in my mind, *Stay-in-the-room,* with some hope she'd re-appear. I got dressed, then looked for any clues that would tell me she was somewhere in the hotel. I looked down hallways, but found nothing. I took the elevator down to the second floor where I could get a good view of the lobby, and saw nothing. I walked around in a frenzy searching, but she was *nowhere* or *somewhere* else.

Perplexed, I went back to the room. Maybe she'll be there, I thought, or possibly there's a clue, something that will tell me what's going on. I explored the room like a hunter after wild game, opening drawers, checking under the bed, in the closet, and after a rigorous search, found nothing, no clues. She had vanished. Is my mind playing tricks on me? Was she really here? Yes, she was! What am I thinking? I saw her. I saw her naked! She was definitely here. I walked over to the window and stared out at the metropolis below, and thought, Samantha, where are you?

About an hour had passed and still no Samantha. I thought about going out into the city to look for her? But where would I start? This city is huge. Should I stay here in the room? I could call the police? That might not be a good idea. If I go out, I might run into Zinty. Ideas rolled over and over in my mind. What's it to me if a detective is hired to follow someone? What . . . what am I thinking, she'll be back. I'll write until she shows up. I took out my laptop; started typing about senses and feelings because I was feeling uneasy about this whole situation, and had a sense of something wrong—something strange.

Chapter Twelve

"*T*hat's alien to me" is an expression used about something we know nothing about, but it could be something others have experienced over and over. Maybe it's said in a situation, or about an action we generally know exists. I think all movements, functions, and mechanisms are realized at an early stage of life, perhaps in the womb.

Our senses, depending how sharp, assist us to discover the world as we know it exists. An example is hot and cold learned through a sense of touch, and along with taste, smell, sight, and sound are powerful associations that contain links to past experiences that exercise our mind. If any sense is hampered, the others will become more keen, and open vistas that enable one to function in a world that does not forgive.

Judgment is related to senses and linked to memories we accumulate throughout life. Any sense may trigger a mechanism that results in a split second decision. Taking advantage of an opportunity can completely change one's existence. Benefits and disadvantages are balanced, influenced and determined by whether we agree or disagree to accept an opportunity at any given moment. There comes a time once in life, or perhaps over and over, when a decision is questioned. There are reasons for events that affect our present state. Some say it's destiny, others affirm repetition of others for success, follow in another's footsteps. Does this function, action, or mechanism allow one to rationalize and see logically?

What's that? I thought, and stopped typing. Is someone in the hall? Who could it be—hotel staff? I sat quietly and listened, then heard it again. What is that? Who is that outside my door? I walked over and put my ear to the door, but didn't hear anything. I peered through the eyehole, but couldn't see anything. I opened the door quickly, looked up and down the hall, but it was empty, nothing there.

My senses are overloaded, I thought, or is it another flashback from the tea the painter gave me? Maybe I feel this way because of the cat and mouse game with Samantha. I sat down and got back to writing.

Why does the inconceivable happen at a given moment? What stops time and space in one's mind as real time continues to flow? This invention, degree of measurement, this endless circle is mysterious and alien to me. Does destiny throw us into a given direction? Do we decide on our own to remain static, nomadic, rich, or poor, wise or foolish? Are life's minutes counted and measured? Do they add up to a value expressed according to what is important, or is our time preordained? Is there a thing as vision; to see beyond, to feel life alive with all its wonderful movement? Is imagination truly the most important expression of all? A fresh creation growing from seeds of thought intercepted by our senses, then planted, waiting to blossom into an idea that we use, share, or save for the right moment in time. A novel idea, may be silly or foolish at the moment of fruition. Shared, it may be accepted or rejected for the same reasons, perhaps if given the opportunity flourishes as a gift.

Again I heard a noise, but this time it came from outside. I walked over to the window, but didn't see anything. I opened the sliding glass door and stepped onto the balcony. The city was bustling as I looked over the railing, the wind blew in my face, then up. My mind must be playing tricks on me, there's nothing out here, and went back into the room and started typing again.

The past and future are parallel, side by side, running to an extreme end in the opposite direction, then vanishing into an umbra that becomes a paradise revolving into a beam on an axis. How do you decide your parallax from sunrise to sunset? By conditions, habit, sentiment, satisfaction, possessions, knowledge? Can a wave on the sea or grain of sand affect the link in the chain of imagination seeking the breath of life?

I see the painter-picture, the instrument-music, the teacher-student, the stranger-friend. We are charmed by sentiment, put at a loss for words. I desire strength and courage at the moment of truth. I wish to rebel against absolute defeat and advance to conquer customs and traditional ideas. I wish to be kind and gentle expressing and sharing the sweetness of life. I wish to give homage to those who have not won a place in history or on any stage. Gracious and thankful just to be in someone's dream.

I stopped typing, *To be in someone's dream,* I whispered, "Didn't Bob Dylan sing that in a song?" I started typing again.

We use our fingers, hands, or tools to fashion and conceive what we imagine. Ideas created with paper and pen, images made into words to be read or spoken for all to drink in, be entertained by, or heed. A trail of thought, straight, round, or angled dots and dashes, ringlets that swim on the paper as our eyes pursue the words to the conclusion. History tangled, twisting, climbing, descending, floating, trembling and changing from black and white into a rainbow of fare to feast on, drawing knowledge from a star, ocean, an experience learned from others, unfolding one person's existence, then casting this bread in our basket.

I stopped again, grabbed a beer from the mini bar, and gulped it down. "Just what I needed," I mumbled, then checked the time; it was late, so I got back to typing.

A log rolling down a hill becomes a wheel, a branch from a tree is fashioned into a spear, a cave converted into shelter, a spark of lightning fire, a floating leaf on the sea takes shape as a ship, a bird on the wind the possibility of flight. The imagination continually exhibits extraordinary capacity, a secret essence that to this day cannot be explained in any basic or systematic method. Along with imagination these tools are used for creating an axiom; principles that one perceives from an environment that encloses, besieges, or embraces. We surrender to all because our senses have programmed us to do so from an early age. They are based on principles of our sanctuary, rejection of our work, love and emotion, hopes and dreams. The seed, flower, fruit, drop of dew, dream, thought, idea, spry and imagination are based on heavenly troth, grandeur and genius—short-lived.

Then, I heard a couple of knocks on the door. Who is that? I thought. Samantha has a key, she could get in if she wanted to, then more knocking on the door. Well, whoever it is must think someone is in the room. I got up, made my way over to the door, looked through the eyehole, and this time saw a guy standing there with a tray of food.

"Who ordered all the food?" I whispered.

I opened the door. "How are you this evening, sir?" the man at the door said in a pleasant voice.

"Fine, thanks," I said, "Uh—who ordered the food?"

"Don't know, sir. Wasn't it you? I was just told to bring it up."

"Oh—okay, bring it in."

He wheeled the cart into the room, "Where would you like it, sir?"

"Right over there by the bed is fine. Here you go," I

said and handed him a few bucks. "When was it ordered?"

"Don't know, sir," he said. "I'm just the delivery boy, and if you need anything else just call."

"Sure, thanks." Well, this is all right, I thought, I was getting hungry. I moved the cart closer to the bed and started eating, then turned on the TV.

The news was about the presidential election. Every election is the same. We choose from two candidates the person we think best qualified to steer the country on to prosperity. We look for a visionary who communicates and displays the natural ability of leadership. The news pundits always use the term horse-race when comparing aspirants for the highest post in government. They always say, *It looks like a horse-race; winner take all,* and maybe that's what these wannabes should actually do, have a bona fide horse-race, I thought as I opened my laptop and typed.

    The candidates all have their
issues, especially those they think
important to save the human race, and
the planet. I say good luck to you.
They mix science, religion, and
politics to make the soup that will
cure the ills of the world. The only
reason anyone would subject themselves
to the anguish of running for president
of a country is to have power and
control beyond what most people will
ever achieve. Influence over other
humans, anything they want just for
the asking, push a button and destroy
paradise—goodbye plumeria.
    We know what happens when one person
has total control. A look into recent

history is an eye opener, world war
duce for example, and the Nazis' plan
to cull humanity from the planet.
There's film footage of what was done
to the Jews, and this didn't happen
thousands of years ago. The Nazis took
eugenics to a new level, not only to
create a super race, but wipe out
entire races or abnormality of any
kind. Many who could have spoken out
turned a blind eye. How and why, we
ask? How an idea turned into such a
disastrous time in human history?

Originally, the eugenics idea was
conceived and practiced in many
countries, supported by many famous and
influential people of the times with
the belief that with proper breeding
and sterilization, we could achieve the
perfect human race. At a laboratory
in a once old whaling town some people
decided that the feeble minded
defectives should not pollute the gene
pool. The United States government got
involved and supported the scientist's
claims with the 1927 supreme-court
ruling, Buck vs. Bell. After many court
cases and speeches by experts in the
field, it was decided and the policy
implemented. The court upheld the
decision for compulsory sterilization,
and thousands of people were sterilized
without consent. People with high IQs
will have more children, and those

with low IQs won't have any. Now that's power to control life, who's born, who's not.

Science progresses at break neck speed these days. Every ten years a new discovery takes place. The design theory is now under discussion, and research is being done on a micro level using instruments that enable us to see the once invisible. We now know there is design in our world. Infinitesimal creatures function and perform in micro-communities much like the world we live in and see every day. The devices we create give us a window to a microscopic universe allowing us to unlock and open this unseen world; perhaps the knowledge could be used for supreme control.

Speeches, communication, the language of DNA, emotion, and what issue will touch the people, make them line up to choose and vote for their candidate. Our senses, how we perceive the world around us, where and how we get our information, on our own terms, or have it forced down our throat. To be enlightened! How to become enlightened? And if I am, does that make me an ally, foe, or narrow minded?

I wrote, drank and ate until I was blind, then woke the next morning confused, with bits and pieces of food everywhere, and the television news blaring about a government plan to tear down old housing and replace it with something more modern. You would think people would be happy to have new and modern housing. According to the TV newscaster the government failed to mention the cost to live there would double. "That's why they're protesting," I shouted at the TV. "They won't be able live there anymore, because it'll be, too expensive." The reporter mentioned gentrification. Gentrification, that's the story of life, isn't it? I thought.

I stood up and looked around the room, but too quickly, and became dizzy, everything was fuzzy. The last thing I remember seeing before hitting the floor was the cat picture on the bed. When I opened my eyes I recalled the dream I had during the night. I slowly got up, switched off the TV, sat on the bed quietly, then typed it as it came back to me.

In the dream I was in first grade, looking at a blackboard, sitting in the first row of the classroom behind an old wooden desk with a lift-up top. The word N-E-C-K-E-R was printed in capital letters on the blackboard. Small ticking clocks were mounted on the top of all the desks. A pencil rolled off my desk, slowly fell, tumbled down, hit, then melted into the floor. Words were carved into the wood of the desk. On the top of the desk was a notebook. I opened it and saw some kind of code. I looked around the classroom—it was empty. The sound of the ticking clocks became louder and louder; a sound like Morse Code. I

```
covered my ears, but it wouldn't go
away, then suddenly, it stopped.
```

Necker was written on the envelope that Samantha gave me, I thought. It had the ticket to Bora Bora. I sat there quietly for a moment, not sure what to make of the dream. Then like at the train station after I drank the tea, the room whirled, distorted, spun, and reordered back into shape. I closed my eyes. When I opened them, everything was back to normal. I got up and went into the shower, turned on the water, and listened to the spray against the glass door of the shower. It felt good to have a hot shower. I watched the water and soap go down the drain, thinking, my dirty DNA is going down the drain.

Chapter Thirteen

*I*t was dawn when I gathered my things and left the hotel room. I took the elevator down to the lobby and walked to the front desk. "Good morning," I said.

"Good morning, sir. Checking out?"

"Yes, I'm ready to check out," I said, "but my wife may have already checked us out. The room was under the name Ray, R-a-y."

"Just a moment," the clerk said, then looked at his computer. "Yes, you're checked out."

"You checked us out?" I asked. "I mean, were you working when my wife checked us out? I was just wondering what time she left the hotel because we're meeting later at a restaurant for lunch."

I watched the clerk punch computer buttons behind the counter, then he said, "Let see she checked out," he looked at the screen again, "almost about an hour ago."

"An hour ago!" I said surprised.

"That's right," he said and nodded. "Is there a problem?"

"Uh—no—no," I said. "Do I need to sign anything?"

"No, sir, you're all set."

I walked through the lobby out of the hotel into the morning sunshine wondering how much Samantha paid for the room, and who checked us out.

It was a beautiful morning, and I had some time to do a little writing before meeting Veronica, so I looked for a place to sit and relax, and have a cup coffee. As I walked I thought about the events of the previous night, about Samantha, about Zinty.

Just ahead I saw an intersection. When I got there I looked down the busy streets. Which way? Just like the Robert Frost poem, take the traveled path, or the less traveled one. It takes longer for concrete to wear out in the city, and makes it difficult to know which path is the less traveled one. There was a park down one street, so I walked in that direction. Opposite the park was a nice hotel that looked inviting, and I was dying for a cup of coffee. I went in hunting for a coffee shop. In the entrance of the hotel I heard the sound of water falling, then around the corner saw a series of waterfalls between the stairs, that went up to the second and third floor.

I followed the stairs up as they went around in a circular pattern above the artificial waterfalls. Walking up the stairs I noticed a gold plaque attached to the wall, and the inscription, *This hotel was designed by the world renowned architect, Samuel Lee Loyde*. Samuel Lee Loyde! Samantha's father? Where are you, Samantha? Where are you? And— why didn't we stay at this hotel?

At the top I spotted some tables opposite the waterfall. That looks like a good place to do some writing,

I thought. And maybe the sound of the water will give me some new ideas, some inspiration, but first I need some black juice to get me going.

"Hello," I said to a waitress at the counter in the cafe across from the waterfall.

"Yes," she said. "What can I get for you?"

"One cup of coffee. Take out, please."

"Sure, what size?"

"A small one."

"Okay, that's Six-sixty."

"Here you are." After handing her the money, I thought, six-sixty for coffee? It must be great stuff, hope it's not like the tea, then walked to a table near the waterfall.

I opened my computer wondering what to write while listening to water falling to the pool below, mesmerized, watching the droplets reflecting in the light, then saw what looked like a face behind the waterfall on the first floor. I couldn't help thinking—I know that face! It was a woman's. I got up and moved closer to the railing. I stood staring through the falling water. Wait a minute, I thought. It's Samantha. I could clearly see her standing there, looking at me and smiling from behind the falling water. I wanted to go down and get a closer look, but I felt eyes on me, so I sat down at the table watching until she vanished.

I scanned the hotel. People were looking in my direction. I just smiled, but inside I wasn't smiling, I was thinking, I saw her—I know I did! What is she doing here? How can I get into the pool and behind the waterfall without attracting attention? Then an idea, drop something into the water, and make a commotion about getting it back. The crowd will go for that; it won't be strange at all, but what can I drop into the water, my computer, no not that, it would never survive. What else do I have? I took an inventory of everything, everything in my bag and pockets.

My wallet! I took it out, held it in my hand, waited a bit, planning, going over in my mind what I was about to do. I stood, walked down the stairs holding my wallet acting clumsily, which for me in my present state wasn't too difficult, then dropped my wallet and went into my act, shouting, "*MY WALLET! MY WALLET! IT FELL INTO THE POOL.*"

I quickly ran to the bottom of the stairs where a few people had gathered, breathing hard and my heart pounding.

"I just dropped my wallet into the pool," I said to a guy standing on the stairs next to me, then pointed. "Right there! See it floating? Over there!"

"Why don't you get someone from the hotel to help you?" he said.

"I have to get it now, before everything is a soggy mess. Can you hold my stuff for me?"

"Okay—sure."

I stepped into the pool, and waded over to the falls with a voice behind me shouting, "There it is—over by the falls." It was the guy who was holding my stuff. "Over there," he repeated, "over there! Straight ahead!"

It's now or never, I thought, and went behind the falls. The water poured down soaking me completely. There was a small space behind the falls, so I followed the narrow passageway touching the wall checking if there was a door, or opening leading somewhere. I fumbled about, and had to hurry before the hotel staff showed up. "It's got to be here. There's got to be a door. I know there's a door," I grumbled, then pushed an Aztec shaped stone; the wall opened like an elevator. I stood surprised, soaked, and stunned. I turned back and looked through the waterfall where the crowd had grown to a large audience. I better get out of here, I thought, and pushed the stone again, watched it close, then waded back through the pool. Some hotel staff muscled their way through the crowd. One guy extended a hand to help me out.

"Are you all right, sir?" the hotel employee said as he pulled me up.

"Yeah, I'm fine, thanks."

"Why did you go into the pool?" a hotel security man asked as he ran over. "Are you okay?"

"I dropped my wallet. See! Here it is." I held up my wallet for him to see. "I was walking down the steps when it fell into the pool. I jumped in to get it back. Sorry for causing such a fuss."

"You should have had one of us get it for you. You might have been injured," the security man said.

"I'm okay, no problem, just a little wet, well—really wet. Completely drenched in fact. Do you think I could get my clothes dried?"

"Sure, follow me." I tagged along after the hotel employee to the elevator leaving a trail of water behind, turning to see the crowd disperse, then he pushed the button for the seventh floor. After a quiet ride up we walked down the hall, then he stopped. "You can use this room," he said gesturing, then opened the door. "Let me have your clothes. I'll have them cleaned for you."

"Room 777—looks like I hit the jackpot. This sure is nice of you. I appreciate all of your help." I went into the bathroom, took off my clothes, and came out wearing a bathrobe. "Here you are," I said and handed my wet clothes to the hotel employee. "I can't thank you enough for this."

"It's our pleasure, sir."

"How long do you think it'll take to get them back?"

"Not long, about an hour. Just enjoy the room."

"Thanks again for everything," I said, closed the door, took a deep breath, and tried to put everything together in my mind. What was all that about? I saw Samantha behind the waterfall? I saw the door. I opened the door. It was there. I know she was there. Maybe I'm being watched right now, I thought. There could be a hidden camera anywhere in this room. I'll act blasé, turn on the TV, just sit here on the bed, and wait for my clothes. Maybe this is where Samantha wanted to go. Why she needed my help to get away from Zinty. What's she mixed up in? Her father must be in on it, too. He designed the hotel. His name is on a plaque in the lobby. What's it about? What's it all about—echoed over and over in my head.

While waiting for my clothes to dry, I watched the news, and part of a movie about a troubled astronaut who had come back from a space mission a little disturbed and acting creepy. Johnny Depp played the main character. The movie was getting to the climax, and intense, when a sudden *sharp rap* on the door made me jump, my heart pound, and my fingers tingle. I took a deep breath, composed myself, walked to the door, and opened it. The same guy who took my wet clothes was standing there, holding them in both hands all nicely folded like a present.

"Hey, thanks for cleaning my clothes," I said as I took them. "Sorry for all the fuss."

"No problem, Mr.— I'm afraid I don't know your name, sir."

"It's Ray, John Bird Ray."

"I see, Mr. Ray. Before you leave, the hotel manager would like to speak with you. Could you spare a moment?"

"Sure, no problem, I've got some time. Let me change, and I'll be right with you." I went into the bathroom, thinking, I'm getting the hell out of this place asap. I dressed, left the room, and walked to the elevator where he was waiting for me with a grin that changed to a smile.

"Okay, I'm ready," I said. The hotel employee followed me into the elevator, then pushed the button for the top floor. "Penthouse," and thought, so that's where the office is, and smiled back at him.

In the elevator I asked, "Do you have any idea what the manager wants to see me about?"

"No, sir, I don't. Maybe he just wants to apologize for the inconvenience."

We got off, walked down the hall, and stopped in front of two huge embossed wooden doors with golden handles reminiscent of the Pomona travel agency. He opened and held the door for me, then gestured with his hand and said, "Go right in, sir."

The manager sat grinning behind a huge wooden desk, and carved in the wood were the same geometric shapes I saw in the stone. Do these people all use the same designer, I thought. As I got closer he stood to greet me.

"Hello, Mr. Ray. I'm George Mulreck, the manager of the hotel, and want to apologize for any trouble you had at our hotel today."

"No problem at all. I have my wallet back, and got my clothes cleaned, too. Do I have to pay you for having them cleaned?" I asked.

"Absolutely not," he said, then let out a nasally, haunting laugh. "Please have a seat."

"Oh, that's good," I said, and sat down in a very comfortable chair. "What did you want to see me about?"

"Well, if possible, could I get some information about what happened in the lobby." He looked at me suspiciously, then said, "So—we can avoid such problems in the future."

I gave him a not-sure-why-you're-asking-me look, "Okay—whatever I can do to help."

"From what I understand, you were trying to retrieve your wallet after it fell into the pool under the waterfall?"

"Yes, that's right."

"How did it fall into the water?"

"What do you mean?"

"What were you doing when you dropped it?"

"Well, I don't know. It just fell out of my hand while I was walking down the stairs."

"You weren't afraid to go into the pool and under the falls?"

"I was more afraid of everything in my wallet getting wet, destroyed, or losing it."

"Perhaps I would have felt the same," he said. "We'll have to put some kind of barrier up so it doesn't happen again. Is today your first time at our hotel?"

"Yes, the first time," I said. "You have a nice hotel."

"Thanks, we like it," he said. "By the way, I have a document I'd like you to sign that releases us from any further responsibility, or damages that you incurred. Could you sign it for me please?"

"Sure, be happy too! I'm fine, just got a little wet is all."

"Well, thanks for meeting with me, and I hope you stay with us sometime in the future. Also, here's a gift certificate that can be used at any of our restaurants in the hotel. We think the food is excellent."

"I don't know what to say. You've been so kind," I said. "Cleaning my clothes, and a free meal, thanks."

"Well, it's the least we could do for all the trouble you've been through today."

We shook hands, and I said goodbye, but I felt he was trying to get me to say something about what I saw behind the waterfall without pushing, too hard.

I turned and waved before getting to the door as I left the office. Mulreck returned the gesture with a nod, then just as I was about to open the door, grabbed air where the handle would have been. Surprised—I said to the same guy who brought me to the office, "Thanks for your help."

As I looked at his eyes, wondered, How did you know I was going to open the door?

"We're happy to be of service, sir. Please, visit us again."

"I'd love to, but this hotel's a little expensive for me, but I'll be back to use this restaurant certificate."

"Oh, please do, the food is excellent."

"Bye," I said and walked out of the hotel, thinking, Maybe I can bring Veronica here for dinner and a swim.

I headed to the park across the street. I've got to go through everything, figure out why there's a secret door behind the waterfalls, why Samantha was there, what she's involved in, and what the hell is going on.

Chapter Fourteen

Was there a way I could get back into the hotel and check it out? Should I just forget about it? I could always go back later, I have a gift certificate for the restaurant. Maybe Samantha's in trouble? Should I tell the police? I'll wait, I thought, it's best to wait a little until I figure this out. As I looked back at the hotel I saw the name of it spelled out in huge blue letters,

"**N-E-C-K-E-R**, the same name was on the envelope, the one Samantha gave me with the ticket to Bora Bora. It's the name of a hotel!" I said enlightened. Is this the only one, or are there more? Maybe there's a chain of these hotels around the world. Why all the secrecy? I thought. What does it all mean?

When I looked back at the hotel again the exterior changed in design, and shape, depending on the angle of my position, and how I looked at it. Somehow this strange phenomenon was built into the design? Now, I was getting nervous. What had I stumbled into? Again, I was regretting meeting Samantha and going along with her hare-brained idea. And, who's Zinty? What's the connection? Are they working together? Did they steal something? Belong to an international crime syndicate? I have to find a place to clear my head and think this through.

I walked in the direction of the train station, or what I thought was the direction of the train station. After all that happened I was becoming paranoid and thought someone was watching, and keeping me under surveillance. So not to be obvious when looking around, I was nonchalant, occasionally checking if I recognized anyone, no one special stood out.

I came across what looked like an interesting bar called *Outsiders Inside*. On the sign below the name there were two pool cues stamped in an **X** pattern under a skull, like on a pirate flag. After opening the door, I walked into a wall of blaring rock music, and couldn't hear myself think. This was a pool bar; just what I needed to forget, and relax.

I walked over where some people were standing at the bar. One tall guy was wearing a faded army field jacket. I overheard someone call him GT. Next to him a sinewy character with a handle-bar moustache, and had the name Wild Bill embossed on his coat. They faced the pool tables, which were occupied by some other guys who looked like bikers, and off to the side was a small stage where others were sitting, talking, and drinking.

These guys were pros! I watched them hold and use a cue-stick like they were born with it in their hand. They made the cue-ball do all kinds of crazy tricks. Amazing and unbelievable shots were made in the short time I was there. I should play a game or two, I thought, try my luck. No—better not, these guys are in a different league.

The bar-keep came over after I sat at the bar.

"What'll you have?"

"A bottle of Corona."

He brought over the Corona, then asked, "Lime?"

"Yeah, thanks."

"Never seen you before," he said. "New around here?"

The barkeep had long hair, a thick moustache that continued, then disappeared under his chin. Under his lower lip a patch of hair, so he looked like the famous gunfighter, Wild Bill Hickock, or the hunter, Buffalo Bill Cody.

"Yeah, got in a few days ago."

"A few days ago," he said and laughed. "Like it here?"

"I guess it's okay," I said. "Say—ever been to the Necker Hotel. It's just down the street?"

"Are you kidding! Costs a fortune to stay there," he said, and laughed once more. "If it cost a dollar to go around the world, I'd be broke after I stepped out that door," he said pointing at the entrance.

I laughed and said, "Let me buy you a drink," then asked, "What's your name?"

"Spratt."

"Spratt," I repeated. "How did you get that name?"

"Don't know. Maybe it's got something to do with coming from a big family."

"A big family?" I asked.

"The youngest runt of ten," he said. "What are you called?"

If he's the smallest I wonder what the biggest looks like, I thought.

"John, John Bird Ray," I said, "I used to be called Birdman in school, but that was long, long ago." *American Pie*, I thought, and gulped down the rest of my Corona.

"You want another one, Birdman?"

"Sure," I said. "And, you have one on me, Spratt."

"Oh," he said in an amplified groan. "You're the kind of customer I like."

"What kind of customer is that?"

Spratt looked at me. "The kind that buys the bartender drinks," then shoved a lime down the throat of his Corona, raised his bottle and said, "To the new guy in town!"

"Say, what's the deal with the name of this place," I asked, "and the pirate design out front?"

"Well, the guy who owns this place is a bit of a strange fellow. He's hard looking, a big bruiser, drinks like a fish, but never gets drunk. I asked him about the name after I started working here. He told me he was a descendant of John, *Calico Jack,* Rackham, the pirate who designed the Jolly Roger, so he has pirate blood in his veins."

"You believe that?" I asked.

"Yeah, I do," Spratt said. "He has dark, cold eyes, meaty arms, and carries a knife that's a foot long."

"When does he come in," I asked.

"We never know! He just shows up, and when does— raises hell."

"Sounds like a fun guy," I said.

"The last time he was here he shot up the place. See those bullet holes in the wall over there," he said and pointed.

"Someone called the police, but he knows people in Police Department. They just talked, and then—left."

"So, he does whatever he wants? You like him?"

"He's interesting, that's for sure," Spratt said. "Hold on, someone needs a beer, be right back."

I watched the pool game and mulled over whether or not to play again, then decided against it because they were just, too good. I finished the last of my beer in one gulp while thinking about all that had happened since arriving in town. Trying to figure out or make some sense of it all, but nothing made any sense. I checked my watch. Time flies when you're having fun, I thought, and when you're not, it stops.

Spratt came over. "Another Corona?"

"No thanks," I said. "I'm heading out, got a date."

"Okay, see you around," he said. "Let's shoot some stick next time."

"We'll play for beers," I said.

"I'll be here." He raised his beer and took a swig.

"Yeah, and I'd like to see this guy, Jack."

"Here's a picture of him," Spratt said, and handed it to me. I couldn't believe my eyes, it was Zinty, a picture of Zinty, but dressed in biker garb.

"I know this guy," I said.

"You know him?" Spratt said surprised. "How?"

"We met on the train," I said. "I've got to go, then stepped out of the *Outsiders Inside* bar, and walked down the street trying to figure out where I was. That building looks familiar, I thought, and turned the corner.

Chapter Fifteen

*O*n the way to the station after leaving *Outsiders Inside* I watched my back and looked around constantly, then thought, I'm being followed, and felt some momentary paranoia. Is this sensation from the tea the painter gave me, the beer, from the situation with Samantha, or a result of having absolutely no idea of where I am? Nothing looked familiar, just a lot of tall buildings, stores, people, and cars everywhere. I'm lost I thought, nothing more, but now what?

After walking for about twenty-five minutes I realized I was standing in front of the same hotel where I had spent the night. I stood there shaking my head in disbelief. How did I get here? I thought. Am I stuck in a time warp? I saw a stairway as I went around another corner, and headed down to what I hoped would be a subway. I heard a train coming, so I hurried, slipping, almost tumbling and falling flat on my face, then made it to the platform in time to see the doors close. I stood there out of breath watching it pull away. "Damn!" I grunted. It was twelve o'clock. "Can I make it to the station in time to meet Veronica?"

While waiting for the next train I took another look at the cat painting. I noticed the painter's phone number written on the bag. I should call him and ask about the tea. It must be why I'm lost and feeling this way. I also had Samantha's number somewhere, and searched my pockets. Where's that piece of paper?

I took out my cell phone and dialed the number. It rang with no answer. I tried again. This time someone answered, but all I heard was heavy breathing. That's what I was doing a few minutes ago, I thought.

"Samantha," I said, and heard the breathing again. "Samantha," I said, then was disconnected. That didn't sound like a woman breathing, I thought.

"I'll try one more time," I muttered.

After it rang once, a timid voice said, "John, is that you? John?"

"Samantha?" I said.

"Yes, it's me," she said.

"Is everything okay?"

"Yes, everything's fine."

"You sound different, Samantha. What's wrong?"

"Nothing's wrong—nothing at all—I'm fine," she said, but her voice was shaky, nervous.

"You're sure?" I asked again. "You sound nervous."

"Yes, I guess you could say that," she said, then there was only silence.

"Samantha," I said. "Samantha! Are you there?"

"Listen, you stay away from Samantha," a rough voice growled.

"Who is this?"

"We met on the train," the voice growled again.

"Who—"

He interrupted, "Well, do you remember seeing my gun?"

"Gun! What?" I said puzzled.

"We talked about writing on the train. Does that jog your memory?" the voice said in a slow, deep whine.

"Gun?" I said then thought, the detective from the train. It's the detective from the train—Zinty!

"Stay away from Samantha," he roared. "If you don't, I'll show what my gun does."

I pulled the phone away from my ear looking at it, whispered forcefully. "What? Are you for real?" I put the phone back to my ear.

"Samantha's part of my family! You get the picture!"

"Is this some kind of joke? Is Samantha okay?"

"She's fine, John Bird Ray, just stay away."

"Zinty . . . I'll call the police."

He laughed in a shallow way and said, "I am the police," and hung up.

"Wait a minute—Zinty!" then only heard a dial tone, and was left scratching my head in disbelief. I'll leave it alone for now. I don't know her that well. She's just a spoiled rich kid. I caught the next train going to Grand, but couldn't get the conversation with Zinty out of my head. What an asshole, and why the sham about writing a book on the train. Why was he following her? I wanted to help Samantha, but also wanted nothing more to do with her. She—left the hotel, she—dragged me into this.

On the train I saw an advertisement for an exhibition of Egyptian History at the Field Museum. What is history? I thought, and took out my laptop.

Chapter Sixteen

*H*istory, the mind, and all that's written, who cares and who'll pass on the knowledge and wisdom that's accumulated throughout the ages? If there's no one to read history, does it end? Perhaps it's happened?

Amazingly, there's little evidence regarding written history; we can only trace our existence back roughly ten thousand years, and a lot of people believe the earth is billions of years old. It's fascinating because there are no credible answers to what took place during these billions of years other than humans were cave-people who wandered the earth hunting for sustenance, and frolicked in the Garden of Eden?

While some fossils have been found, nothing directly links humans of today to any of the creatures that were on the earth billions of years ago. We desire knowledge and reason, continue to ask the big question, and hunt for the answer. Experts in this field who speculate on human origin have come up with a hodge-podge of formulas and theories. Will we have an answer someday? The minds that work on these puzzles and conundrums vary.

In the case of minds for instance, take the precocious William John Sidinoy. Who is he? Some say the most intelligent human who ever lived; a phenomenon with many achievements unsurpassed by anyone. It's said he spoke at six months, read soon after, typed his own work at four, entered a prestigious university at twelve, and graduated before he was fifteen. He spoke and read, English, French, German, Russian, Greek, Latin, Armenian, Turkish, and many other languages. He astounded students, and scientists alike, when he wrote about black holes long before anyone heard of them. His IQ was estimated to be 300, or higher. What became of him? He got involved with a group that protested for social change and was arrested. The press wrote negatively about him, hounded, and labeled him as weird, some kind of freak, which resulted in an extreme animosity toward the media. Eventually he had a falling out with his parents, who were both educators at the university he attended, after they tried having him sent away. He worked at odd jobs until his employers found out who he was, then moved on. It's possible he wrote and published many articles and books under aliases, ones that you've possibly read, to avoid any attention or fame.

William John Sidinoy died from a stroke in his early forties. Was he a burned out genius, learn, too much, too quickly? Is it possible to overload a mind with facts and information, or was he a guy who got a raw deal, and just wanted to be left alone? In one of the last letters William John Sidinoy wrote something like this.

We have many super-humans among us today. End the struggle within your magnificent mind, and communicate with the cosmos.

We have many super-humans among us today? What! Super-humans live among us today? If so, what are they up to? Do they control the world with furtive communication and create scenarios for domination? Is there a diabolical plan conceived by evil super-human geniuses battling with good super-human geniuses to help the poor unfortunate inhabitants? History is replete with good versus evil stories; positive and negative forces fighting each other. Stories from the Bible to Stephen King address this basic idea, and we're left to speculate on who let the genii out of the bottle.

Then I remembered a verse in the Bible mentioning something about sons of God, so I checked my notes. I found it, and got back to typing.

Genesis 6:4. There were giants in the earth in those days; and also after that, when the sons of God came unto the daughters of men, and they bore children to them, the same became mighty men which were of old, men of renown.

What does it mean? I thought, and typed.

Are the son's of God, angels? Does it infer there's a connection between angels and humans? A relationship that created super-humans, a remnant of the past that springs up every so often to give the ordinary a special gift, to create and share brilliance with the mundane inhabitants of our minuscule world? Are the stories of legends and myth true? Are some people born with a special talent? Is there such a thing as a Star Child?

There are many people we consider gifted. Albert Einstein's name is known worldwide. He's a giant known for his theories of relativity. Where did his ideas come from? What secrets does space hide? When will they be uncovered? Do groups with members from around the world get together and discuss these issues. Maybe they know something we don't? Are they superhuman?

I stopped typing and looked up from my laptop because the train had stopped at the station where I had met Veronica the day before. I scrambled to gather my things and got off.

Chapter Seventeen

We planned to meet at one o'clock, and now it was one, but I didn't see her anywhere in the station. Maybe she forgot, I thought, or perhaps she didn't mean it. She's not going to show up, then I turned quickly after feeling a nudge at my back and saw Veronica's radiant smile, and cheerful brown eyes.

"Hey, for a while there, I didn't think you were going to show up."

"Why would you think that? Don't you trust me?" she asked. "We're soul mates now, John."

"I just thought you may have changed your mind."

"Oh, don't say that!" she said. "Let's have some fun. Come on, let's go"

"Where are we going?" I asked. It really doesn't matter, I thought, as long as I'm with you.

"You like Mexican food, don't you?"

I looked at her bright eyes and said, "Love it! That sounds great. Have a place in mind?"

"How about this place?" she said, and took a business card out of her wallet and showed it to me. "It's called Charlie's. I hear the food's great, and it's not far from here."

"Okay, Mexican food it is. Which way do we go?"

"Follow me." She grabbed my arm and we were off.

"How was your day? Get any writing done?"

I looked at Veronica and smiled because I felt like I was floating on air.

"I wrote a little this morning."

"The same topic?" she asked. "Bullshit?"

"No, I've moved on to another topic."

"What's the new topic?"

"It's about life in general, our senses, how people learn from their environment, and a bit about aliens," I said. "Don't know how I'm going to work that into my book."

"Aliens?" she said. "Now, what do you know about aliens?"

"I don't know anything about aliens. I'm making it up, and it's not really about aliens. I had some tea from this painter—didn't I tell you this? I've been feeling strange ever since. I'm sure it was spiked." I looked at Veronica and smiled. "Back to the book, I've got to somehow connect the stories I'm writing, together. I was sure I'd have more done by now, but got sidetracked last night."

"What happened last night?"

"Oh, it's a long story, a long—long—story."

"We've got all evening."

"Okay, let's see." We continued walking while I thought of where to start about the previous night, meeting Samantha, the night at the hotel, and Zinty. I didn't want to get Veronica into any trouble by being connected with me and what happened with Samantha.

She looked at me and smiled. "Well, are you going to tell me about your long night?"

"Okay. Let's see," I said. "Where do I start? Okay, I was walking down the street, then saw a travel agency." Veronica listened intently. "You know how travel agencies have brochures and pictures of places to go in the window?"

"Yes—yes! I know," Veronica said trying to coax more out of me.

"Well, I stopped to take a look at the brochures, and pictures at a travel agency. As I was looking in the window, a woman in the travel agency motioned for me to come in. I thought, okay why not, so I went into the travel agency. First we talked about places to go, then she told me she owned the travel agency, her father was rich, and a guy was following her, but didn't say why, or know why."

"Are you making this up?" Veronica asked.

"No, I'm not making any of it up. It's true. She pointed this guy out who was sitting at a coffee shop across the street from the travel agency, and I recognized him.

"What?" Veronica said. "Who was he?"

"A guy I met on the train earlier that evening. He told me he was a detective, and we talked about writing."

Veronica had the look of disbelief on her face, raising her eyebrows, her head cocked to one side. "So, this guy, he was a real cop?" she asked.

"Yes, he was—and had a *real* gun," I said. "At the travel agency we concocted a plan. We decided to call two taxis, then meet at a hotel. She had one of her employees, a guy named, James, call for the taxis."

Veronica looked at me. "This really happened?" she said, sounding like she didn't believe any of what I was telling her. Then thought, I wouldn't have believed it either.

"Yes, to get away from the detective."

"You took taxis," she said, "to where?"

"Samantha told me she had an apartment, but we decided to go to a hotel first, and see if she'd be followed by Zinty. The idea was to check into a room, stay there for a while, then leave."

"A hotel?" she said. "Which one?"

"The White House Hotel."

"The White House Hotel? That place is expensive. You're making this up, aren't you?"

"No, I'm not. It's all true."

"You checked into a room there?"

"No," I said, "we checked into a really nice room there."

"What happened next?"

"We decided to stay the night because the detective was at the hotel and wouldn't leave."

"You stayed the night with her in the room?" Veronica said with a staggered, beguiled look.

"I had to! Zinty, the detective followed us," I said. "I saw him in the lobby. Nothing happened, she took a shower, I took a shower."

"Together!" Veronica said in a raised voice.

"No, no—not together," I said. "She took a shower first, and when I came out of the shower she was gone."

"She wasn't in the room?"

"Nope, she was gone, disappeared. First, I thought, to get some ice or food, but she never came back. I searched the hotel, but couldn't find her, so I went back to the room and worked on my book for a while, then I heard a knock on the door."

"Was it her?"

"No, it was a guy from room service with a huge tray of food I didn't order. I ate what I could, fell asleep, then checked out the next day. She, or someone checked us out the next day, paid for the room, and I haven't seen her since."

I almost told Veronica about the Necker Hotel, seeing Samantha behind the waterfall, and the picture of pirate Zinty. She'll never believe me, I thought, and left it alone.

"You haven't seen her since?"

"No, but I have her telephone number. We met on the train. Well, actually not on the train, she sat opposite from me on the train reading a book. Do you remember when I told you I was writing about bullshit? She was the one who had the book, and gave me the phone number."

"Okay, I remember," Veronica said.

"Well, I called her number, at first I wasn't sure that I had it, but remembered putting it in my pocket. I called not really knowing who would answer. It turned out to be Zinty the detective, and he wasn't so pleasant. He basically said, *Stay away from Samantha or I'll make your life a living hell.* I'm not sure whether to take him seriously, but he flashes his gun around," I said gesturing with my hand. "He wants people to know he's a tough guy."

"This all sounds so far fetched. Why did you go to the hotel?"

"I don't know, just wanted to help. She came across as vulnerable, and thought I could use the experience in my book. She also tempted me with a trip to Bora Bora."

"A trip to where?"

"Bora Bora."

Veronica looked surprised, then concerned. "What are you going to do?" she said.

"What can I do? Zinty's a pretty big guy, and I don't know Samantha. We've just met once," I said. "Only once!"

"You spent the night with her in a hotel," Veronica said.

"Nothing happened," I said. "She took a shower, I took a shower. She left and never came back. I spent the night alone, eating and writing."

"I think we should do something. Call the police—or do something to help," Veronica said.

"What am I going to say to the police? Hello, I know a girl who may be in trouble. Then they'll ask, *What's your relationship with her?* and I'll say, oh—we met on the train. She asked me to help her get away from a detective. Maybe you know him, his name is Zinty. Oh yeah, then we went to a hotel. Come on, Veronica, they'll think I'm nuts."

"You could call Zinty again."

Shaking my head, I responded, "And say what? Hi, Zinty, it's me again. Let's get together for lunch, and talk about writing a book together. No way," I said, "that guy's crazy. I want to forget all of this. Let's talk about something else. Let's talk about you."

"Okay, okay," she said, "but what happened to you is just—so—strange."

"What do you do?" I asked.

"I work for a flooring wholesaler."

"You mean, a carpet company?"

"We sell everything to cover a floor, carpet, ceramic tile, vinyl."

"What do you do there," I asked. "Install carpet?"

"No," she said with a direct stare. "Do I look like a carpet installer? I do office work, take care of ordering, shipping, that kind of stuff."

"Do you like it?"

"It's a job," she said and smiled, "and the pays okay."

"Ever go out to any clubs?" I asked.

"Yeah, sometimes, went to one last week."

"What's the name of it?"

"It's called, *Outsiders Inside*," she said.

"I know that place. I had a beer there a little while ago. The bartender's name is Spratt. The guy who owns it claims he's a descendant of a pirate."

"You're kidding about this, right?" she said.

"No, it's true, according to the bartender."

"What about you, John? What do you do other than write?"

"I've had jobs that anyone can do."

"Well, what kind of jobs?" she asked again.

"I was in the army for a while."

"In the army?" she said surprised. "What did you do in the army?"

"I was a photographer," I said.

"A photographer," she said with interest and leaned toward me. What did you take pictures of for the army? Something secret?"

"Just events, nothing special or secret," I said. "It was a little boring. I remember once I was taking pictures at an event when this officer walked up to me. At first, I thought he was going to say something about my camera, or ask a question about photography."

"What did he say?"

"He told me to get a haircut," I said and we burst out laughing.

After we settled down, Veronica said, "That's funny. How long were you in the army?"

"For three years, then I got a job at a studio."

"So you're a photographer?" she said.

"Yeah, photographer, slash writer," I said, "and eventually opened a studio. I was excited to work for myself. It was slow at first, but things picked up after a while."

"Are you still in photography?" she asked.

"Sure, I shoot weddings, do some commercial work, had a job shooting handmade wooden clocks a few weeks ago, and do portrait work, too. I closed my studio for a while to come here to be in the city. I thought it would help me write. You know, adventure, inspiration, meet some people, and make some connections," I said. "How long have you been at your company?"

"Just a few years, but I like acting," she said. "Someday—"

"Well, if you need any pictures for your portfolio, I'm your man. Have camera will travel," I said. "So, where's this restaurant you've been talking about?"

Veronica lifted her arm and pointed across the street. "Right over there."

"Oh, looks like an interesting place," I said sizing up the two-story white stucco building with a sign at the top that read—**CHARLIE'S CANTINA**

Chapter Eighteen

We stood opposite the restaurant watching people eating on a balcony that spanned the entire length of the building. "Sitting up there looks fun," I said.

"It looks lively, too," Veronica said, then pointed at the balcony. "Look! Up there!" We watched some people letting balloons go. They floated wildly, unfettered, up with the breeze they went, dancing away along with the music.

"Yeah, I think everyone's having a good time at Charlie's. They're celebrating something; can't wait to go in." Whenever the door opened I saw people dancing in the bar as we crossed the street. We walked into a wall of flesh as we stepped through the door, then snaked our way through the mob on the first floor.

"That's nice," I said. "Look at that!" then tapped Veronica on the shoulder and pointed. "That old wooden bar and mirror must be worth a fortune." The mirror behind the bar was lined with bottles of booze, sombreros, cow horns and cactus.

"What?" Veronica asked, and shrugged because she couldn't hear me over the music.

"We should check out the bar and the band after we eat. What's the name of the band?" I said raising my voice a notch while pointed in the direction of the stage.

"I don't know—let's ask someone." Veronica said.

"Good idea," I shouted back and nodded.

We continued to muscle our way through the crowd in the direction of a staircase that led to the restaurant on the second floor. Over the blaring music a waitress at the top of the staircase said, "Hi, table for two?"

"Yes," I said. "Do we have to wait a long time?"

"No, no, I have a table, follow me," the waitress said. "How's this one? It faces the street."

The table was small, but we didn't mind. "It's cozy. Thanks," I said.

"What can I get you to drink?"

"Can we think about it a minute?" Veronica said.

"Sure, take your time," the waitress said. "Just give me a wave when you're ready."

"What's the name of the band," I asked.

"Hands & Feet," the waitress said.

"Hands & Feet," I repeated, "Thanks. They sound great."

"Yeah, I think so, too," the waitress said and smiled. "They play here a lot."

"I like this place, Veronica. It has character."

The ceramic tile on the table was covered with images of peppers, cactus, and horses.

"Nice table," I said, "and those are nice pictures," then gestured at the horse images on the wall. "Ever go horseback riding, Veronica?"

"Sure, I love horses," Veronica said. "Do you?"

"Sometimes," I said. "I grew up in the country, and used to ride a lot."

"Nice atmosphere, great music, this place is terrific," then she took a deep breath and said, "the food smells really good, too."

The waitress came over to our table to take our order. "We like the band, and your restaurant."

"Thanks," the waitress said and smiled.

"Is there some sort of celebration going on?" I asked.

"Yeah, it's a birthday party."

"I guess we came on the right day," I said.

"What'll you have?"

"Let's see." I looked at the menu. "What're you having, Veronica?"

"A margarita."

"That's what I'll have," I said, and smiled at Veronica. "What are you going to order?"

"I'll have a chimmachanga with beef," Veronica said.

"Let's see, I'll have a fajita."

"Anything else?" the waitress asked.

"How about an order of guacamole," I said. "Can you leave the menu? We'll probably order more later."

"Sure, I'll be right back with your drinks," the waitress said and went down to the bar.

"You chose a nice place, Veronica."

After a few minutes the waitress returned; drinks in hand. "Here you go," she said, smiled, and set our drinks on the table.

"Thanks, that was fast. Let's have a toast." I raised my glass. "Here's to Chicago! Where I met a beautiful woman."

"I have one," Veronica said. "Here's to an exciting night in Chicago with a new friend."

Our glasses touched with the familiar clink! We took a sip; I leaned over the table kissed her on the lips, and was surprised when she laid one back on me.

"This day is turning out to be fantastic," I said.

"Nothing can top this," Veronica said.

"What do you like doing for fun, Veronica?"

"All kinds of things," she said. "Going to movies, going out to eat—with a nice guy," she laughed, then her face became sincere. "And sometimes I write poetry."

I sat back surprised. "You write poetry!"

"That's why I was interested about what you were writing on the train," she said.

"Tell me one," I said.

"I'm not good at reciting them," then closed her eyes for a moment, "but here goes."

We're part of the ocean and part of the sky
Part of a joke and part of a lie
I see on your face when you laugh and cry
The gleam of your smile and twinkle in your eye
Part of the ocean and part of the sky

"That's just the beginning," she said and looked at me, smiled, and asked, "Do you like it?"

"It's nice," I said. "Tell me another one."

Not with a crystal ball - Not with cards on the table
Not with tea leaves - Not read from the stars
Not told in stories from a dream where everything passes soon
But in the eyes - the moment of truth
Bright as the midnight moon
That's where I saw love

"That . . . remarkable!"

"I've got some others with me," she said, "Here take a look," and handed me an embossed brown leather journal.

I took the journal, opened it to the first page, and read.

CHIMBORAZO

Wet, moist, steamy rain water
Falling, rolling onto the leaves
I now hold in my hand
On my port and starboard sides
In front and right behind
Glistening drops of radiant beads
Thunderous as they dive to earth
Sliding and rolling down my face
Over my eyes, across my lips
Down and off my fingertips
Falling in time with the beat
Of millions of other raindrops
A sound rumbles through my soul
Hear and feel drum humming waves
Tickling the bottom of my feet
Taste of heaven on my tongue
I feel each drop rise up through me
Now how can this be done
No mind on earth can conceive
Who knows the secret long kept
That drops through the trees

"Like that one?"

"It's great, Veronica, you're a real poet."

"Thanks, I'm glad you really like them."

"Who wouldn't like this?" I said. "It's great!"

"I'd like to read your poems sometime," she said.

I flipped to another page.

"Yours are much better than mine."

SAINT REMY
A wall that surrounds
Exhausted come to rest
But there is no rest
Only a schedule to keep
Love breaks free from life
Becomes unrelenting passion
Day and night—twists—turns
Visions suspended in air
Change what's seen by all
To an image in mind
Slice of a moment in time
Painted on canvas
Hung on a wall
Colors flowing in a frame

I read while watching her smile, "Saint Remy is about Vincent Van Gogh," she said. "His passion was off the scale. All of his energy went into expression, and trying to make the paint come alive."

"He lopped off a piece of his ear, didn't he? Don't know if that's passion or—well—I don't know," I said then looked at the next one. "Blink. What's this one about?"

"It's about someone saying goodbye because they'll be away a long time; a moment that seems to last forever."

"I'm beginning to feel that way about you, Veronica."

She reached over and held my hand. "But it's not all sad because we always have the other person in our heart. And—no matter how long you're apart, you're still together."

"We always have the memories of the time spent together," I said.

"That's right!"

"I really want to read this poem."

BLINK
In the blink of an eye
The tear that falls
Has a love that holds on tight
In the blink of an eye
The smile I see
Has joy that fills an empty heart
In the blink of an eye
The hardest thing I ever said
Was goodbye
No matter how far or how long
We are apart
We stand together
You're forever in my heart

"That one's heavy," I said. "Here's your book, Veronica. I'll read more, later, okay?"

"Do you really like them?"

Nodding, I said, "I think your poems are truly amazing!" then I looked at her, "You should publish it."

"I want to, but I don't have enough work for a book."

"A book doesn't have to be long, poetry can be any length or any number of pages. I can help you," I said. "Never know, you might become famous, then I can tell everyone I know the famous poet, Veronica Wrigley." I picked up my margarita. "A toast to poetry!"

Veronica said, "To poetry, and to poets!"

"I write poetry, too. Well, I've already told you that."

"Yeah, you did," she said. "I'd like to hear one."

"I can't remember any of them," I said. For some reason my memory is short. I can't remember things. How about the next time we go out, okay?"

"Here you go," the waitress said as she set the food on the table.

"Everything looks delicious," I said. We ate and listened to the band play while we looked at each other, our minds linked, our thoughts flowing.

Then I said, "What else should we order? Where's that menu?"

"Right here," Veronica said and handed me the menu.

"Let's see, how about some quesadillas, and two more margaritas?"

"I like how that sounds," she said

"Excuse me," I said to the waitress. "Could we order more food?"

"Of course," the waitress said. "What would you like?"

"We'll have the quesadillas, and two more margaritas, please."

"Sure," the waitress said. "Do you want the margaritas right away?"

"Yes, thanks," I said then turned to see what was going on in the restaurant, and was surprised, in fact couldn't believe my eyes. The painter who had sold me the cat painting was being shown to a table. He spotted me, raised his hand and nodded, so I waved back, then he came over to our table.

"Well, my friend, we meet again. How are you?" Then he saw Veronica, and his face lit up like a jukebox. "Who is this lovely senorita?"

When I bought the painting I didn't notice, but seeing him now reminded me of Zorro. He was wearing black clothes, had a thin moustache, and a small patch of beard under his lip, just like Zorro. I wanted to call him Zorro.

"Why don't you join us?" I asked. You know, it just hit me, I don't know your name. I've been calling you the painter since we met. So, what's your name?"

"Just go on calling me the painter," he said. "I like that. It sounds nice."

"Okay," I said. "This is Veronica."

"Hello, senorita, it's a pleasure. You look ravishing. Have you seen the painting our friend bought from me?"

"Yes, I have. It's very nice—interesting," Veronica said as she shook his hand.

"Let me guess, you two have recently met, yes?" the painter said. "You make a great couple."

"That's right! We've just met," Veronica said. "How did you know?"

"Ah—it's my business to know people, and what they want," he said. "I'm a painter! I paint with my heart, imagination, and love. You two are in love, aren't you?"

I looked at Veronica, our eyes met as I watched her hand reach out and touch mine, then we both smiled.

"Ah—" the painter said, and thumped his chest with his fist. "I knew it!"

After a sip of my margarita, I said, "I stopped by a shop on my way here today. As I walked around saw some paintings that looked like yours, so I asked, Hector, the owner about them. I gave him my telephone number. You may be getting a call from him. I need written permission to use your painting for the cover of my book."

"Oh, yes, Hector, a great guy. He lets me put my paintings in his store until they're sold. I make some money, he makes a little money, and someone gets a great piece of art. You know, I can't remember your name. What is it again?"

"John Bird Ray," I said.

"John Bird Ray," he laughed. "Birds and cats don't get along so well my friend. Maybe, I'll start painting birds. I tell you what—the first bird I paint is for you, John Bird Ray. We'll consider it a gift; no charge."

"Thanks," I said. "I'd like to know about the tea you gave me. Strange things have been happening ever since drinking it. What was in it?"

"Just tea my friend, just tea," he said and held up his arms to show he was innocent, and repeated, "Nothing my friend—nothing—really!"

"No," I said, "it was more than just tea."

"Okay, it was a special drink," he said. "Do you know ayahuasca?" (a.ja.wa.ska)

"No—What's that?" I asked, then said, "A—special drink?" in a naive way.

He held up his hands and explained. "It's tea made from the root of a giant vine that grows in the South American rainforest." He gestured with his arms wide open to show how big the root was. "It gives you a feeling of what is really around you. A person deeply knows things that are seen, perhaps have some old memories come back, maybe some experiences that are not memories, but from your mind trying to figure out life. I'm sorry I offended you. I feel badly now, John," he said. "Please forgive me."

"Why give it to me?" I asked.

"Well, you said you were a writer and wanted to use the painting you bought for the cover of your book. I was moved by that. I thought it would help inspire you. After drinking ayahuasca, some gain insight and wisdom in the area they that interests them, the mind works faster, and ones reflective and creative abilities are enhanced. Were you inspired?" he asked.

"Yeah, and I'm still being inspired," I said sharply. "Does it stop?"

"That's up to you, my friend," he said.

"Up to me!" I said. "What do you mean?"

Veronica jumped in, "What does this special drink look and taste like?"

"There are different ayahuasca. There's the black, the heaven, the star, and the chacruna leaf—to make it work.

Just a moment," he said and looked up and waved. "I see some friends. I'll be right back okay." The painter walked to the other side of the restaurant near the stairs and spoke with two guys and a young lady, and must have known them well because they were hugging, kissing, and shaking hands. While he was talking to them with his back toward us I saw his face, and he smiled at me. "Wow! Weird!" I said to Veronica. "Did you see that?"

She looked at me and said, "See what?"

"Didn't you see that?" I said again. "Like in a dream when something weird happens."

"Maybe this stuff," Veronica looked, and pointed at my margarita, "or that tea you had is kicking in again."

"Yeah, my second one. Wow!" I said. "I guess it takes time for the tequila to hit, but once it does, wham, like a hammer. Let's get out of here," I said.

"Could we have our check please?" Veronica said as the waitress walked by our table.

"Sure, I'll bring it right over."

"I'll take care of this," I said and grabbed the check as the waitress handed it to Veronica.

"I should pay for some of that, I invited you,"

"No, it's on me. I had the best time. Let's do it again, and again, and again."

"Okay, when?" she smiled.

"How about next weekend?" I said, "but I'll choose the restaurant, okay?"

"How much of a tip should I leave, John?"

"How about twenty bucks? She was really nice." We left the restaurant and headed downstairs.

"Let's listen to the music for a while, Veronica, since we're here, unless you want to get going. What do you think?"

"They sound pretty good don't they?"

"Yeah, they do," I said.

"There's your friend the painter dancing with that young woman he was talking to."

"Yeah— and look at him go," I said.

The painter was dancing up a storm. We watched them dance for a while, then ordered a couple of drinks. We found an empty table and sat down to enjoy the music.

"This band is really good, aren't they? I'm getting into the music," I said while tapping my hands and feet.

"Yeah, they're great!" Veronica said.

Just then the music stopped, and the lead singer of the band announced they were taking a break.

"You've got to dance my friends. It makes your blood hot," the painter said breathing heavily as he staggered to where we were sitting. "I need a drink."

"You look pretty hot out there on the dance floor. Who's the young lady?" I asked.

"This is Maria, my dance partner."

"Yeah, you both sure look good out there. Do you come here a lot?" Veronica asked.

"Yes, I love this place, and today is my birthday!"

"Oh, congratulations! Well—it's getting late, so we're heading out, see you around," I said as we shook hands.

While shaking hands he said, "Oh, too bad you're leaving so soon, my friend. Remember—I'm going to paint you a picture with birds."

"What's your number again?" I asked.

"I think you have it on the bag—right here," he said and pointed. "It's right here," he repeated, then shook Veronica's hand. "John, today you spent the afternoon with a lovely girl. Have a good night, too." Then, he turned toward Veronica. "It was lovely meeting you, Veronica. Don't get into any trouble." Just then the band started playing again. The painter looked at Maria and said, "Are you ready to go, Chiquita?" and they floated across floor.

Chapter Nineteen

We left Charlie's hand in hand for the wide open city. The music faded until only the clamor of traffic, and rumbling trains broke the soft evening air.

"So, where are you going now, John?"

"I should work on my book," I said. "I'd like to get as much done as possible before I leave. Going back to the bed and breakfast, I guess. What about you, Veronica?"

"I'll tag along with you," she said. "I'm taking the same train. You can tell me about your book."

We jumped on the train looking for a seat. "Let's sit over there," I said.

We sat down, and I moaned, "Man—am I full!" as I patted, and rubbed my stomach.

"Me, too," Veronica agreed, nodded, then put her hand on my face, and kissed me.

"Oh—I like that," I said.

"Are you planning to call Samantha again?"

"I don't know? I should just to make sure she's all right," I said. "I'll try later."

"Let's call her right now," Veronica said.

"Why now?" I asked.

"Just to know if she's all right."

"Okay, we'll give her a call when we get off the train. Let me read more of your poetry."

"You really like it?"

"Yeah," I said nodding, "I do! Very much."

She smiled, and handed me her leather journal as the train rattled down the track. I opened the journal to a poem called Sweet Music.

SWEET MUSIC
Whistle a natural sound
Hum a morning tune
Vibration in the afternoon
Drum when night comes
Becoming my voice
Laughter, cries, beating heart
Made from a piece of wood
Or steel, that glows
Spreading through and filling the room
Looking for an ear to feed
An echo floating on the wind
Then silence that grows
Hungry for more
I catch a dancing note
Before it hits the floor
And there is no way
To set it free
In the end
It must die with me

I looked at her. "It's sad, but beautiful," I said. "I think you're right about music. If it's not written down or recorded it's forgotten. What's this next one about?"

WATER
Glass raised to the lips;
Water trickles on the tongue!
Cold, refreshing sensation;
Held by the hands!
Ice cubes rattle;
Up the glass tips!
Into the body flows;
From the foundation of life!
To cleanse and purify;
The great need!
Pure crystal clear liquid of life;
Quench my thirst!
Just the sight of it flowing;
Fills me with joy!
Let me be first;
To wish you cheer!

"They're all great!" I said. "You have to publish this, you have to put it in print, I'll help you."

"My stop is coming up, she said."

I handed her the journal. "They're all fantastic, Veronica."

"We're here," she said, "this is my stop. You can read more on our next date, okay?"

We got off the train together. "Let's look for a pay phone to call Samantha," I said. "I don't want to use my cell phone. Never know what might happen if my number is connected with her somehow."

"I don't see any phones," Veronica said.

"There's one," I said and pointed, "next to that vending machine over there."

I dug in my pockets for some coins, and Samantha's number. "Here it is," I said. "Hope she's all right. Well, here goes," I said and dialed.

It rang and rang. I finnally hung up the phone. "There's no answer, maybe she's asleep."

"Try again," Veronica said as we both watched a train pull into the station and screech to a halt. I called the number again. "It's ringing," I said, then heard a sound, and said, "Hello, Samantha? Is that you?"

A faint whisper was all I heard, then a quiet, timid voice. "John, is that you?"

"Yes," I said, "are you okay?"

"I'm locked in a room at the travel agency," she said, "and I can't get out."

"Was it Zinty?" I asked.

"Yes, and he'll be back soon," she said mournfully. "Can you get me out?"

"Why did he lock you up at the travel agency?"

"I don't know," she said desperately. "Maybe you were right," she hesitated, "to get money from my father."

"He spotted us at the hotel," she said, "and somehow got into the room while you were in the shower and forced me to go with him," I could hear her voice crack. "After that he brought me here." I was wide awake now, and puzzled, as I looked at Veronica.

"What is she saying?" Veronica asked.

"Zinty snapped, and kidnapped Samantha to get money from her father," I said, holding my hand over the receiver. "I don't believe this guy. I told you he was nuts!"

"Listen, stay calm and just wait. We'll come and get you out."

"Who's we?" Samantha asked.

"I had dinner with a friend tonight. We're going there together, don't worry."

"Okay, but hurry before he gets back."

"We're on our way," I said. "Hold on!" I hung up the phone and looked at Veronica. "Still want to tag along?"

"Yes, I do."

"Well, let's get back on the train."

We went to the platform and waited for a train downtown. After we got on, Veronica didn't say much on the way to the *Pomona Travel Agency*. My heart was racing along with the clanging train as it rumbled down the tracks. I didn't know what to expect once we got to the travel agency. I looked at my watch. Eight-thirty in the evening, and felt like time had come to a standstill.

Chapter Twenty

"**W**e're almost there Veronica," I said, and turned to the hypnotizing lights of the city that reflected in glass as we drifted through the wind and down the iron track.

"How are you feeling?" I asked, then took her hand and held it firmly. "You're not saying much."

"Okay," Veronica said. "Just thinking about Samantha. I hope she's all right."

"I'm sure she's fine, Zinty's probably not even there," I said. "She's dramatic—that's how I read her, and likes to put on a performance. Her family's got a lot of money, so she's has a lot of time on her hands." I looked at Veronica and smiled. It's funny how life can be so unpredictable, I thought. One hour ago I was having dinner with a great looking girl, reading poetry, now I'm on my way to rescue someone. Am I dreaming? Is this all for real? I just got here yesterday, and now I'm going to rescue a girl.

"Is this actually happening, Veronica?" I asked. She looked at me and smiled. I stared out the window of the train again as the layout of the Pomona travel agency flashed in my mind along with different scenarios and possibilities of what could happen. I thought of the best way to get in, how to get Samantha out before Zinty shows up, and if he's at the travel agency—what to do then.

The train came to a screeching halt, and that was followed by an announcement, *Passengers please be careful when the doors open,* as the train reverberated in the loneliness of the empty evening train station. The noise from the iron wheels squealed in my ears when we stepped off the train, then we let out a gasp and jumped when the train's air brakes let out a blast behind us.

"We're getting edgy, John," Veronica said.

"I know." I closed my eyes for a moment and thought, calm down—relax.

"This is it, Veronica," I said. "The travel agency is a short walk from here, right across the street from a cafe."

"What's the plan, John Bird?"

"John Bird? You're calling me John Bird, now."

"It sounds like James Bond, and I feel like we're on a secret mission."

"Okay, right," I said, then thought, Man—oh—man, what are we doing? We're acting like children playing a game, this is serious business, and Zinty has a gun.

"I see some lockers over there. I'm putting my bag in one. How about you? There's enough room for yours, too." I said as I put the money in the coin slot.

"No, it's okay, I'll carry it."

"Done, let's go," I said and put the key in my pocket. "Let me give you an idea of the layout. When we got rid of Zinty the last time, I left through the back door, maybe we can get back in the same way." I looked at Veronica for a response, but she didn't say anything. I grabbed and nudged her shoulder, "Are you okay, Veronica?" I asked because she looked paralyzed.

"Yeah, I'm ready," she said anxiously then took a couple of deep breaths.

"Okay, so let's go around to the back. Follow me."

"Got it," Veronica took a few more deep breaths.

I turned and said, "Let's try to be quiet," then tripped and fell before I finished what I was saying.

"You, okay, John?" she asked, rushing over with a look of panic. "Okay?" she asked again.

"Yeah, I think so," I said and picked myself up off the ground. "I'm all right! Just got caught on something sticking up over there." I touched my leg where it hurt, then looked at my hand and saw blood. "Hell, I'm bleeding, I must have cut my leg on whatever it was, but I'll be okay." I brushed myself off. "Let's go."

"Is it bad? Do you want to stop? Go back?"

"No, I'll be all right." then let out a moan as I stood. "Let's keep going."

I took the lead with Veronica right behind, then looked up. "What was that?" I said and wiped my face, the sky dark and heavy. "It's not going to rain, is it?" As the words, *It's not going to rain,* rolled off my tongue heaven's tears slowly fell, tapping the leaves, painting the street, and soon turning into an intense cascading downburst that fell so hard I held my breath. We ducked under the overhang of a building in the alley. "I'm soaked," I said, "How about you, Veronica?"

Veronica looked at me, rain rolling down her cheeks and said, "What do you think?"

"Yeah, I guess you are, too," I said. "Having fun?"

"Yeah—most fun I've had this year," she said.

"We could wait it out?"

"Whatever you say, John Bird, you're in charge. I go where you go," she said and sneezed.

"Sorry, don't have anything to wipe your face."

"I'm okay," Veronica took a scarf from her bag, and wiped the water from her face.

"All right, we'll wait for a little while," I said watching the rain fall in buckets. "Let me tell you what I remember about the travel agency." I held up my hand pointing to it like a map. "When I left out the back door last time, I walked down a narrow dirt path between a fence, and a building that looked like a garage. I remember vines hanging down. We'll go down that path, and try to get in through the back door, okay?"

"What if we can't open the door?" she said.

"Then we'll try a window," I said, "or break one."

"That sounds like a good plan."

"I remember the back room being small, and connected to a larger room," I said. "We'll take it step by step because everything always looks different in the dark."

Veronica looked at me as I watched raindrops run down her face. I raised my hand and wiped them away as she said, "Thanks."

"I think once we're in the agency we should wait a bit, and get a feeling for what's happening just to be safe. I don't know much about Zinty, but he sounded like a lunatic on the phone. He's a cop, and used to these circumstances," I said. "We'll just take it slow and easy first, find Samantha, and get her out."

"That all sounds good," Veronica said. "Play it safe, I get it. I'm with you, John."

"Okay, let's go," I said. "Ready?"

She gave me the thumbs up and said, "Yes."

"This is the way to the back of the agency," I said, "Follow me."

The rain echoed off the street drenching us while lightning bolts grazed the sky, then both of us jumped after a massive clap of thunder exploded like cannon fire.

"Man," I yelled. "That scared the crap out of me."

"And that felt pretty close, too," Veronica said, "and went right through my body."

"I hate all of this sneaking around," I said.

"It's for Samantha," Veronica said. "You're doing it for her, and she needs our help."

"Yeah, we're almost there," I said and stopped for a moment, then turned, looked at Veronica, and gave her a kiss on the lips. "You okay?"

"Yeah, I'm okay. What was that for?" she asked.

"For good luck!" I said then she kissed me.

"What was that for?" I asked.

She smiled. "More good luck!"

A steady stream of rain fell from the roof first hitting us, then forming puddles at our feet. Veronica cupped her hands under the pouring rain, collecting some, and splashing it on her face. I did the same.

"It's not letting up, but let's keep going," I said. "Maybe the storm will make good cover. We won't have to be as quiet, and it'll drown out our movements." I looked at Veronica and said, "What do you think?"

"Now, or never, I guess," Veronica said.

A lightning bolt struck and shook the ground as we made our way down the small alley. I stopped again and turned. "All right, Veronica?"

"Fine," she mumbled, "keep moving." We dodged the vines that hung from a lattice above which blocked some rain, but the path was slippery, and we were soaked.

"I wish we had a light," I said.

"I have a small light in my bag. Just a second."

I looked at her. "You're amazing."

"Here it is," she said, then turned on the light, and pointed it at the ground. "Better than nothing."

"Great, now we can at least see where we're walking." We moved slowly measuring our steps. "There's the door over there. Let's try to open it," I whispered, and turned the door handle. "It won't budge," I said, and tried again. "It must be locked." I turned toward Veronica. "Well, that didn't work."

We were turning into dripping wet sponges soaking up everything, and there was no space left for anymore water. I tried pulling on the door one more time without any luck.

"Let's try this window over here," Veronica said. "I think we can get it open; it feels loose. Let's push together and maybe it'll give." We pushed, but with wet hands couldn't get a good grip.

"Try, one more time," we grabbed the window. I grunted, "Push hard!" it gave way, then slid up with a bang.

"Do you think anyone heard that?" Veronica said.

"Don't know," I said, "I hope not."

"Me, too," and gave me a raised shoulders, I don't know, worried look.

I crawled through the window first, then as quietly as possible dropped to the floor. Water splattered all over, and I was soaked to the bone. My clothes were completely saturated with a virtual lake was rising around me.

"Are you in?" Veronica whispered. "John?" she whispered, "Okay?"

"I am now," I said. "Your turn give me your hand."

Veronica climbed in and said, "It's really dark, isn't it?" We sat quietly huddled together in the small dark room. "This reminds me of a movie I saw where people go into a house, and no one gets out alive."

I looked at Veronica and said, "That's something I

didn't need to hear." The Door's song, "Five to One" rang in my head as a flash of lightning lit the room, and we could see each other's face clearly for a split second.

"Spooky, isn't it?" Veronica whispered.

Other than the rain and thunder, it was quiet. "How long are we going to stay here, I'm cold?"

I whispered back, "I don't know, just a little longer to see what's going on, let's make sure it's safe."

"Okay," she whispered.

In the back room where we were I saw some shelves to the right of the door that led to a bigger room. "I'm going to crawl over to the door," I whispered, "Stay here. I'll check if it's clear, okay?"

"Okay," she whispered back.

On hands and knees I crawled across the floor, grabbed the door knob, turned it, and slightly pushed open the door. I could just barely see into the next room. I looked at Veronica and whispered, "I don't hear or see anything. I think it's okay, come on over." and signaled with a wave of my hand. Except for the occasional thunder and rumbles that rattled the windows it seemed safe.

"Is it a good sign that it's so quiet?" Veronica asked.

"Don't know, but any noise we make will be covered up by the rain and thunder, so the storm turned out to be a blessing in disguise," I said. "How are you holding up?"

"I'm okay. What now?"

Since the door was open only a crack my view was narrow and obscure. "Let's just wait a few minutes for our eyes to adjust to the dark," I whispered to Veronica, "so we can judge the landscape better. After a moment I asked, "Hear anything, Veronica? Do you think it's safe?"

"I don't know. I guess it's okay," she whispered back. "My legs are getting sore from crouching."

"Okay, here we go," I said and opened the door a

little more. "It still looks okay," I whispered. "Let's open it wide enough to get through, and crawl across the room?"

"That sounds good to me," she whispered. "Who's going first?"

"I'll go first, and you stay here until I give you the thumbs up. If anything strange happens—run like hell!" I whispered.

"Run where?" Veronica nervously whispered back.

"Go out the window if you have to," I said, and pointed to the one we had just crawled through.

I moved across the floor through a room that led out to the front office. I opened another door, but didn't hear a peep. Now, I thought it was strange. "What's going on here? Where's Samantha?" I turned to Veronica puzzled and shrugged.

Then, Veronica looked at me, her mouth wide open, screaming my name, "John—John!" I watched stunned, thinking, What the hell's going on? "Help!," she cried.

She hit the floor, her head bounced, and her eyes were wide with fright. She clawed and scratched at the floor with her outstretched arms trying to stop herself from being dragged behind the door. After a solid slamming thud, it closed on one more muffled shriek of Veronica calling my name, then she vanished in the darkness.

"Veronica—" I yelled, and was on my feet faster than you can say mixed biscuits three times. I ran to the door, twisted and turned the door knob, but it was locked. I stood back and kicked the door again and again with the bottom of my foot, but it wouldn't budge.

"John!" she screamed through the door, "Help!" in a wild, shrieking voice heavy with pain.

"Veronica—Veronica," I shouted wildly.

I threw my shoulder into the door like a hammer, a wrecking ball tearing down a highrise building. I winced as

I crashed into it again and again, until it broke free. "Veronica," I yelled, sifting through the shadows untangling the silent air, armed only with a marching pulse.

"Veronica! Are you all right?" I said in a sorrowful tone. "Where are you?"

"Over here by the window," I heard her moan. "Someone grabbed my leg and pulled me back. He was powerful, John, so strong," her breathing suffocating, and mixed with cries. "Let's get out of here."

"It's okay, it's okay. I'll get you out," I said. "Can you stand?"

"I'll try."

"Here, put your arm over my shoulder."

"What's wrong?" I asked because she had trouble keeping her balance and was struggling to walk.

"My knee! I can't walk," she said losing her balance.

"Not at all?" I asked. "Just a little bit? Come on. I'll help you. We can't stay here. Let's head out the back door."

"I have to stop, John, please!" her face radiated agony.

"Rest here while I unlock the door." Veronica leaned against the wall holding onto a file cabinet, but as I watched, thought, She'll crumble soon. I got the door open, and put Veronica's arm around my neck again supporting her.

"You can do it, Veronica," I said as we stepped out through the door, and into rain that poured down on us like water over stones in a stream.

"We'll be out of this soon," I said taking deep breaths.

The darkness was consuming, and I felt Zinty in the shadows. His presence rising around us like sulfur being expelled from the earth's crust.

"I'll be okay, she said."

As we stepped through the door to make our way toward the alley I growled in pain, and agony, after a sharp sting cut through my back followed by a force that propelled us forward. Hapless, we fell to the ground like a pair trees that had been chopped down. I landed on my chest with a thud leaving me breathless, the wind knocked out, coughing and spitting up water and mud. As I tried catching my breath I saw Veronica covered in mud lying on her back, holding her leg. Something solid had struck us *hard* from behind. On the ground in shock, weary, trying to come to my senses, I heard the hollow clunking sound of something fall. With my right arm wiped the mud from my eyes, turned, and saw a 2x4 with spikes on one end, glistening in the rain. Luckily we were only hit by the board.

"I told you to stay away from Samantha," the same voice I'd heard on the phone barked. "She's part of my family!" As the shadowy figure got closer, and after a flash of lightning, I saw Zinty's ragged faced, then heard a click. What's that sound? I thought, then realized it was a gun being cocked. Once more I brushed the water and mud from my face, looked up, and saw a gun barrel pointed squarely between my eyes. Bob Dylan's "Knockin' on Heaven's Door" went through my head as I watched the wet dripping gun barrel glimmering in the rain.

In the next moment my reflexes took over. With my hands behind me I braced myself, rolled to the right, picked up the board he had used on me, and swung it like a sledge hammer. I fell again, but heard, and felt the solid thud of the board making contact with the front of his shins. I let go of the board. As he backed away, I saw it stuck to his legs. The spikes at end pierced, and were buried deep, through and out the back of his legs.

He howled in agony as lightning lit the sky. He screamed, "You son of—" His face ugly with hate and agony as thunder exploded, and vibrated through my bones. The board still stuck to his legs as the gun slipped from his hand, fell to the ground, and into mud. He let out more painful moans as I watched him grab, rotate, then pry the board off. Blood mixed with rain dripped to the ground. Under the lightning I saw Zinty's cold grey eyes, and clearly knew he was going to kill us. An injured animal fighting for its life, he stumbled and fell, water splashing, mud covering him. He stood slowly and growled, "I'm going to rip out your heart—you . . ." as his legs gave way he fell again before finishing his rant. He picked himself up and came toward me dragging his feet through the mud.

This is our last chance, I thought. If he gets hold of me I'm a dead man, and Veronica a dead woman. Scrambling, I blindly ran my hands along the ground in the mud and water to find the gun. "There you are," I muttered, under what I thought would be my last breath my breath.

I jumped. "Got it!" Mud and water splashed in my face stinging my eyes, filling my mouth, then as quickly as I could with the back of my hand, wiped my face. When I opened my eyes I saw Veronica lying on the ground. "Veronica," I yelled as I watched her holding her knee, crying in pain, and trying to get up. "Stay there!" I shouted, then turned toward Zinty who was limping toward me. He looked confused, shaken, and was bleeding, but wasn't backing down. I had to do something.

"When I get my hands on you I'm going to rip your face off," he said, and came closer, slowly inching along.

"Stop!" I yelled. "Stop!"

"I'm going to take my gun back," he barked! "Use it to blow your brains out, then she's next," he said, and pointed to Veronica as he stumbled closer.

There was no talking with Zinty. It was him or me. One of us was getting shot, I had the gun, and decided it wasn't going to be me. I raised it—aimed—and—pulled the trigger. There was a flash; a thunderous crack from the barrel. It lit the night and blinded me for a second. Again, I pulled the trigger, again and again, "You're going to stop now," I said. I wasn't taking any chances and emptied the gun. The shots echoed like a bass drum as spent shells flew in the air, until the only sound was the clicking of the trigger, and the falling rain. Zinty wobbled, fell backwards crashing against the door knocking it open. He ending up flat on his back on the threshold making gurgling sounds, his feet gesticulating wildly as I watched him die.

I stumbled over to Veronica. "Are you okay?" was all I could manage to get out because I was breathing like a steam engine, and my heart was pounding like a jack-hammer all the way down to my toes.

"I think so," Veronica said panting, trying to catch her breath.

The rain continued to fall while the lightning occasionally broke the night. We were soaked, covered in mud, blood, and cold, but we were alive—Zinty wasn't. I walked over and studied him as he lay in the doorway. His feet were still shaking, his body jerking as I held the gun to his face. His head came up a little, then he lifted his torso bracing himself with his arms. He was looking directly at me trying to mumble something.

"You . . ." thunder cracked, ". . . asshole," I said and pulled the trigger, but had forgotten that the gun was empty. There was only a clicking sound like fingers snapping, then I lowered the gun. He wasn't moving at all, and was finished. I wasn't sure how many times I had shot him, but there was blood everywhere on the door, floor, and windows. I didn't move. I stood silent looking up to the dark sky as the Bob Marley song, "I Shot the Sheriff" looped over and over in my mind. I stood over Zinty, wiped the rain from my face, and thought, You asshole, then screamed, "This is bullshit! Why is this happening?"

Chapter Twenty-one

I walked over to Veronica, she looked at me as rain rolled down her cheeks, and asked, "What about Samantha? Do you think . . .? Do you think . . ." she paused, the words wouldn't come out. Veronica couldn't say it, so I finished the sentence.

"Dead? I don't know," I said breathing hard. "I'm sorry you had to get involved in this Veronica."

"What are we going to do?" Veronica's voice was shaky, she was holding her knee, deeply in pain, trying to calm herself by keeping in her tears.

"First, let's get out of the rain," I said.

I grabbed her arm, picked her up, and carried her inside out of the rain. We stepped over Zinty, who was blocking the doorway, his body halfway in the building, his legs outside floating in a pool of rainwater and blood. We made our way through the door, looking down at him, careful not to step on the body or slip on the wet floor. Then, Veronica screamed, "His eyes . . . his eyes are open! He's moving! He's still alive!"

"Impossible! I shot him, so many times," I said. He could be wearing a bullet-proof vest. Hurry, get inside." With my help, Veronica hobbled in while I kept my eyes locked on Zinty.

I got a chair for her, but she felt more comfortable on the floor. Veronica rested as I checked Zinty, holding the gun on him all the time, even though it was empty. I kicked his lifeless body a few times, but there was no movement, or reaction. I stepped closer and jabbed him with the barrel of the gun, no sign of life. I put my hand on his neck and felt for a pulse; there was none, just his blood on my hand. I wiped it off on my pants, like paint, and looked at Veronica. "Should I bring him in or leave him outside?"

Veronica looked at me, our eyes met, then after taking a deep breath she said, "What! No, leave him outside."

"Okay, I'll pull him outside." I put the gun on the floor, grabbed Zinty by his feet, and dragged him under a table near an overhang in the back of the building. His head bounced on the ground after falling from the threshold of the door. "Sorry, Zinty," I said, then added, "You asshole."

Under a pouring cascade of rain I quickly went through his pockets, thinking I might find something to help us. There was a wallet, a wad of hundred dollar bills, and a picture of Samantha that fell out of his shirt pocket when I turned him over. His right hand landed palm up, and that's when I noticed something odd. What are those marks on his fingertips? I thought, and touched them. Just like the blind guy, and like the homeless guy. I ran back into the building and brushed off the rain, "How are you, Veronica?" I asked. "Look! I found this wallet, some money, and this picture of Samantha. I handed the photo to Veronica.

"It's too dark. I can't see it very well," she said, and tried looking at it again, moving it near the window. "Can we turn on a light?"

"Let's talk about what we're going to do before we turn on any lights," I said.

"We have to call the police. That guy out there is dead."

"What'll we say to the police?"

"We tell them the truth. That you shot him because he was attacking us, and going to kill us."

"Yeah, and then I spend the rest of my life in prison for murder."

"You won't go to jail. He was trying to kill us. They'll understand."

"Maybe we should just leave before anyone comes."

"We can't," then Veronica looked up at me. "Did you hear that?"

"Yeah! Where's it coming from?" I walked over behind a counter. "There's a door over here." I said.

"Where does it go?" Veronica asked.

I turned the door knob. "It looks like it goes downstairs to a basement."

After I opened the door we clearly heard someone groaning and whimpering.

"It sounds like a women crying for help," Veronica said.

"I'll go down and check it out," I said.

"Be careful."

"Just give me a minute to take a look. I'll be right back, don't move," I whispered forcefully while holding up my hand like a traffic cop. "Stay there!"

I touched, and rubbed my hand along the wall where I thought a light switch might be.

"Here's one!" I switched it on. "Well that's not much of a light," I said as a soft glow cast its way up to the top of the stairs. After a few steps down I could smell the nasty mildew rising from the damp basement. I imagined a ghoul or zombie lurking in a corner, jumping out, but it was quiet except for the squeaky steps, and the faraway lonely murmurs. I should have a club or something, I thought, or Zinty's gun.

"Shit!" I groaned, closed my eyes, then tore off the cobwebs that covered my face like a dry silky mask. "I hate spiders, damn," I said brushing off the rest of the web. I stood still on the old staircase bracing against the wall to keep my balance. The murmuring grew louder as I followed the worn out stairway down, listening to the old wood creak with every step, this was odd because from the outside the place looked so elegant. In the darkness, I felt and measured each step moving my feet back and forth over the width of each one, testing its strength before proceeding. Now at the bottom, the small glow was the sole source of light. I fought off more cobwebs, then under the halo of light to the left saw an old gargantuan furnace, beyond that another dark space where the cries originated.

From the top of the stairs I heard Veronica's hollow echo. "Everything okay?"

I turned, and saw her at the top of the staircase.

"Stay there! It's too dangerous for you to come down. I'm walking over to a door on the other side. Stay there."

"Okay," she said, "I'll wait."

"There's got be another light switch," I muttered as I searched up and down, groping the walls in the dark. Then I found one and flipped it on. Nothing happened. I flipped it on and off again and again, still nothing happened. I felt another switch next to the one I was turning on and off. Maybe this one will work, I thought. "All right," I said and looked up, "The light's bright enough to see all around," and continued down the narrow hallway.

On the right was a door which I tried opening. It was locked. More sounds came from behind the door. "Samantha?" I said, then heard a crashing sound like a chair falling over. My right shoulder was sore from knocking the other door down, so I rammed into this one with my left side. It wouldn't budge. I need something to open the door? I thought, and looked around.

"Samantha, are you okay?" I said through the door.

"Yes, I'm fine, but the door is locked."

"Okay, hold on,'" I said. "I'm going to find something to knock down the door."

"Hurry, please," she said, "before Zinty gets back."

"Oh—we don't have to worry about him," I said in a calm relaxed tone.

"Yes we do! He's crazy—he'll kill us," she said, her voice excited, and filled with fear.

"Trust me," I said. "We don't have to worry about Zinty."

I went over by the furnace and looked around. I picked up a board, but it felt, too light, then found a big heavy piece of pipe that I gripped like a baseball bat. This should do the job, and swung it, ready to hit a home-run.

"Stand back, Samantha," I said. "I'm going to start bashing on the door. You don't want to get hurt."

I lifted the pipe and started to clobber the door. "It's working," I said with splinters of the door flying through the air. "I'll have it open soon." After I swung a few more times the door flew open. I saw her on the floor in the corner of the room. "Samantha!"

She stood, ran over, and held on to me while whispering my name, then collapsed in my arms.

"You'll be okay," I said. "Everything's okay now."

She looked exhausted, held on tightly, and wouldn't let go, then cried, "He grabbed me, brought me here, and locked me in this room!" She was catching her breath, crying, and talking all at the same time, "I didn't know what was going to happen. Where is he? Where is he?" she repeated, then she rested her head on my shoulder.

"Don't worry," I said, "Zinty's not a problem anymore, and he'll never bother you again."

"Yes, he will. He'll never stop. We've got to get out before he gets back."

"Everything's okay, don't worry, I took care of Zinty."

She looked at me troubled, and asked, "What do you mean?"

"Not now, let's go upstairs, Veronica's waiting."

"Who's Veronica?"

"You don't know her, she's a friend, and hurt. We've got to call the police, and get her some medical attention."

"Does Zinty need a doctor?" she asked.

"No, he needs an undertaker," I said.

"He's—"

"Yes, he's dead," I said. "As dead as a thing can be, dead, forever and ever!"

"How?" she asked.

"I shot him," I said, "with his gun."

"He was a cop, John, he has friends, cop friends, and knows important people."

"It was self-defense. Veronica saw everything, he was trying to kill us, and there was nothing else I could do. We'd be dead now if—" Samantha started crying. "It's okay, Samantha. It'll be okay, let's go upstairs."

We saw Veronica sitting on the top step waiting for us. She stood, leaned, and braced against the wall when she saw us. "John . . ." Veronica said, and smiled at Samantha as we made our way up the stairs. "You, all right?"

"Go ahead, Samantha, then I'll follow." I looked at Veronica and asked, "Can you walk?" as I helped Samantha to a chair.

Veronica tried to walk, but couldn't. "My leg feels as heavy as lead," she said as she sat on the floor holding it outstretched; cringing. "My knee's in bad shape. I can hardly move it."

"Samantha," I said, "is there a light in here that we can turn on?"

She pointed to a switch behind the door. I turned it on, and saw blood on the floor near the back door where I had shot Zinty. Samantha walked over to the window, and stood next to the door in a puddle of it, looking down at the floor, at her shoes, then—at me.

Shoes, something Zinty won't need anymore, I thought, not where he's going, then said, "Why don't you come over here, Samantha?" I watched her for a moment. She looked confused, looking around imagining what had happened, then a long stare out the window. She was trying to find Zinty, but she couldn't see through the darkness.

"Where is he?" Samantha asked compassionately.

The rain slammed against the window like machine gun fire as I walked over and stood next to her, "Don't worry. He can't hurt you now." Then lightning set the sky ablaze and we saw his body lying outside near the table. She jumped back into my arms, turned, and buried her head in my chest, "It's okay. Everything's okay," I said, and looked out the window watching Zinty's body being pummeled with rain, then a streak of lightning, and burst of thunder rattled through the window, and us. Samantha grabbed and held me tight. I looked over at Veronica watching us embrace by the window. I shook my head and shrugged, as if to say, What—am I supposed to do?

"Let's get away from the window. Sit here while I help

Veronica." Veronica's face was filled with pain as she clutched her knee.

"How can I make you more comfortable?"

"I don't think you can," she said, her anxious eyes flaring. "I need a doctor. You've got to get me to a hospital. The pain's getting worse."

I walked over to Samantha. "We've got to do something," I said. "Veronica's hurt, and needs a doctor. I've got to call an ambulance, and the police. This is going to be a big deal! Lots of news reporters, cameras, questions. Are you going to be all right? Can you handle it, Samantha? Is there anything you want me to do, or anyone you want me to call?"

"Do what you have to. Make the call."

"Veronica," I said as she looked at me her face tight with anguish and pain, "I'm calling a doctor for you. Hold on." I grabbed the phone. A million thoughts went through my mind. "What do I tell them?" I said, then dialed 9-1-1.

The phone rang, and a woman's voice asked, "What is the nature of your emergency?"

"I need an ambulance, and the police. A man's been shot, and he's dead. The ambulance is for two women, one has an injured leg, and she's in a lot of pain."

"What's the address?"

"I don't know just a second."

"Samantha, I've got the 911 dispatcher on the line, and I need the address for this place."

Samantha looked at me and said, "It's 1600 Chandler Street."

"Okay."

"Sir, are you there?" the dispatcher asked.

"Yes," I said. "It's 1600 Chandler Street."

"Is anyone else hurt?"

"No, I mean, yes, there's a girl with an injured knee."

"Where was the man shot? And, how do you know he's dead?"

"He was shot more than once—I checked—he's definitely dead."

"Is the person who shot him still there?"

"Yes, I shot him."

"Was the shooting an accident?"

"No, it wasn't an accident. I shot him in self-defense because he was trying to kill me."

"What's the name of the victim who was shot?"

"His name is Nick Zinty."

"What's your name, sir?"

"My name is John Bird Ray."

"Is the weapon still on the premises?"

"Yes it is, and I've got it."

"What are the injuries again?"

"There are two women, one has an injured leg, it's her knee and ankle. The other woman was locked in a room for a long time. I don't think she has any serious injuries. She's just upset and in shock."

"Sir, an ambulance is on the way," the dispatcher said. "Just stay there and remain calm."

"Okay," I said, and there was only a dial tone. I looked at the girls.

"They're going to be here soon, so now we just wait." I sat down at the counter. Samantha was over by Veronica trying to make her comfortable. Lightning struck, flashed across the sky, and I caught another glimpse of Zinty's body floating in a puddle. I'm glad it's over, I thought. Wow, what a night, what—a—night!

Chapter Twenty-two

We felt apprehensive and restless waiting for the police. The silence in the room painful, and haunting, as we listened to each other breathing over the rain-smacked windows and occasional groan of thunder. It became so agonizing that I held my breath as long as I could, then the Simon & Garfunkel song, "Sounds of Silence" was in my mind along with the thumping of my heart. Veronica was in obvious pain and continually moving around on the floor to get comfortable. Samantha stood by the window peering into the blackness, *and me*, I sat on a stool at the counter still reeling from blowing Zinty away. As I moved, it squeaked, irritatingm, like an old wound or blister being torn off. On the counter in front of me was the vehicle of destruction, but also our savior. Emanating from it, and floating in the air, was a whiff of gun powder spurring an instant replay of hazy images evoking the ghosts of what I had just done. I suppose it's true, I thought, what I had read and written about the sense of smell as more images of gunfire, and Zinty dead in the mud, flipped in my mind.

My fingertips were felt numb, so I rubbed my hands, clenched my fists, then cracked my knuckles. What's going to happen to us now? I covered my face with my hands, then looked up at the ceiling and muttered, "How did this happen?" then let out a sigh as I thought about what I would say to the police. I looked at Veronica and Samantha, they were watching me, and the moment our eyes met, and locked in—I knew how they felt.

I stood, and walked over to Samantha. "Are you okay?" then, as lightning lit the darkness we saw Zinty outside under the table. His water-logged body floating in a pool of water and mud like a stranded whale.

"Everything—will be okay, Samantha," I said. She looked at me and smiled, then I asked Veronica how she was feeling, but before she could answer, the silence between the rumbles of thunder was broken by the shrill cry of sirens echoing outside.

"Here they come," Samantha said.

First, we heard some muffled thumping on the wooden doors in the front of the travel agency. "Sounds like they're trying to get in through the front," I said.

We heard something collide into the door, then a loud crash. As we watched toward the front where the pounding noise drummed, the police burst through the back door dripping wet, guns in hand—pointed straight at us. An officer's face flaring as he shouted, "Everyone, put your hands behind your head." Then he commanded, "Right now! And—don't move."

My hands shot up as police swarmed in from everywhere like bees. Soon the room was overflowing with uniforms and suits. "What's your name? "Identify yourself!"

"I'm the one who called," I said with my hands raised behind my head. "I made the 911 call."

Still pointing his gun, ready to fire, the officer looked at me, then ordered, "Stand over there, put your hands flat against the wall, and don't move."

"Okay—okay," I repeated, following his instructions precisely, and stood against the wall.

"This guy's okay," the officer said after searching me then asked, "What's your name?"

"John Bird Ray," I mumble, "and that's Veronica Wrigley on the floor over there, she needs an ambulance. Her knee's injured and she can't walk at all," I said with my face hammered against the wall. The officer had his forearm buried into the back of my neck, but I could turn my head enough to see another cop talking to Samantha.

"It's okay, the place is clear," I heard someone say from the other side of the room. "Send in the paramedics."

"Can I speak to Veronica?" I asked the officer.

"Sure," he said, "go ahead."

I put my hands down when the officer released his grip, turned, and saw a parade of people dripping a trail of water on the floor. A continuous caravan hauling in equipment from the front door to the back, where Zinty was floating in his private pool.

Through the window I saw more and more flashlights shining, glaring, and camera flashes flickering as a small group of police investigators gathered around his body.

"It looks like they're putting up, or building a structure over Zinty's body," I said.

The hypnotizing camera flashes combined with lightning was quite a show. This is all for you, Zinty, I thought, then wondered what would happen to us.

"What are they doing out there in the rain?" Veronica asked as she leaned against the wall, and closed her eyes.

"They're collecting evidence before taking away Zinty's carcass," I said.

Veronica opened her eyes, and looked at me. "Don't worry, John," she said. "It was self defense. We'll tell them."

"I know—I know," I said.

Then, a rain soaked gray haired guy wearing a long beige coat, maybe in his fifties, walked into the room. I could tell he was in charge by the way he directed the show. In a gravely voice he said, "I want to see the body, but first talk to the witnesses, and the person who made the 911 call."

As he turned, the officer gave me an intense stare. I couldn't hear, but read the officer's lips as he pointed at me, *That's him over there.* Great, now I'm famous, I thought.

"Okay, I'll start with him," the man in the beige raincoat said, then took out a notepad, jotted some notes down, and marched my way. I whispered, "*My Way,* Frank Sinatra sang that song, and he looks a little like him, too." The melody of it danced through my mind while a guy with a camera started to carefully take pictures of everything in the room. Then, Mr. My Way, introduced himself, "I'm Detective Mussear," he said, "I'm in charge of the case. What's your name?"

"Hello, I'm John Bird Ray," I said, then wondered if I should shake hands—better not, I thought.

"I have to inform you that before you say anything, you can have a lawyer present."

"Okay, I understand, but I don't have anything to hide," I said. "I want to be up front and open."

He looked at me with his steady clear blue eyes, and asked, "Can you tell me what happened here tonight?"

I looked at the lines of experience frozen on his face.

"It was self defense! I was saving my life, and Veronica's. That's her over there on the floor, and her leg needs attention. She can't walk," I said, "that's why she's on the floor. The other girl is Samantha, and I found her locked in the basement. We came here to help her."

"Okay," he said with a probing stare. "Let's start with how you know the dead guy?"

"I don't really!" I said wide eyed. "We met on the train, then I helped Samantha get away from him."

"How did you meet her?" he asked.

"She's just an acquaintance. We met on the train a day ago, then here at the agency."

"She invited you here?" he asked.

"No, not exactly," I mumbled slowly and quietly, "not really. I was walking down the street and noticed the brochures in the window," I said, then pointed to the front of the travel agency.

"You were walking by and stopped to look at the pictures in the window?"

"Yeah, I was standing over there outside looking in, when she asked me to come into the travel agency. First we talked about traveling, then she told me about Zinty. At first I didn't recognize her, but then remembered her from the train, she gave me her telephone number."

"Zinty's the big guy floating in the puddle outside?" he asked.

"Yeah, he's the guy outside," I said. "The guy who tried to kill us. Am I being arrested?"

"Let's determine what happened before I arrest you," he said. "Tell me more."

"So, you are going to arrest me?"

"Well, I'm leaning in that direction," he said with a broad grin, "with everything I've heard so far. You don't have to tell me anymore until you have a lawyer present."

"I don't have a lawyer, and if I did," I said, "it wouldn't change the fact that I shot him."

"You shot him?"

"Yes, yes, I shot him," I said frustrated, "because he was going to kill us."

"Are you sure you want to tell me this," he asked as he wrote in his notepad.

"Yes," I said, "I want to! I'm not involved in any conspiracy. It's what happened." Then I told him in one breath. "Samantha was reading a book on the train. I wanted to talk to her, but she got off the train before I had the chance to say anything to her."

"Who was reading the book on the train?" he asked.

"Samantha," I said. "That's her over there by the window."

"And, you two met recently?"

"Yes, that's right. Just yesterday. after I got into town."

"She told you about Zinty?"

"Yes," I said. "She thought someone had hired him to follow her, and wanted to get away, and asked me to help. That's all I know about Zinty."

"Whose idea was it?" he asked. "Yours?"

"Idea?" I asked. "You mean to get away from Zinty?"

"Yeah, who came up with the idea?"

"I guess we both did."

"So, you wanted to play detective?"

"I don't know—it just happened. Like I said, I just got here a few days ago, and came to Chicago for inspiration. I'm writing a book."

"You're a writer?"

"It's my first book—first novel," I said. "I thought I could meet some people, check out some places that would inspire me, but never imagined that anything like this would happen."

"Where are you from?"

"I'm from Lacrosse."

"Where's that?"

"South of Minneapolis, on the Mississippi River."

"You do anything else other than write?"

"I'm a photographer."

"What kind of pictures do you take?"

"Mostly weddings and portraits, but any photography work I can round up."

"Is this your gun?" he said as he held it up to show me.

"Yes, I—mean—no! That's it—but it's not mine."

"Whose gun is it?" he asked.

"It's Zinty's gun," I said, and went on painting a picture of the shooting. "He dropped it. I saw it in the mud after I hit him in the knees with the board. He charged me like a maniac, like a linebacker sacking a QB, an unstoppable tank. I grabbed the gun, started squeezing the trigger, and let him have it! Emptied it . . . he finally stopped."

"You had no other choice?"

"Choice—choice!" I repeated. "Have you seen how big he is? He's was going to kill me. I had to defend myself."

"But he was unarmed, right?" Mussear said. "He didn't have a gun, did he?"

"No, he didn't," I said, "I did," and ended my defense with, "and wasn't taking any chances."

"Maybe I would have done the same thing," Mussear said and nodded.

"He hurt Veronica's leg when he dragged her out of the office—I erupted. It all happened, so fast, it's a blur, like a dream," I said. "There was nothing else I could do."

"I know what you mean," he said. "Everyone says the same thing when they try to recall events from the past. You'll recall more, later."

"Yeah, you're probably right." I said, and turned to watch the paramedics who were taking care of Veronica.

While he wrapped her injured leg, one paramedic said, "Miss! We're going to lift you up on a gurney, just remain still, okay. I've immobilized your leg." While working fast he told her, "I've given you something for the pain. You're in good hands. Now, here we go," the same paramedic said as they did some last minute preparations before lifting her, and checking to make sure everything was secure. "Okay, are you ready?"

Veronica managed to mumble, "Yes, I'm ready," as the painkiller started taking affect leaving her glassy eyed, and incoherent.

"Okay, one, two, three, and lift," he said, and in one quick motion, they had her safe on the gurney. I watched the paramedics take Veronica out to the ambulance. Samantha followed with one last look toward me. I couldn't hear, but I read her lips. *Bye, John,* as they carried her out of the travel agency.

"I'd like to go the hospital with them, if it's all right with you, detective?" I said.

He looked at me with serious eyes, and after a moment of silence said, "Sorry, I can't let you do that," then added, "these two officers will escort you downtown. You'll have to stay in custody until we finish our investigation."

"Am I being arrested?" I asked again.

"Well, not exactly, you're a suspect in a shooting, and it's procedure," he said. "We've got to take you in for questioning. You should be able to get out on bail, but that's up to a judge." Mussear turned toward an officer with a square face and said, "Take Mr. Ray downtown."

Shaking my head I muttered, "I don't believe this is happening." I felt like I'd been crushed under the wheels of a car, and dragged away. My body was numb as I watched the detective, and other police. I wondered what he's thinking. "Sorry, I can't remember your name," I said.

"Lieutenant Mussear," he said, "and I'm in charge of the case. If you have any questions, I'll answer them for you later, okay? These officers will take you to headquarters, I'll see you there." That was the last word from him as he walked outside into the pouring rain where Zinty floated face down in a pool of black water.

How's the view at the bottom of the world, Zinty? I thought.

"Okay, let's go," the officer standing next to me said in a commanding voice, then motioned with his hand for me to walk in front. "That way—to the car."

I watched the rain dance on the showroom windows as we walked to the front of the agency. "Is your car parked nearby?" I asked.

"Right outside in front," the officer said.

As we got closer to the front of the agency I saw the red flashing lights from the patrol cars, and ambulances, reflecting off the street, and in the raindrop covered display windows of the agency. We walked out through the arched doors into a cluster of officers holding back a small crowd of people. Amazing, I thought, watching them trying to get closer. Pouring rain and still they come out to see the circus. It feels like a turkey shoot with all of the lights and cameras.

Some people in the crowd were snapping pictures as I watched the ambulance with Veronica and Samantha drive away. Then, like in a Sam Peckenpah movie, everything was one long moment on the way to the patrol car, all in slow motion. The two officers looked at me and smiled, their heads moving in slow motion. One spoke in a husky, deep slow motion voice, *That's the car over there*, his arm moving slowly, fighting gravity as he pointed to the patrol car. *Right over there*, then he motioned for me to get in. I watched the traffic pass in slow motion under the driving rain, water purling down my face and into my mouth, every detail slow and clear. People in the street were phantoms glowing under dripping street lights. Others were gawking and howling out of their car windows as they drove by. I turned for one last look at the travel agency as the Jimi Hendrix song "Purple Haze" flooded my head.

Chapter Twenty-three

I got into the back seat of the patrol car watching the reflections of the red revolving lights in the travel agency's windows. Raindrops echoed as they dropped from the coal-black sky like massive clear stones exploding on impact with the ground. From the patrol car I saw the police moving in a hypnotic whirling motion, going in and out of the building with boxes and bags. As we drove between the hordes, the nauseating, pulsating red glowing waves of light washed away the darkness.

"Give them a blast of the siren," the officer in the passenger seat said. When the siren erupted the multitude parted like the Red Sea, but muscled closer for a peek of the passenger. I turned for one last look of the travel agency when I heard a rumble, then a dark heavy grumble vibrated through the stark falling rain. First, I thought it was thunder, but the sky lit up in a violent red glow that hovered above the city like an alien space ship preparing for landing.

"What was that?" I said, while looking at the officers in the front seat of the patrol car.

"Yeah, what was that?" both of them said simultaneously. Both officers rolled down their windows, stuck their heads out, and looked back at the travel agency.

The driver turned toward his partner, and said in a tortured voice, "Explosion!"

"Look at that!" the other officer said after the blast.

My first reflex was to duck and cover. "What's hitting the car?" I shouted as wood, metal, and pieces of glass struck the patrol car. "Oh, man—what the . . ." I yelled, and was thrown into the barrier that divided the front seat from the back of the patrol car when the officer hit the brakes. I crumpled on the floor, then a shockwave pushed the car forward. I looked up through the rear window of the car and saw a steady flow of glowing embers raining all around, and turning to mist as they hit the ground, reminding me of the lava flow I saw in Hawaii.

"Let's go back and see what's going on," one officer said, then he looked at me. "You stay here!" They scrambled out of the car, and back to the travel agency on foot, dodging the debris in street.

"Stay here," I repeated. "No way." I got out of the car and followed them back to the travel agency. A guy walked up to me and asked, "What happened? Was it an explosion? What blew up?"

"The Pomona Travel Agency," I said.

"Should I call the police?" he asked.

"The police are already here," I said. "I think you should call the fire department."

I watched the two officers run between traffic, and people, to get back to the travel agency. There was chaos and screaming from the throng that had gathered from out of nowhere. Most of the people that in the street looked like regular folks who lived in the area.

"Look at that guy—he's on fire!" someone yelled. More luminous figures covered in flames; looking like dancing torches, burst from the travel agency, and into the street. They were screaming.

From the crowd another voice shouted, "Help him!"

"There's another one," a man said, and pointed. "Over there, look over there," he said. "That guy's on fire, too!"

I waited until the pieces of glass, wood, and other shards stopped falling before going closer.

"Look at that fire! I've got to get some pictures of this," a tall skinny kid said, and started snapping away with his camera. "Wow! I don't believe it! What great timing. I can send these pictures to a TV station."

A TV station, I thought, they'll be happy to get pictures of this for the evening news.

On the street, embers glowed, and smoldered all around. People on the ground cried for help as their burned bodies were pummeled by cold black rain. Is this what hell looks like? I thought. Ambulance sirens screamed on the edge of the city followed by fire truck after fire truck, then a caravan of patrol cars. It was pure disorder as I watched the paramedics and firefighters work to control the situation. The street was filled with charred bodies and burned fragments. More sirens rang and echoed through the city. Finally it dawned on me that I was just in that building, and could have been blown to bits. What is this all about? I thought as I watched the flames climb higher, up, and over to the building across the street. Shaking my head, I mumbled, "What's going on?"

"BRING THAT HOSE OVER HERE—OVER HERE!" a firefighter yelled. After he sprayed the fire a huge steam cloud emerged. He shouted again, "KEEP IT

RIGHT THERE—RIGHT THERE!" Screams and howls echoed all around as the devastation unfolded. A long ladder extended from one fire truck high to the top of the building, then another ladder was raised as the firefighters flooded the fire from different angles.

"I think we've got it," a fireman said. "We've got it under control."

"Looks like we've got it licked," one said. "Keep spraying," another said.

The police put up barriers to keep the crowd back, and direct traffic away from the area. I moved closer and heard them ordering the crowd, "STAY BACK—STAY BACK."

I walked to the barrier as the rain let up a little. "Can I get a little closer," I asked a police officer.

"No! You can't cross the line. Stay back! Everyone's got to stay back."

I watched the travel agency burn, and crumble into a heap. Utterly obliterated to a pile of scrap. There's no way to get people out, I thought. They're dead, burned alive, but Samantha and Veronica are safe, and on their way, or already at the hospital. There's nothing I can do here. I'll head for the hospital, I thought, but first I'll get my laptop and painting from the locker.

On the way, I saw police milling around in front of the station. I ignored them, and headed for the lockers to pick up my stuff.

Just as I entered, I was greeted by an officer who said, "Sorry, the train's shut down."

I looked him in the eye. "Because of the fire?"

"Yeah, the fire's real close, so we had to shut it down."

"How long?" I asked.

"Don't know, sorry."

"I left my bag in a locker," I said. "Can I get it?"

"Sure, go ahead."

I went to the locker, grabbed my bag, and started walking out of the station when the police officer said, "Sir, excuse me, sir,"

I kept on walking.

"Excuse me, sir?" he said again as he caught up to me.

I thought this is it! He knows I shot Zinty, and is going to arrest me.

"Sir," he repeated.

Thinking the worst I turned, and said, "Yes!" Ready to raise my arms and swallowed surrender.

"I've just heard the trains will be down for an hour, maybe two, could be three. You might want to take a taxi, or call someone to pick you up."

"Oh—okay, thanks for the tip," I said, then let out a sigh of relief.

"Sure no problem," he said.

It was probably just my imagination, but his tone sounded suspicious, and he threw one last curious look at me. I smiled, shouldered my bag, and walked out of the station. First looking left, then right, I decided to walk straight up the street, looking for a taxi or a way to the hospital. The clamor from the commotion at the travel agency became faint and distant, and the night peaceful. I walked past a park, heard dogs barking, and some people talking. Soon there was only the sound of the city, a door closing, some laughing, garbage trucks loading trash, and footsteps on the pavement.

Chapter Twenty-four

I walked at a casual pace hoping to catch a ride to the hospital, a taxi, car, bus, anything, as I replayed the events in my mind one image at a time. Having dinner, shooting Zinty, the travel agency blowing up, then I noticed a black SUV drive around the corner and follow me. Carefully, without being obvious, I tried to see who was driving, or in the car, but the windows were dark and reflective, I only saw shadows, and lights.

I turned, and went around the corner, the car turned trailing me. I walked a bit, looked over my shoulder, then turned again, so did the SUV. I stopped and looked in a store window display. It pulled over and stopped. This cat and mouse charade continued until I realized I was lost; no longer heard sirens or saw the fire. I didn't know which direction to go, had no sense whatsoever of how to get to the hospital, anxiousness overwhelmed me, sweat poured down my face and into my eyes. A voice in my mind shouted, *Run!* But answered, *Which way?* I scanned the maze of streets and alleys, looking for an escape route. I saw my reflection creep along with the shadow of the black SUV in the store windows as I walked.

Should I confront whoever is in the car? Questions about the people in the car were stinging. Were the people in the SUV involved with the explosion at the Pomona Travel Agency? Do they know me, Samantha, or Veronica? Work with Zinty?

I turned at the next corner, walked a bit, then thought, I've had enough of this, and ready to give'em hell. When I looked back, there was no SUV. They're after Samantha! I've got to get to the hospital. My mind raced to figure out where I was and get my bearings. I looked up and down endless dark streets. I must be walking away from the city, then in the distance I saw a taxi. There's my ride, great, but it didn't stop. "HEY—HEY—STOP!" I yelled waving my arms, running, chasing after the taxi as it breezed by.

Finally it pulled over. A guy poked his head out of the window. "Need a ride?" the driver asked, his boyish gleaming grin a welcoming image.

"Yes! Yes, I do," I moaned out of breath. "This running is hard work." I stood on the street for a minute holding on to the car out of breath ready to keel over, coughing, and choking for air. "Give me a second to catch my breath," I said. "I'm glad I found you."

As I opened the door he asked, "Where to?"

"I need to get to the hospital." I jumped in, but we didn't move. "What are we waiting for?"

He turned and looked at me. "Which hospital?"

"Which hospital?" I said with a blank look. "I don't know? How many hospitals are there around here? "

"There are five I can think of right off hand. You

have to tell me where to go—that's the way it works, pal."

"There was a huge explosion about thirty minutes ago, a lot of fire trucks, ambulances. They took a lot of people to the hospital because they were badly burned," I said panting, rills of sweat running down my face. "The fire was huge, flames everywhere, they even closed down the train! Didn't you see, or hear anything about it?"

"No, I didn't," he said. "Didn't hear anything about a fire." Then in a calm voice he said, "Take it easy, I was listening to music, and working out at the airport all night."

My voice was tense. "Where would they take people after a fire and explosion?"

"Don't know, that's a tough question."

"Which hospital is the closest?" I asked.

"The nearest one is County, and about twenty minutes from here."

"Take me there," I said. "I've got to get there quick. Hurry! Step on it."

"Okay—okay," the driver said. "Don't worry, pal, I'll get you there."

As we drove, I held my head in my hands, rubbed my eyes, then looked up at the rearview mirror, and saw the driver eyes in the reflection, his penetrating stare unnerving.

"You're probably wondering why I want to go to the hospital."

"Hey, I meet a lot of weird people in this job. Your story is just another one I'll add to my collection. I really don't care, but if you want to tell me—go ahead."

Should I tell him? Where do I start? I thought "You know the explosion I mentioned?"

"Yeah, the explosion," he echoed then asked, "You blow something up?"

"Not me!" I said. "I don't know what's going on, but I was there when it happened."

"You were there?"

I could feel skepticism in his voice. "Yeah, I was there," I said resolutely.

"Why?"

"I was helping a girl—well, actually two girls."

"Oh wow," he said. "This is getting better all the time."

I leaned forward and grabbed the metal screen divider. "There's more," I said, "before the explosion, I killed a cop. Shot him so many times he looked like a screen door."

"You're not going to get weird on me, are you?" the driver said. "I'll dump you on the street! I have enough problems of my own."

"No, it all just happened so fast," I said. "I was helping these girls. Well, let's see! Where do I start? Tonight, I had dinner with a friend, who I met on the train—yesterday. We went to help another girl, I met on the train. She owns the travel agency. Yeah, it was yesterday at a travel agency."

"Yesterday? Travel agency?" the driver said. "You've lost me, pal, I can't follow what you're saying."

"Samantha, the girl who owns the travel agency was in trouble, so I went there with another friend, Veronica, to help," I said. "We had to break into the place because it was closed. I called her after we had dinner. She told me about this guy who was following her, and how he locked her up at the travel agency."

"He's the one you killed?"

"Yeah, and the girls were put in an ambulance, and taken to a hospital. I don't which one, but it must be near here. The girl I had dinner with has a knee injury, and they took her out of the travel agency on stretcher. The other girl, Samantha, was in shock, and afraid of Zinty."

"That's some wild story, man," the driver said in a doubtful tone. "Some story."

If he doesn't believe me, who will? I thought. "The police started investigating. I left the agency with two officers who were escorting me to their patrol car when the whole place exploded into a ball of fire! We had just started driving away." I said gesturing wildly. "It was surreal. Fire was shooting out of the windows, doors, and building. Pieces of glass and metal were falling out of the sky and landing on the car. I didn't know what to make of it at first. Even the cops were surprised, then more police arrived, more fire trucks, more ambulances, a crowd gathered. It was nuts—like a dream or a movie."

"It sounds like the movie I saw last week."

I laughed and said, "Yeah, that's exactly what I thought. Am I in a movie or dreaming? The officers ran back to the building, so I followed them. People were running out of the building on fire, screaming and crying," I said recalling the images. "The firefighters yelled for them to lie on the ground—then tried to help—but they were burned. I'm sure one guy on fire was the detective who interviewed me twenty minutes earlier before the place blew up."

"This all happen tonight?" the driver asked.

"Yeah, tonight, it was crazy. I still don't believe it," I said and sat back trying to relax.

"So—what was this guy doing with the girl? Why kidnap her? What's deal with him?"

"That's strange, too," I said. "His name's Zinty, and I met him on the train."

"You've met a lot of people on the train."

"He told me he was a detective. I saw Samantha, the girl he was following at the travel agency later. It's a bizarre story—all mixed up," I said.

"Yeah, that's a good story. I'll move it to the top of my list," the driver said. "Here's the hospital."

"Thanks, for listening."

"What's your name?" he asked.

"John Bird Ray," I said. "Thanks, for picking me up. I've got to go in, and see if they're in trouble."

The driver turned toward me as I sat in the back seat of the cab and asked, "Need any help—or want me to go in the hospital with you? I wouldn't usually offer, but my shift is over. I'll give you a hand, if you like."

"Hey, thanks for the concern. There was a black SUV following me before you stopped," I said, "then it vanished. I have no idea who was driving, but maybe it has something to do with, Zinty."

We drove to the entrance. "Okay, I'll watch your back."

"I don't know how to repay you for this."

"You can start by paying me the fare," he said laughing.

"That's right. How much do I owe you?"

"Why don't you just buy me dinner sometime?"

"Okay. I know a great Mexican restaurant."

"Oh, yeah—so do I," he said. "Do you think these guys might come to the hospital today?"

"I've thought about it. Just watch for anything that's odd," I said. "I remember seeing a movie with a hit-man who went to a hospital to kill a witness, and not sure if that's what's going to happen, but let's play it safe."

"Here's a spot," he said, then parked in the taxi pick up area in front of the hospital.

"How long can you park here?"

"Just as long as I like," he said. "I'm a cab driver; this is a taxi stop. Sometimes we wait a long time for patients."

We got out of the car and walked into the hospital.

Chapter Twenty-five

"You know, we've been talking all this time, and I don't know your name," I said. "What is it?"

"Dominic," he said. "Dominic Wrigley."

"Wrigley?" I said. "That's interesting, the girl I met on the train, and had dinner with tonight, has the same last name, Veronica Wrigley."

I opened the door of the hospital. He looked at me stunned, staggered back for a moment like he had been hit over the head with a club. After a long silent moment of looking at each other while standing in the doorway of the hospital he said, "My twin sister's name is Veronica."

My jaw dropped. "Your twin sister!" I said, swirling, and dizzy like after getting off a roller coaster.

"I don't know how many Veronica Wrigleys there are in this city," he said, "but it could be her. We haven't talked in a few weeks."

"What are the odds of me catching a cab with the brother of the girl that I had dinner with tonight?" I said. Why am I caught up in the middle of this mess? I thought. "These last few days have been unbelievable."

"You know, at first I thought you were the one who needed help, but after listening to that story I believe you. Let's go see," Dominic said. Now, he was the one in a frenzy, racing in front of me into the hospital, and to the counter asking if Veronica Wrigley had been admitted.

"Hi," Dominic said to the nurse on duty.

"Yes, can I help you?" the nurse asked.

"I think my sister may have been admitted a little while ago. Could you check for me, please?"

"What's her name?"

"Her name's Veronica Wrigley."

"Okay, let's see what we have," the nurse said, then typed the name, and looked at the computer screen. "Yes, Veronica Wrigley was in ER, but she's been moved. It says she's in orthopedics now."

"Where's that?"

"Orthopedics is on the fifth floor," she said. "I'll ring, and see if she's been given a room yet, just a moment."

"Thanks," Dominic said.

"Excuse me," the nurse said. "She's in room 1154. You can wait in the room or go to orthopedics on the fifth floor. Ask the nurse on duty if you can see her."

"Okay, thanks," Dominic said.

Now that we knew where Veronica was I asked about Samantha. "Excuse me, there was another girl who came here in the same ambulance. Could you tell me if she's here, too?"

Dominic walked to the elevator ahead of me. The door opened, he stood there holding it, excited, his hands up in the air beckoning. "Are you coming?"

"Go up without me," I said, and waved him on, then just before the door closed, he gave me the thumbs up.

I looked back at the nurse. "What's her name?" she asked. "Her name is Samantha Loyde," I said.

"Yes, she was in ER, but not admitted. I don't know where she is right now," the nurse said, "maybe on the fifth floor with your friend's sister or in the room."

"Okay, great! You've been a big help. I'll see if I can find her." I walked to the elevator, got in, and pushed the eleventh floor button. I watched the numbers above the door change as the events of the past few days rolled over in my mind. Meeting the girls on the train, having dinner, the explosion, meeting Dominic, and topping off the night by killing Zinty. The elevator stopped. It was quiet as I stepped out looking for Dominic. I didn't see him anywhere, so I went to the nurse's counter.

"Hi, could you steer me to room 1154?"

The nurse pointed. "Right down there at the end of the hall on the left."

"Thanks."

I marched down the hall checking room numbers looking for room 1154. Patients were sitting or sleeping in their beds. "Hi, how are you?" I said to a skinny goofy looking kid with tousled, disheveled hair. He just stared into space without saying a thing. I continued down the hall looking for room 1154, greeting patients as I walked, repeating, "Hello, how are you?" I found room 1154, and the door was open, so I strolled in. Samantha was sleeping in a chair. Dominic nowhere in sight.

"Samantha," I whispered, touching her shoulder.

She turned, and looked up at me with a glazed look. "John, you're here," she said, and closed her eyes again.

"Got here a few minutes ago," I said. "Don't get up."

"John, you're here," she mumbled again.

She moved around in the chair rubbing her eyes and face, then stood. She looked a little shaky as I watched her take a drink of water from a cup that was on the hospital tray next to the chair.

"How are you feeling, Samantha?"

"Wiped out," she said. "They gave me some medicine to relax when I checked in, so I'm a bit dizzy. What about you, John? What's going on with you?" she asked, stumbled a little, then sat in the chair again.

"You'd better stay in that chair for now, Samantha," I said, and didn't know what to think. Yesterday was bizarre, but it was getting stranger, and more and more weird.

"How's Veronica?" I asked.

"She's fine," Samantha said, her speech garbled from the medicine she had been given. "Are you okay, John?" she asked again.

"Just fine, just fine," I said. "You just rest, don't talk, just relax."

"Veronica's going to have knee surgery," she said. "They're going to do it right away in the morning because she's in a lot of pain, otherwise she's fine."

"When are they going to start?" I asked.

"Don't know," she said. "I've lost track of time. What time is it, anyway?"

"Close your eyes, relax, and don't worry about anything," I said. "I'll ask the nurse." Then, I leaned over and kissed her on the head. "I'll be right back, just rest."

I went out into the hall and walked to the nurse's station. There were a few nurses sitting behind the counter.

"Hi, excuse me."

"Yes, can I help you?"

"I hope so," I said. "How do I get an update on the status of a friend of mine who was admitted tonight?"

"What's your friend's name?"

"Veronica Wrigley, and I think she's having surgery in the morning."

"Okay, I'll take a look, hold on a moment."

She picked up the phone and had a short conversation with someone about Veronica, then put down the phone and said, "Sir, she'll be in surgery another hour, then they'll bring her to the room. You can wait there if you like."

Surprised, I said, "I thought she was having surgery tomorrow morning?"

"The doctor thought it was best to do the surgery as soon as possible. Also, there are some policemen downstairs, I think to see you, if your name is John Bird Ray?"

"Yes, it is."

"They asked for you by name, then told me they were going downstairs to the cafeteria."

"Police?" I said. "Okay, I'll go talk to them, and if you see a guy named Dominic Wrigley, could you tell him that I'll be right back?"

"Sure, let me write down the name. Can you spell it for me, please?"

"Dominic Wrigley," I said. "W-r-i-g-l-e-y, like the stadium, or the gum."

"Okay, I'll pass on the message."

"Thanks," I said, and headed to the elevator, then down to the cafeteria to meet the police.

It was a quiet, but every so often a voice or sound of something echoed through the hallways as I walked to the cafeteria. I went to the vending machine and bought a Coke. I turned around startled, tossing my drink in the air, after seeing two guys who appeared from nowhere.

"You guys scared the crap out of me."

"John Bird Ray," one man said in a deep voice.

"Yes," I said.

"We're from the police."

Halleluiah, I thought, but lousy timing. "A nurse said you were looking for me," then while wiping the drink from my shirt told them. "That's why I came down here. How's everything at the travel agency?"

"Not good, fire's out, but the building's a pile of rubble, and a lot of people are dead or burned," he said. "We need to make a report of the incident. I'm afraid you'll have to come with us, Mr. Ray. We need to ask you some questions."

"I'll help in any way I can, but my friend is having surgery right now, and I'd like to be here when she wakes up. Can't we do this tomorrow?" I pleaded. "I was on my way to the police station before the explosion. I talked to a detective at the travel agency—his name—was—Mussear—I think. Where's he?"

"Didn't make it; he was in the building during the explosion, and trapped in the fire. Tell you what, I'm going to let you stay here tonight, Mr. Ray, but you come to the station and talk to me tomorrow. My name is Woodstone, Detective Mark Woodstone. This is my case now, and I have a lot questions to ask you about the explosion, and the shooting."

"Okay, I'll be there," I said. "What time?"

"Be in my office tomorrow at noon."

"Okay, I'll be there." We shook hands. "Bye—tomorrow—at noon," I repeated and nodded as they left, then went back to Veronica's room.

Chapter Twenty-six

Dominic was sitting in the chair next to Veronica's bed when I walked into the room. "How is she?"

"She's still knocked out from the surgery," Dominic said. "I don't think she'll wake up until tomorrow."

Sprawled out asleep on the other bed in the room, with her toes sticking out from under the blanket was Samantha. "It looks like she's out, too."

Then a doctor walked into the room. "Hello, my name is Dr. Honda. I performed the surgery. I came down to check how Veronica is doing, and explain what I did during surgery. Who is Veronica's closest relative? "

"Hi, I'm Dominic, Veronica's brother."

"Let me tell you how the surgery went." In his hand was a miniature plastic model of a knee joint. "Veronica had torn ligaments in the knee joint. There are two ligaments," he then held up the plastic model showing us.

"These two, the anterior and the posterior, or commonly called the ACL and the PCL." He pointed to the plastic ligaments on the plastic model. "They were both torn, and surgically reconstructed."

We walked over to Veronica's bed, then Dr. Honda pointed at Veronica's knee. "There are three small incisions which you can see now, but will be gone after a bit of time. We've started icing her knee," he said and pointed to the blue ice cast on Veronica's knee. "When she wakes up, and the anesthesia wears off, she'll feel some discomfort. We want her to rest today, but try walking tomorrow."

"That seems so soon," I said.

"It's best to keep the muscle strong by moving it right away. This injury takes time to recover, but she's young, Veronica should be walking soon, and active in a month."

"It only takes a month to recover from this kind of injury?" Dominic asked.

"Recovery is a step-by-step process," he said. "First, a physical therapist will help her walk, massage and ice the knee, then put together an exercise program for her to follow. Are there any other questions?"

"How long does it take for the knee to completely heal?" I asked.

At least three-months before she's comfortable putting weight on the knee, twisting, jumping, turning, and running."

"How long will she have to stay in the hospital?" Dominic asked.

"Well, maybe three to five days at the most barring any complications," he said. "This surgery has a high success rate, and most everyone can go back to a normal life. She has to start slowly, then gradually do more and more, but she'll be walking tomorrow. Of course there's always a chance of sustaining another injury down the road."

"Will there be anything she can't do?" I asked.

"If she follows the advice of the therapist, she'll recover nicely.

"Thanks, Doctor Honda," I said as we shook hands. "Thanks a lot, for everything."

"Have a nice night," Doctor Honda said, and walked out of the room with Dominic.

As I looked over at the bed I saw Veronica moving.

"You're up!" I stood at the foot of the bed as she tried sitting, but she didn't have the strength, so I grabbed the remote and raised the bed. "How do you feel?" I asked as the bed eased up.

"I'm numb from the waist down."

"Can you move your toes?"

Veronica locked her elbows, and struggled to sit up. "It's tough!" she said. "Are my toes moving?"

"Yes, they are!" I said. "Good job."

"Soon you'll be able to move all of your toes, and before you know it, raise your leg, then be walking, and running." I said. "Just take it easy today. The doctor said a therapist is coming by to tell you about some special exercises, and give you routine to follow."

Veronica smiled, then asked, "What's the doctor's name?"

"A nurse said it was Dr. Honda, and that he was from Japan."

"Dr. Honda," she mumbled, and smiled. "Like a car, fixing people up . . . in a body shop."

"Are you hungry at all?"

"I'm thirsty," she said softly, her voice drained of energy. "Is there anything to drink?"

I filled a glass, "Have some water," and held it to her lips.

"Thanks, I think I'll rest now," she said, closing and

opening her eyes, groaning, "Oh—my leg's so sore."

"The anesthesia is wearing off. Just relax and don't worry about anything. I'll change the water in the ice pack." I held Veronica's hand. "I'll be here if you need anything."

"I think I'll do that right now," she said, and this time closed her eyes, and fell asleep.

"Hello," a man said in a friendly way as he walked into the room. "I'll be helping Veronica get back on her feet." He was a muscular guy who looked like a body builder. He was so big that his white hospital uniform was skin tight, and his muscles bulged from everywhere.

"Hi," I said. "She just fell asleep," then introduced myself. "I'm, John, Veronica's friend."

"Nice to meet you, I'm Boris. Okay, we'll just let her rest today. I'll come back tomorrow," then he handed me a file. "Could you give this to her? It's a schedule and program for her rehabilitation."

"Sure, I'll tell her you stopped by."

"Okay, see you," he said.

"Bye," I said, and watched him as he left the room. That guy looks a little like Zinty, I thought.

Then, Dominic came back into the room in a happy mood. "How's she doing?"

"She seems okay," I said. "Woke up for a minute, then went back to sleep."

"I've been talking to the nurses, and they all say she'll recover pretty fast. This kind of knee surgery's been perfected on athletes, and the doctors here are all specialists, they do a lot of knee operations. What's the plan? Are we all staying in the hospital tonight?"

"I guess we are," I said. "There's one extra bed, and two chairs."

I looked at Dominic, then at Samantha asleep on the bed. "It looks like we're sleeping on chairs tonight."

We all dozed off, but I woke during the night when a nurse came into the room to check on Veronica, the last time with a stiff neck. Sleeping in this chair is the same as flying twelve hours in economy, I thought, and cracked my neck. I looked around the room—it was quiet. Hospitals are all alike at night, and every sound amplified. I changed the water in Veronica's ice cast, then headed to the cafeteria. In the hallway my footsteps echoed like a tap dancer on stage. Patients were snoring and moving in their beds as I walked down the hall. Hospitals are eerie at night, I thought, and the smell, that special hospital smell that makes you feel like you're swimming in a jar of alcohol takes your breath away.

I walked to the elevator, pushed the button for the first floor, then listened to the cables grind and moan as it went down, and finally stopped with a thud. The doors opened, Safe and sound, I thought. I headed toward the vending machines, dropped some coins in the slot and listened to them rattle as they fell into the coin box. I pushed a button and watched a candy bar tumble down in slow motion. I just stared at the candy bar for a moment, "Dazed and Confused" like the Led Zeppelin song that was rattling around in my noodle. I heard a loud bang as the candy bar landed in the tray below. I opened it, took a bite, and went back to the room. That tea the painter gave me must have kicked in for a moment, I thought.

When I got back to the room everyone was asleep. I needed sleep, too. I sat in the chair across from Veronica's bed, closed my eyes, tried to get comfortable, and dreamed of Bora, Bora.

Chapter Twenty-seven

*F*lashing lights burst on blinding me for a moment, then there was an announcement for everyone to wake up, and get ready for breakfast. How long did I sleep, I thought, two, three hours? Veronica was sitting up in bed, and a gal brought in her food, and it looked pretty good.

"How's the knee feeling this morning?" I asked and stretched the *kinks* out of my body.

"Sore," she said, her face pale with pain. "There's so much pressure. I think it's going to explode if I don't get some ice on it."

I dragged myself over to the small round blue cooler next to the bed that held the ice. "Hold on," I said. "I'll do that for you." I lowered the cooler, drained out the water, shook the ice around, and raised it so the cold water could flow back into the ice cast.

"How does that thing work?" Veronica asked.

"With gravity. I place this container lower than the ice cast, and water flows out, and into the cooler. Raise it above the ice cast, the water flows back into the ice cast.

"Thank you, *Isaac Newton*," she said.

I laughed and said, "There you are, Veronica, all set for a while. Does your knee feel any better?"

"Yes, much better," she said. "Who would think that plain old ice would give that much relief. I hope the swelling goes down soon."

"It's only the first day. You'll heal fast, and be up and around in no time. The doctor should be coming back this morning to talk to you, and let you know how everything went during the surgery."

Someone came in to take Veronica's tray. "Are you finished with your food?" she asked.

"Yes, thanks."

"Okay, I'll take this for you," she said.

Then a nurse came into the room. "Good morning, Ms. Wrigley," she said. "How are you feeling this morning?"

"Tired." Veronica said. "My knee hurts, but the ice makes it feel better."

"Let's look at your knee," the nurse said, and took off the ice cast. "It looks fine. You know we're taking you to rehabilitation this afternoon. You'll work with a therapist and start bending that knee. It's best to get it moving right away, and put weight on it.

"That's what I've been hearing."

"Okay, I'll take your temperature. First, put this under your arm, please, and hold out your other arm," the nurse said. "Now, I'll check your blood pressure."

"Do you know anyone who's had this kind of surgery?" Veronica asked.

"My brother had knee surgery last year. Now he's riding a bike, and walking with no problem, you'll be fine too," the nurse said. "Your blood pressure's fine, let's see that thermometer. Oh, your temperature is a little high. I'm going to change your IV." The nurse put a new bag on the post. "The doctor should be here soon, and I'll see you this afternoon. Do you have any other questions?"

"No, thanks very much, see you later," Veronica said. "Oh, by the way, what's your name?"

"My name's Debra," the nurse said.

As the nurse was leaving the doctor came into the room. "How are you today, Ms. Wrigley?"

"A little sore," she said. "When does the swelling go down, Doctor Honda?"

"That's going to take a little while," he said. "Let's have a look at your knee." Doctor Honda held her knee, and bent the joint. "Good! It looks fine. You'll be running laps in no time, and you're going to start re-hab this afternoon. It'll be painful at first, but you'll get your knee iced down, and massaged after the session."

"I'm looking forward to the maasage part."

"I'll see you tomorrow."

"Bye, doctor."

"I'm going downstairs to get some coffee. Anybody want anything?" I asked.

Dominic got up. "I'll go down with you. I need to stretch my legs."

"Can I get you anything, Samantha?" Dominic asked.

"No, I'd just like to go home," Samantha said. "I don't think I can take another night here."

"Where do you live?"

"I guess, I'll go to my father's place. John, can you call a cab for me?"

"Sure," I said. Where does he live?"

"In Highland Park," she said. "Or, I could go to Buffalo City; our place in the country."

"Okay, I'll call a cab, but I need an address."

"Why don't I give Samantha a ride home, my taxi's right downstairs. We drove here last night, remember?" Dominic said.

"That's right, what am I thinking, you have a taxi. How about it, Samantha? Dominic can give you a ride home, or take you wherever you'd like to go."

"Sure, okay."

"We can head out anytime, Samantha?"

"Can we leave, now?" she asked.

"Sure, just tell me the way," Dominic said.

"Okay, I'll give you directions in the car."

"See you, John, Veronica, I'll be back—when I get back," Dominic said, then asked, "Sure you guys don't need anything?"

"No, we're fine."

"See you tomorrow, then," Samantha said.

"Bye," I said.

They waved once more, and left the room.

"I think, I'm going to rest," Veronica said.

"I'll change the water in your ice cast," I said. "When's the physical therapist coming?"

"This afternoon," Veronica said, and closed her eyes.

"Oh yeah, the nurse said that, didn't she?"

"Don't worry about me; go ahead and write something. I'll be okay, really."

"Okay, Veronica," I said. "Where's an outlet?"

I sat down, plugged in my laptop, smiled at Veronica, and thought of Dominic and Samantha. I wonder what they're talking about right now. How we all met?

Chapter Twenty-eight

*M*eeting people is easy because they're everywhere. It happens randomly or sometimes is planned. Can we imagine what will be said during an encounter before it happens? Does it ever occur that way.

What are Dominic and Samantha talking about right now while driving to her house—can I make it sound real?

Dominic looked at Samantha who sat relaxed in the passenger seat, the window down, her deep dark red hair floating in the wind like flames of a fire. She brushed it away from her face with a nonchalant toss, then tilted her head back against the seat.

"So, Samantha, where did you first meet, John?"

"We met on the train."

"When?"

"A few days ago."

"A lot can happen in a few days," Dominic said nodding.

Samantha looked at Dominic. "We noticed each other on the train, but didn't talk. The next time was at my travel agency. John happened to be walking by and stopped to have a look at the travel ads in the window. I recognized him, and asked for his help."

"You two met just by chance?" Dominic asked.

"Yes," she said. "Just by coincidence."

"That's remarkable, running into someone twice on the same day," Dominic said.

"I hadn't thought about it," she said. "I guess you're right."

"How long have you been in the travel business?"

"About five years."

"Five years," he said. "That's quite a while. I'm really sorry to hear what happened," then asked. "Do you want to open your business again?"

"I don't know," she said. "Maybe someday."

"How did you get into the travel business, Samantha?"

"My father helped me."

"Did you like it?"

"I rarely worked regular hours," she said, then leaned toward Dominic, and smiled. "My staff managed the office for me. I just went there occasionally to see how things were going."

"I see, a hands-off boss." Then Dominic said, "So, you guys had a rough time the other night?"

"You can say that again."

"So, you guys had a rough time the other night? Sorry, bad joke," Dominic said. He was just trying to cheer her up, but Samantha wasn't laughing. The tree-lined road ahead became narrow, then separated. "Which way do I go?"

"Turn right, and just follow the road. It's the last place."

"Okay, will do."

As Dominic drove, he saw the lavish homes behind the stone walls and iron gates. A lot of wealthy people live here, he thought, and followed the winding road up the valley.

"How about listening to some music, Samantha?"

"Sure," Samantha said.

Dominic turned on the radio. "How's this?"

"I like it," she said. A slow solo sax tone flowed from the radio. Soon it was accompanied by a subtle bass sounding like the heart beat of the engine as the car twisted around the corners. The music floating up-up in time with the turns as they drove, then a piano joined in, and finally the light beat of drums. The music relaxed her. Her eyes were closed while he gazed and explored her stunning body. He watched her dark red satin hair dance around her face.

They continued up the narrow road until they came to a large gate, but there was no house in sight. Dominic imagined what it would be like living in a huge mansion protected from the ordinary outside world, not a care or worry for the staples of life. They stopped and waited in front of the gate for a moment, then it buzzed, snapped, and slowly opened.

"They knew we were coming," Dominic said surprised.

"They know everything," Samantha said.

Dominic drove through the gate down a long tree-lined driveway, then the house came into view. It was a real piece of architecture, built of stone and brick, a palace for a king.

"Samantha, your father must be one wealthy individual."

"I suppose so," she said. "Park over there by the entrance."

"What do you mean? You, think so?" Dominic said and drove to the front of the house. "You don't know if he's rich?" Dominic stopped the car in front of the house next to massive columns that looked like two giant white legs.

Samantha turned toward Dominic and asked, "Would you like to come in?"

"Love to," Dominic said without giving it a second thought. They got out of the car, walked up the long wide steps that led into the splendid cornerstone mansion. It stood there before them, built for men of renown.

Where did story that come from? It's a familiar, but faint picture in my mind. What else can I write about people meeting? I thought for a moment, and typed.

A cruise ship is an interesting place, of course it's not all wine and roses. There are stories of passengers falling overboard and never seen again. Passengers catching strange viruses that spread throughout the ship; leaving everyone helplessly ill, and we all know the story of the Titanic.

{Cruise Ship}
"Tell me what happened?" the captain asked.

"It was . . . It was . . . a huge long tentacle with claws," the passenger said.

"What did you see," the captain asked again.

"It was dark, cold, black as night," the passenger said.

"Yes—yes . . . then what?"

"It shot out of the water and bit off a crew member's head, like biting into a popsicle," the passenger said.

"Here it comes again . . ." they shrieked and were dragged to the murky depths below.

People meet in the military while they're learning soldiering. They live together, train together, party together; and they get close. Soldiers depend on their buddies in dire situations; a fellow soldier's life may be decided in a split second. Of course, some clash in the service, and never get along.

A quote from a soldier. "*I was a soldier; it was tough, but I always ate all of the food on my plate, and kept my eyes open for a country to take over.*"

{Boot Camp}

"Why did you join," one recruit asked another.

"Oh you know—travel, learn something. What about you? Why did you join up?"

"I couldn't find a job; at least not one that was fun."

The bus stops in front of the barracks. "Well—here we are. What's going to happen next?"

"I don't know."

"That's the Drill Instructor over there."

"Yeah—he looks like a tough guy."

"I think he looks like an asshole."

"What have I gotten myself into?"

School is a melting pot, a brilliant place to meet. Students start rock bands, companies that become conglomerates, a few become multi-billionaires, and some become drug dealers and addicts. This is the radical group of youngsters who bring change to the world.

Most people want a comfortable lifestyle first, then consider saving the world. Money is power; wealth is freedom, so all the financial gurus who follow the golden rule preach. He who has the gold, rules.

{School}

"Why is this school such a boring place?" one student asked.

"Because it's filled with boring people," the other student said.

"Yeah . . . I bet the Army is more fun."

"Yeah! I bet it is!"

"Let's join up!"

I stopped typing. Will I finish this book? I thought. What's it about, and how will I ever put it into a story? I started typing more about how people meet.

An airport or train station is a good meeting place. Regular travelers know and become friends, with the people who work in the airport restaurants and bars, when there's a long wait between flights. Travelers meet travelers, talk about themselves, where they're going, what they're doing. Obviously, you can't help but meet the passenger sitting beside you on a plane.

{Airport}
"Hello, how are you?" a passenger said.
"Fine," the other passenger replied, then asked, "How about you?"
"Great! This is my first flight."
"You're kidding?"
"No, never been on a flight in my life, I'm a virgin. Get it? Virgin."
"Good one. I travel a lot."
"Why?"
"For business."
"What kind of business are you in?"
"I work for the government."
"What do you do for the government?"
"Actually, between you and me, my job is a little boring."
"What do you do?"

"I fly around the country meeting and interviewing people who say they've seen a UFO."

"What do they talk about? Are they a little bit crazy?"

"No, most are quite interesting, but I've been doing this for such a long time now, it's become a little boring."

"How about you . . . ever seen a UFO?" the first time flyer asked.

"Just between you and me, I've seen a lot of. . . everywhere!"

"Well—nice talking to you, bye." The first time flyer got up and walked away muttering."

There's always curiosity, an interest about others, and the face is truly remarkable. It tells all and hides all. When we see a face, our mind begins collecting information from ambiguity we slowly assemble information as we need and desire.

Now and then emotion sets in, love at first sight, electrified mind and body burn, tingle, explode into a marvel, into a phenomenon that may change the world. "*Change the World*" that's a song, I thought.

A hospital, where I am at this moment is a place for a chance meeting, or a bookstore, a coffee shop, church, wedding or funeral, police station.

Police Station! Police Station echoed in my head.

I stopped typing as panic set in. What time is it? I thought, and looked at my watch. Woodstone, I have an appointment with Detective Woodstone at twelve today. I thought the worst. They'll come looking for me if I don't show up. I'll be arrested and be sent to Devil's Island.

I looked over at Veronica. She was asleep, her arm black and blue from being a pin cushion for the IV, her leg resting on a pillow. I don't want to wake her, and Dominic will be back soon, I thought. She'll only be alone for a short time. I left a note for her on the table next to the bed.

Veronica, I forgot about going to the police station. A detective was at the hospital yesterday. He wants me to answer some questions about Zinty, and the night at the travel agency. I promised him that I'd stop by his office at noon. I didn't want to wake you. If all goes well, I'll be back later today. John

Chapter Twenty-nine

I headed for the elevator and down to admissions in the lobby. It was busy with the young and old in wheelchairs, on crutches, people bandaged, and some who were in obvious pain. I don't know how anyone can work in a hospital, I thought, they're tough. I walked into a beautiful day. It sure feels good to be outside, healthy, free, and hope it stays that way. I waited a few minutes at the front entrance, then got into the first cab that pulled up.

"Where to?" the driver asked.

"Can you take me to this address?" I asked, then handed him a piece of paper.

He looked at the paper and muttered, "Daley Plaza, City Hall building," then at me. "Okay, hop in."

"Do you . . . " I asked as I got in, "or—can you—take a scenic way? How about driving up Lake Shore Drive?"

"It'll cost more."

"No problem," I said. "I have time, and may not see daylight for a while, so let's take it. Go that way."

"You're the boss," he said and drove off.

I sat back, turned, and watched buildings and people fuse into the backdrop of the city. A taxi, I thought, now there's a place to meet someone, and how I met Dominic.

"How long is the drive to City Hall?" I asked.

"The trip downtown to Daley Plaza is about thirty minutes," he said, "but it'll take us a little longer going this way, about an hour."

"That's perfect," I said. "Up to now, I haven't seen the lake, just spent most of my time on subways, and trains." As we drove, I saw everything as new, but I couldn't get the last few days out of my mind. What's going to happen next? I closed my eyes and dreamed of Bora Bora.

Suddenly I woke—when the driver said, "Hey, pal, we're here, Daley Plaza."

I woke bleary eyed. "Already, I was out," I said, and reached for my wallet. "What do I owe you?"

"Sixty-six bucks."

I handed him seventy dollars. "Keep the change."

"Thanks, good luck."

"Yeah, you're welcome, thanks for the ride," I said, but he was *already gone* before I finished my sentence. "Already Gone" That's a song by the Eagles.

I turned and saw a huge-old-gray hulk of a building, and measured the bulky round columns and capitals that rose to the sky, but nothing identified it as City Hall. Is this the police station? I thought, then wondered if I was in the right place until I saw some police officers in uniform.

In the distance children played on a huge metal sculpture. Curious I walked over, and saw it was the Picasso I'd read about. I looked at it for a while trying to figure out what it was, a horse, a woman, maybe a little of everything all mixed up, and shaped into a new form.

I returned to the stone monument of law and hustled up the steps. The doors opened to a lot of action, people talking, moving quickly. Now, I was nervous with second thoughts, but knew I had no choice, and had to get this over with. I walked to the counter to ask the person standing there for directions, and information.

"Excuse me," I said.

"Yes," the officer said. "What do you need?"

"I have an appointment to meet a police detective today. Could you tell me where I go?"

"Sure," he said. "Go up to the fifth floor. You'll see an information counter. Just ask someone when you get there."

"Okay, thanks," I said. As I stepped into the elevator, the events of the previous night came back to me again. I watched the numbers above the door light up, 1-2-3 . . . I wondered what Woodstone might ask or tell me about the night at the travel agency. The elevator door opened. I looked around, then stepped out, headed down the hall, and walked to the closest desk.

"Excuse me," I said. "I'm looking for Detective Woodstone. A man downstairs told me to come up here. Is he on this floor?"

"What's your name?"

"John Bird Ray."

"Just a moment," he said. "Go wait over there," and pointed to some chairs, then picked up the phone. I sat by the door waiting and watching. This is a busy place, I thought, there must be a lot of crime in the world. After a few minutes he signaled for me to come back to the counter. "Go down the hall, then off to the right, that's the detective's office. He's in there—somewhere."

"Ask for him when you get there."

"Okay, thanks." I made my way toward the office down the hall looking at my shoes, they were in control, and stepping stones to my destiny.

"Excuse me," I said to a man behind another desk. "Do you know where I can find Detective Woodstone?"

"Sorry?" he asked, so I repeated the question. "Detective Woodstone? Where can I find him?"

"Sure, that's Woodstone's desk over by the window. You can wait for him there. He just stepped out for a moment, he'll be right back."

As I walked over, and sat in the wooden chair in front of Woodstone's desk, I noticed a stack of files. The one on the top, labeled Pomona, caught my attention. That was the name of Samantha's travel agency. I was tempted to sneak a quick peek, but as I looked around the office the detectives had their eye on me, so there was no chance of opening the file without being noticed. Then, when Woodstone finally arrived, I stood and said, "Hello, hope this is a good time." He seemed younger than the first time we met. He was well dressed, dark suit, tie, and looked like a clerk who worked in the men's department of a store. His eyes were always on me, and I felt like we were having a staring contest.

He greeted me with a firm hand. "Hello, Mr. Ray." We both looked over at the Pomona file as we shook hands and sat down. "I'm going to ask you some questions about the night at the travel agency," then he grabbed the Pomona file from his desk.

"Well, I have to get this over with sooner or later," I said. "The last few days have been crazy. I don't have any answers to why any of this happened, but I hope I can help. I keep thinking I'm having a long, weird dream."

"I understand," Woodstone said. "We're in the same

boat, Mr. Ray, trying to sort out, and fill in the gaps of what happened at the Pomona Travel Agency."

"What would you like to know?"

"Okay, first question. Why were you there?"

"Just like I told the detective at the travel agency that night after I called 911, his name was Mussear. I went there with my friend, Veronica Wrigley, to help Samantha."

"You're talking about helping Samantha Loyde?"

"Yeah, that's right."

"How do know Samantha Loyde?"

"That's another long story, but basically we met a few days ago on the train, then at the travel agency."

"You didn't know her before that?"

"No, never met, or saw her before that."

"What about Zinty? Ever meet him before?"

"I talked to him the other day on the train. At first I thought he was just another passenger, and found out later he was hounding Samantha," then in an excited voice said, "and threatening me on the phone."

"Do you remember what he said, or told you?"

"No, not exactly, something like, *Stay away from her, she's part of my family—you'll be sorry*, that's all I can remember."

"That's good enough for now, don't worry, I know it's hard to remember things like that."

"Yeah," I said, "maybe more will come back to me later."

Woodstone came around to the front of the desk, sat on the corner, then moved around trying to get comfortable. "We have this problem with Zinty. He was a detective—he's dead—and you're the one who killed him, so we have some loose ends, Mr. Ray. A detective getting shot and killed is a big problem."

I looked at Woodstone, "Zinty told me he was a cop

when we met on the train. He was friendly, downright cordial, and warned me about pick-pockets. We talked about writing. He told me that he wanted to write a book about a case he was on. I told him that it was a good idea, and gave him my card. He wrote down his number and gave it to me."

"Do you think he was following you?" Woodstone asked.

"Don't know," I said. "It wasn't until I spoke to him on the phone that he turned from *Dr. Jekyll* into *Mr. Hyde*. Telling me to stay away, threatening he would do something—like kill me. That's when I understood that he was serious, and a little disturbed."

"Tell me about the night at the Pomona travel agency."

"That night at the travel agency was self-defense. I shot him with his gun."

"Why did you shoot him?"

"Zinty was crazy, out of his mind. He just kept coming and wouldn't stop. It was him or me. He was going to kill Veronica, and he locked Samantha in the basement."

I wanted to know what information the police had, so I asked, "What do you guys know about Zinty, and Samantha?"

"Sorry, I can't talk about details of the case, but let's see what we know about Samantha Loyde and her father."

He grabbed the file off the desk again, looked through it, then at me.

"I saw that file on your desk while I was waiting," I said, "and I recognized the name, Pomona."

"Any information that you have on this situation would help immensely," Woodstone said.

"I can't tell you much about Zinty or Samantha because I just met them a few days ago. I don't know much, why or how Zinty is involved—but the police must know something? You guys are investigating. You must have some ideas, right?"

He paged through the file again, looked up and asked, "Have you ever heard of Samuel Lee Loyde?" He turned the file around and showed me an 8x10 glossy black and white picture. "We believe this man is involved in the case somehow," he said. "We're just not sure how."

It was a picture of Samuel Loyde. He looked distinguished, intelligent, had a square jaw, gray hair, and inquisitive eyes. His hands were folded under his chin in a thinking pose. "That's a nice picture," I said. "I know because I'm a photographer, very nice light. The name's familiar, but we've never met."

Woodstone looked at the file. "He's a famous architect, and designed buildings all over the world. He had a school for architects in the country; a place called Buffalo City," Woodstone said and turned the page. "Listen to this. One night at the school long ago while Loyde was away the caretaker went on a rampage. He killed Samuel Loyde's wife, son, daughter, and a few other people who lived there," he said, "then started a fire, and burned the place down. There's evidence the fire was started by an explosion. That night people reported seeing a huge fireball, and hearing a blast that echoed for miles."

"Sounds like what happened at the Pomona Travel Agency," I said.

"This place was an architectural school, but in the report they list some sort of lab equipment found at the school," Woodstone said.

"That sounds strange," I said. "What kind of lab equipment?"

"We don't really know," Woodstone said. "According to the report, everything was charred beyond recognition, including the people. When the police and paramedics arrived there was nothing but ashes. The whole case is bizarre and doesn't make any sense," he said. "Finally, Loyde returned to Buffalo City, rebuilt the school, and made it bigger than ever."

"Okay," I said wondering where this story was going.

"Well, the caretaker was arrested, found guilty, and sent to prison," he said. "Do you know what his name is?" Woodstone said slowly and quietly.

"No, what's his name?" I asked.

"Peter Zinty."

"Is Nick Zinty related to Peter Zinty," I asked apprehensively.

"Nick Zinty was his son," Woodstone said. "Peter Zinty had no criminal record as far as we know before the incident at Buffalo City. I haven't found any evidence to show that he was violent, emotionally unstable, or on any drugs at the time of the murders."

Woodstone turned the page in the file.

"We're trying to track down Zinty's wife," he said. "She was at Buffalo City when all of this happened. We believed she survived, and may have information."

"We're just not sure about anything at this point. Why do you think Zinty attacked you, and kidnapped Samantha Loyde?"

"I've told you everything I know," I said. "If I had any information, I'd pass it on." Then asked, "So, if his children were killed, who is Samantha? I thought she was Loyde's daughter."

"She was adopted by Samuel Loyde after the Buffalo City incident. We don't know who her biological parents are because we can't find any records. We really don't know much about her. It's as if she just dropped out of the sky, and ended up with Loyde," Woodstone said.

"Never heard any of that," I said, and like I told you,

I just met her a yesterday."

"Loyde is very wealthy and travels frequently in his private jet. He's hard to locate, so it's tough getting any information from him. Buffalo City is a huge estate in the hills near a small town. As far we know his daughter spends her time there, in Highland Park, or at the travel agency."

"Well, she won't be spending any time at the travel agency any more," I said.

"No, guess not." Woodstone turned to another page in the file. "Do you know what else it says here?"

"What?" I asked.

"Peter Zinty got out of jail after a retrial. He was acquitted of all charges, and according to this file the evidence showed there was some doubt as to whether he was responsible at all. DNA evidence shows that someone else was there, but the investigation turned into a dead end."

Everything about this situation with Samantha and her father was getting bizarre. I believed the police knew more, and were trying to find out what I knew, if anything.

I wanted to know what the next step was going to be regarding my situation, so I asked, "What's going to happen with me? Am I being arrested?"

"Yes, I'm afraid I have to take you into custody until a judge resolves the case." Woodstone closed the Pomona file, then looked at me. "Have you got a lawyer, Mr. Ray?"

I looked at his emotionless face and said, "No, I don't. Do you know any?"

"Yes, I know a few, but can't recommend any, sorry. Is there anyone you can call?"

"I can try calling Veronica, but she's in the hospital," I said. "Her brother, Dominic, could help."

"Give her a call right now if you like," he said. "You're allowed one phone call."

"Thanks. Have you got a phone book?"

"Sure, I have one right here in my desk. Here you are," Woodstone said, and handed me the phone book.

I looked up the number for the hospital, called, and was connected to Veronica's room. The phone rang a few times, then she answered, "Hello."

"Hi Veronica," I said. "How's the knee? Are you feeling better? Sorry, I left without saying goodbye."

"Hi John," she said. "Yes a little better. Where are you?"

"You found my note, right?" then said, "I'm at the police station waiting to be arrested." I heard her sigh. "Do know a good lawyer, Veronica?"

"They arrested you?"

"Yes, but according to the detective it's all a formality, and I could get out tomorrow, but I need a lawyer."

"The only lawyer I know does my income tax, but maybe there's someone from his firm who can represent you. I'll call their office," Veronica said. "How do I get in touch with you?"

"Just call the police station, the number should be in the phone book. Wait, better yet, let me ask the detective."

"Okay, John."

"Excuse me, Detective."

"Yes."

"Is there a number I can give to my friend, so she can contact me?"

"Here, tell her to call this number," he said and handed me his card.

"Veronica, are you there?"

"Yes, John."

"Here's the number, if you need to contact me, 666-777-6101." I took a deep breath. "You can get a message to me if something comes up. I'll see you in a few days. Can you let Samantha know what's going on," I said. "I'm not certain, but you both may have to testify in court about what happened at the travel agency. Ask Samantha if she knows a good lawyer, okay?"

"Sure, I'll call her," she said. "Take care, John."

"See you soon, Veronica, bye." I hung up, and sat there trying to make sense of it, but nothing made any sense,
especially the part about me being arrested.

Woodstone came back with a stack of documents for me to look at and sign. "You don't have to do anything until your lawyer looks it all over," he said.

"Okay, I'll wait until later when I have a lawyer."

Two other uniformed officers came in to escort me to the jailhouse. Woodstone said he had to officially arrest me. This was the first step on my criminal journey.

"Okay, you have the right to an attorney. Anything you say . . . " he went through a long list of items, but my mind was somewhere else—it was just noise.

Chapter Thirty

*T*hey took me to a small spartan room with a little table and two chairs. There was a camera in the corner of the ceiling to right of the door, but no clock, so I had no idea of the time. Woodstone and another officer grilled me over and over, asking the same questions, again and again. I was nervous, and breathing became difficult because they took turns bombarding me with questions. I answered, yes or no, mostly, to everything they asked. My voice was tight and shaky, but I guess they were satisfied.

I was taken to another room for a profile and head shot picture, fingerprinted, then all of my valuables, computer, keys, loose change, were bagged. I was strip searched, checked by a doctor, who said I was in excellent health, then given a pair of fatigues, and taken to a small cell with cold concrete walls. It had a small cot, a toilet, and one small light in the ceiling covered by a metal bird-like cage. When I heard the cell door slam shut I knew I wasn't at the White House Hotel.

What am I doing here? I thought, as I looked through the small window in the door of the cell. I rested my head against it, then turned, scanned and measured the cell's space. It was about the size of a large closet. I walked over and sat on the lumpy gray cot. Bora Bora seemed pretty appealing right now.

A few minutes later I heard a voice say, "Here's your dinner." A metal tray was pushed through an opening in the cell door. The food was basic, and smelled okay. In fact, it looked a lot like the food at the hospital.

"Excuse me guard," I said. "What time is it?"

"Six o'clock."

"Thanks." Six o'clock I said, then gobbled everything down like a horse, and finished in record time. I pushed the tray through the slot in the door, sat on the cot for a moment, then put my head on the small pillow they'd given me and fell asleep.

The sun rose, I woke feeling stiff, and felt like I'd aged ten years overnight. Falling asleep in a jail cell is the same as waking up in one, and smells about as bad as the hospital. This was the day I had to go through the gauntlet, the red tape, the system. I hope today goes well, and works out the way, Woodstone said, I thought. After breakfast I waited, and waited. I didn't have my laptop, but had a lot of time to think. The last topic I wrote about was how people meet. People meet in so many different places, and sometimes in jail. There was a guy in the cell next to me who had an Irish twang. He rambled on and on about Irish whisky. Quite the talker he was, and said he liked to start drinking early, so he could drink all day. Actually, I could use a drink right now, I thought.

The guards were professional and treated me according to the book. One appeared in front of the cell door. "John Bird Ray, your lawyer's here."

"Great," I replied. Veronica came through with a lawyer, and now I can get out of this place. I followed the officer to a small interview room where I met a man in an expensive dark blue suit, white shirt, and yellow tie. He had perfectly combed dark brown hair, not a strand out of place, a dark thick moustache, and very nice teeth.

He introduced himself as he stood. "Hi, I'm Harry Bliss. Nice to meet you Mr. Ray."

We shook hands. "Call me, John," I said.

"Okay, John, call me, Harry. Let's talk about what's going to happen today." He opened his briefcase and took out some files. "First, we'll go in and have a seat in front of the judge. Second, I'll present your case. Third, give our reasons for dismissal. I'm sure he's already examined the case, so it should be quick. I've looked at all of the documents relevant to your case, and there's nothing that incriminates you. It's a pure case of self defense. You'll be free to go as long as there aren't any problems that derail us," he said. "You don't have a criminal record do you?"

"No, I don't," I said. "Never been arrested, until yesterday."

"Good," he said, then continued to tell me what would happen. "We shouldn't have any problems getting you out because you have no criminal record, your life, and the lives of the two women were at risk. You were just defending yourself. Do you have any questions?"

"No, not really. None that I can think of," I said. "I don't know what questions to ask." I had no idea what was going on, so I thought it best to find out what my options were. "You're prepared, but what if they don't let me out, what if I'm found guilty?"

"Then you go to prison, and rot in a cell for the rest of your life!" he said, and laughed. "Just kidding, John, your case is cut and dried, and you'll be out today," he said. "I guarantee it! Of course, there will be a date set for trial, and you'll have to return to court, but that shouldn't be a problem either because the evidence is clear."

"That's what I want to hear," I said, and felt confidant that Harry had everything under control, but he did scare the crap out of me for a moment with the prison comment.

"Okay, we'll be leaving in about twenty minutes," he said, and put the papers back into his briefcase. "I'll see you in court."

"Oh, just one question, how much is your fee?"

"Don't worry it's been taken care of. Samantha Loyde is covering all the fees."

"Samantha's paying for everything?" I said unexpectedly. "I thought Veronica hired you."

"I don't know who Veronica is, but you don't have to worry about a thing. Samantha told me to make sure you were well taken care of, and had the best representation."

Thank you, Samantha, I thought, then asked, "Is she coming to the courthouse today?"

"I don't know, she didn't say when I spoke to her on the phone."

"Do you work for Samantha or her father?"

"I work for the Loyde family," Harry said, "and she must like you because they usually don't hire me out."

"What's her father like?" I asked.

"You never heard of Samuel Loyde?"

"I've heard the name," I said, "and I've seen his picture, but don't know much about him, and wondering what kind of guy he is."

"He's very busy, travels a lot, serious about his work, and about taking care of his family."

"I'm sure Samantha will introduce you. As I said before, she must like you. Okay, that's about it, so I'll see you in court. Do you have any questions at all?"

"No, I guess not," I said. "See you there."

A bailiff came into the lockup area and asked, "Ready to go?"

"Yes, I'm ready."

"Follow me, then."

"Okay," I said. We walked down a long narrow hall, up two flights of stairs, then entered a small room. I sat there about thirty minutes, waiting, thinking about life, and if the fat lady really sings when the show is over.

Before we left the room the bailiff unlocked the cuffs, and took me to the courtroom where Harry was sitting. Harry looked at me, smiled and said, "Have a seat."

The only sound in the courtroom was paper shuffling, breathing, and the occasional closing door. "How does everything look?" I asked in a low, quiet voice as I sat down.

"Everything's going to be fine," he whispered. "You'll be out today."

The judge entered the courtroom. "Everyone rise, his honor, Judge Robert Candle presiding," the bailiff said.

Everyone stood until the judge took his seat. He sat down, opened a file and said, "For the record, I spoke with counsel in my chambers before this proceeding today. I'd like to note that we discussed the defendant's case, and the motion submitted by the defense. The defendant will stand trial for the charges against him, but the court will allow the defendant, John Bird Ray, to be released today without bail. Does the state have anything to add?"

"No, your honor, we agree with the court and counsel's request that John Bird Ray be released without bail."

"Will the defendant please rise," Judge Candle said.

I stood, my lawyer stood, then everyone stood.

"You're free to go, Mr. Ray, but must return to this court on the date specified, and stand trial for the charges against you. Do you understand, Mr. Ray?"

"Yes, your honor," I said, "I understand." Tom Petty's song "Free Falling" tumbled around in my head—then I had the feeling of floating on a cloud, free in the wind.

"Harry—thanks for all your help." I wanted to hug him, but we gave each other a hearty handshake instead.

"Thank you your honor," I said, nodded, then thought, I have to thank Samantha when I see her.

Everything at the courthouse proceeded as Harry said, then he turned and whispered, "I have to speak with the judge, then we'll set out for the jail, collect your things, sign some release documents, after that you'll be free to go."

"Great!" I said rejoicing deep inside. I felt like going to church, donating some money, or going to a pet shop and setting all the animals free. My body tingled when I heard the judge say—*Free to go!* Even though lawyers have an unpleasant reputation, I had to admire how Harry took control of my case, and got me out so quickly.

Chapter Thirty-one

We left the courthouse together and walked down to a noisy and hectic street. "I've never been through anything like this before in my life," I said, then looked at Harry. This guy knows how to work the system, I thought.

"Yes, it's quite an experience the first time around," he said with a triumphant smile. "I always feel euphoric, and hungry for more after a trial."

"More? More what?" I asked.

"Winning! Winning of course! More winning—like an addict who needs a fix," he said with overwhelming passion and zeal.

This guy's talking about the law like a sport, but that's okay because I'm out, then looked up, relishing the sunlight, the spice of liberty, seeing the blue sky, and took a deep breath—the fragrance of freedom is beautiful. I was in jail only one night, but now screaming with delight inside to be on the outside of that cold steel cage, and institutional box of rules and laws. In the courtroom, I only watched and listened to people talk about and discuss what should be done in my regard, I had no power.

Harry slapped me on the back, and asked, "Well, how does it feel to be a free man?"

"I can't explain the feeling," and grinning said, "and can't thank you enough for all of your help."

"Think nothing of it," he said. "I don't do this for free, or out of compassion. I'm compensated quite well by the Loydes," then he looked at me, "and that's the way I like it, paid well for a hard days work."

"I see," I said nodding, wondering how much he's being paid for this case. I bet it's a lot, and thought, I should change professions and forget about writing a novel.

"I'll contact you when we have to be back in court for the hearing. I might be able to take care of everything without you," he said. "Perhaps you won't have to come in at all."

"You can do that?"

"Well, don't get too excited, I don't know yet, we'll have to wait and see. I'll keep you posted on what's happening." We walked down the street a few blocks, then Harry gestured and said, "This is my car. Well, like I said, I'll keep you updated, nice meeting you, John, bye."

We shook hands once again. "Thanks," then pointing at his car I said, "That's a nice rig you have."

"I like it," he said, then got into the car, started the engine, closed his eyes and made a face like he'd just eaten something delicious. He revved the engine a few times. "Oh—how I love the sound of rawpower."

I listened to the engine sing with hopes he might offer me a ride, but he just smiled, gave a wave from his brow, and drove away in his red Porsche. Our short farewell was nonchalant as he let me standing on the sidewalk in front of the courthouse in the midst of the city. A few hours ago I was in front of a judge charged with murder, Harry by my side, and now, I'm on the street abandoned like an old piece of furniture. The Beatles song, "Hello Goodbye" popped into my head. Perhaps I was feeling down because I was tired, or still in a state of shock, but relieved knowing the charges would likely be dropped. I guess the events of the past few days were slowly seeping in too. What now? I looked up and down the street watching the cars and the people, then was startled by an ambulance's siren, howling. My mind was cloudy, like waking up after a dream, as if none of this had happened. I shook off the cobwebs and walked to a taxi stand.

"Excuse me," I said, then gave a piece of paper to the driver parked at the corner. "Can you take me to this address?"

"1120 W. Dickens Ave." he mumbled. "Sure," the driver said. "Hop in."

After driving a few minutes the driver asked, "What kind of place is this—a house?"

"It's a bed and breakfast," I said.

"Oh, okay," he said, "a bed and breakfast."

"I want to stop there just to pick up my things, and after that can you take me to County Hospital."

"No problem," he said, and drove off.

I noticed some familiar places because we were on same route I'd used to get to City Hall. It was odd going back to the hospital after going through this nightmare. I stuck my head out of the window of the cab and yelled, "Is this really happening?" I yelled it again, as the wind caressed my face.

"What's that?" the driver said.

"Nothing, just talking to myself," I said, then thought,

I'm taking Veronica out to dinner after she's discharged. As we drove my mood changed completely; now I was happy and excited at the same time. We pulled up to the bed and breakfast. "Just wait for me, okay? I'll be right back." I went in, packed my things, and left the room to look for Tracy.

"Hi, Tracy," I said as I stood at the top of the stairs holding my bag. We smiled, then I walked down the steps, and followed her into the living room.

"How was the festival?" she asked. "Have fun?"

"It's been crazy," I said flustered, "and a long story."

"Are you all right?"

"Yeah, I'm fine," I said. "I have a cab waiting, so I'm in a bit of a hurry. How much do I owe you?"

"You were here for three nights, right?"

"Well, not really, but yes, that's right," I said. "I reserved three nights."

"That's one-hundred and one dollars. Do you want to keep it on the same credit card?"

"Sure," I said, but thought, $101.00, why so cheap?

"Here's your receipt, and you take care."

"Thanks," I said as I signed the receipt. "I'll keep in touch, and let you know how the book's going." I picked up my bag and headed toward the door. "I'll write something about you in the book."

"Okay," she said. "Good luck!"

I rushed out of the bed and breakfast, jumped into the waiting taxi, and took one last look, then whispered, "Bye," and closed the door. I felt like I was leaving home. "Okay, let's go to County Hospital."

We drove through neighborhoods, some nice, some not so nice. For a while I wondered if the driver knew where he was going, or if he was lost. "Are you sure this is the right way?" I asked. "We seem to be on the same road."

The driver looked at me and said, "Yeah, this is the right way. Don't worry, pal, we'll be there soon."

We continued driving down the neighborhood streets stopping at every intersection because there were no stop signs. It was taking a long time, and I was getting worried.

"How much farther is it to the hospital?" I asked.

"Should be there—in about twenty minutes."

"Great," I said, and thought, Twenty minutes, and I'll see Veronica. I feel like I've been away for years."

My hands were tense. I began tapping my feet, and slapping my knee to the beat of "Sweet Home Chicago" then saw the hospital come into view.

"Here we are," the driver said, "safe and sound." He chuckled, then stopped in the front of the hospital.

"How much do I owe you?" I asked.

"Sixty-six, dollars," he said. "You look like you're in a pretty good mood."

"Going to see a girl," I said. "Here you go," I handed him seventy bucks. "Keep the change."

"Good luck with the girl," the driver said, then laughed again.

"Yeah, thanks." I got a strange feeling from the driver. Does he know me? Why does he look so familiar?

Chapter Thirty-two

I got out of the cab and walked through the lobby of the hospital floating on air, feeling invincible having escaped death and punishment. I headed for the elevator, pushed the button for the eleventh floor, the *Robert Johnson* tune still in my head. When the door opened I saw it was filled with patients in hospital robes, holding and connected to IVs, and one guy in a wheelchair. As the familiar smell of hospital antiseptic filled my nostrils I felt sorry for them, but was happy, and nothing was getting me down today. I waited for everyone to get off, then stepped into the elevator followed in by nurses and doctors, and was squeezed into the corner listening to them talk about medical procedures. After they got off I had some breathing space, and eventually made it to Veronica's floor. I went to her room thinking of how to break the news, and thought, I can't wait to see the look on her face when I walk in.

I went in smiling, grinning. "Hi, Veronica!" I said, thinking she'd be happy to see me, but her face was red, and she'd been crying. "What's wrong?" I asked. "Why the tears? Something about your knee, or the surgery?" I sat down on the bed next to her.

"My knee is fine," she said, crying, holding a tissue, wiping her tears.

"What's wrong then?" I asked. Veronica was reticent, holding back. "I've got great news," I said trying to cheer her up. "The Zinty case will probably be thrown out. Loyde's lawyer, Harry Bliss, helped, and Loyde paid."

Veronica looked away and cried. I couldn't understand why, so finally I said, "Tell me what's wrong, can I help? What can I do?"

"There was an accident," she said, and wiped the tears from her cheek.

"Accident?" I said. "Who, what . . .?"

"A car accident," she said, before I could finish my sentence, and broke out in tears again.

"What accident? Who was in an accident?" I asked again bewildered.

She looked at me mournfully, and said, "Dominic and Samantha," then cried again.

I stood there speechless for a moment then finally said, "Dominic and Samantha?"

"The police came this morning. They told me it happened on the road to her father's place in the country. They said, Dominic was driving too fast, and lost control of the car. It rolled over, and crashed into a crevice, exploded, then burned." She covered her face still crying. "Horrible, so horrible."

"Dominic was a good driver. A professional driver. He drove off the road?" I said, "That doesn't fit, does it? Do you really think that's what happened?"

"I don't know what to think," Veronica said. "The past few days have been insane. It's too much for me to absorb—I'm exhausted."

We sat on the bed silent. I held Veronica in my arms, caressing her, trying to reassure and comfort her. With all the horrific news about her brother, pain from her knee the surgery, and seeing Zinty shot, she was torn up inside. This was the last straw, the camel was dead.

While I held Veronica in my arms, I happened to glance in the direction of the door in time to catch a glimpse of a tall old stocky man standing in the hall just outside the doorway. He seemed to be watching us, but I had no idea how long he'd been standing there. He walked away as soon as our eyes met. In that moment I thought, He reminds me of Nick Zinty. I wanted to go after him, but Veronica was resting in my arms, so I stayed in the hospital room rocking her to sleep. I caught myself dozing off from being still so long, and my legs were stinging from numbness. I put Veronica on the bed. She tossed back and forth for a moment, then I covered her with the blanket.

I walked to the chair next to the window and sat down. Watching Veronica I thought about Dominic. He had nothing to do with any of this. Samantha's the one who got us into it. He just wanted to help. Images of Dominic's taxi driving off the road, and exploding jumped through my mind. How did it happen? The same images looped over and over, this is crazy, they're gone, and not coming back.

I dozed off a few times, but always woke up because I couldn't get the images of the Dominic's car exploding out of my mind. I had a gut feeling that something wasn't quite right. A feeling that it wasn't an accident, and caused by someone because of what Samantha knew. Why else would the travel agency have been blown up? Someone set-off the explosion, but who? None of this makes sense, I thought, then nodded-off into dreamland as the sun set.

I woke during the night, and got up to see how Veronica was doing, then dozed off again. I was exhausted. A nurse came into the room almost every hour, checking the IV, taking Veronica's pulse. I opened my eyes every time she came in, but just slightly, then fell back to sleep.

In the middle of the night I let out a painful moan, and jumped to my feet with a charlie-horse in my leg. "Man—that hurts." I growled, grunted, and hobbled around the room trying to shake off the pain.

I checked the time. "Three-thirty. So early," I said, and sat back down in the chair for a few minutes, but couldn't go back to sleep. Still feeling a tinge of stiffness I stepped into the hall, stretched, then went into the bathroom, closed the door, but didn't turn on any lights. As I sat there on the ivory throne the hospital room door squeaked opened. I heard light footsteps brushing the floor. Probably the nurse checking Veronica, I thought, so I didn't bother getting up. I just sat there taking care of business, listening to the whispering voices, but it didn't sound like nurses or doctors—it was someone else. What are they saying? I couldn't understand, so I kept still not making a sound, and just listened intently.

Then, as the bathroom door-knob turned slowly, my heart raced, then pounded! I could hear it beating and thumping in my head. Who was trying to open the door? Was it the old guy I saw earlier? I watched as the door-knob turned back and forth again. I sat there with my pants around my ankles, then stood slowly, and pulled them up. My heart raced faster than ever while thinking of a plan. I'll charge out, tackle, and beat whoever it is—but I need a weapon. I picked up the tiny gray metal trash can from the corner. "This'll have to do." I waited a moment. "Here goes," I whispered, then took a deep breath. "Now, or never," I said holding up the can, and threw open the door ready to swing.

"Dominic!" I said stunned. There he was big as life. "You're not dead. What . . . is going on?"

"That's not a bad thing is it?" he said nonchalantly, and grinned. "Sorry, for bothering—interrupting you," and turned from the door."

"You scared the crap out of me," I said. "Well you know what I mean. Tell me what happened. How did you get here?" Excited and mystified I fired off question after question. "Samantha, what happened on the highway?" I asked. "We heard you guys were dead."

We all looked at Veronica because she was awake, and sitting up in bed with a surprised look on her face. Dominic walked over and gave her a hug. "Why are you crying?" Dominic asked.

"Because I'm happy! I'm so happy," then she smiled and looked at Dominic. "Are you real?" she asked and touched his face. "You are real! It's not a dream!" They hugged again, and Veronica wouldn't let go.

I looked at Samantha, "Nice to have you back," I said. "What happened to you on the way home?" I asked. "Tell me about the accident."

"We were driving up the road to my father's place when I noticed a truck in the rearview mirror," Samantha said. "It came out of nowhere."

"What happened next?" Veronica asked.

"It was getting closer, and wasn't slowing down, then crashed into us, so Dominic drove faster. We were going really fast, and able to get ahead of it on the corners."

Dominic turned, looked at me and said, "Yeah,

then Samantha told me the road ahead was a dead end with no way out. So, on the next curve, I pulled over. We got out, and the car rolled ahead as we ran across the road to a small clump trees. We waited to see what would happen." Dominic's eyes got bigger while he told the story.

"The truck came around the corner, rammed my cab, and pushed it off the cliff," he said in an excited voice, gesturing with his fist—punching his hand.

"It rolled down the hill, exploded into a huge ball of fire, then landed in the crevice below. After a moment, there was another huge explosion, and everything shook off the Richter Scale, like an earthquake."

Dominic sat on the chair next to Veronica's bed, then said, "I need a drink." He grabbed a cup and poured himself some water, took a drink, then continued his story.

"We decided that it was better to let whoever was driving the truck believe we were dead. Instead of going to Samantha's house we got a room at a hotel for a while, until we could figure out what to do. Samantha knows what's going on, don't you?" Dominic said, and looked at her with assurance.

"What's going on, Samantha?" I gave her a probing look as I remembered the night I spent with her at a hotel. "What do you know?"

"I don't know much," she said.

"Just tell us what you do know," I said, then looked at Dominic, "What did she tell you?"

Dominic shrugged, turned to Samantha and said, "Tell them, Samantha"

"There are people doing things," then asked in a fearful tone, "Are you sure you want to know?"

"People doing what?" I said. "Is your father involved in this?"

"Samuel's not my father."

"Samuel Lee Loyde is not your father." Veronica said. Samantha choked up, "Samuel worked for a group."

"What kind of group?" I asked.

"A very powerful group," she said as she sat down.

"Tell us what you know," I said. "I saw you behind the waterfall at the Necker hotel."

"I know," she said. "I saw you, too."

"Where does the elevator behind the waterfalls lead? And who is Zinty?"

"Peter Zinty worked at Buffalo City with my father."

"I've already heard this story from Woodstone at the police station," I said. "There's a file on what happened that night, how Zinty went berserk, killed everyone, then started the place on fire."

"He wasn't the caretaker of the school," she said. "He was in charge of the laboratory in the school, and the secret program they were working on."

"What kind of laboratory?" I asked.

"Microbiological," she said. "They tested people for immunity to disease, conducted biological research for cures and remedies."

"Who did they test?" I asked.

"My family was one group," she said, and cried. "They tested my family, and I watched them all die horribly," then she wiped away her tears.

"Zinty used me in the program. I was given injections, and the molecules in my body only age one year for every ten now. According to the last examination it's progressing, soon I'll stop aging altogether, and don't know what happens after that . . . live . . . die. "

"This is incredible," Dominic said.

"I think that's why Zinty's after me. Everything was destroyed in the fire, so he wants to find out if he can replicate the anti-aging process, and sell it. Samuel Loyde saved me from Zinty. That's why Zinty killed Samuel's family and the scientists working on the project."

"Who got these scientists together?" I asked.

"Zinty was in charge of finding scientists who were experts in microbiological research. He hired them to work on the project, but they discovered what was happening, and wanted to leave. Zinty threatened to murder their families if they didn't cooperate. Samuel heard about it, and used his influence to get rid of him. Zinty snapped, went on a rampage, and burned the school down."

"Just like his son snapped," I said. "Why was your family chosen for testing?"

"We needed money to pay off debts. My real father was in the military. That's how he found out about the program. He thought it would be a way to pay off our bills, so he volunteered, then was asked if our family could participate."

"He did it for the money?" I asked.

"So much money was offered. He thought we would be set for life, but not about the danger. He agreed to their offer, and we all were taken to Buffalo City."

"Where's Buffalo City?" I asked.

"It's located in the country," Samantha said.

"Is it still open?" I asked.

"It's been rebuilt," Samantha said.

"Is testing going on there now?" I asked.

"No, Samuel uses it as a safe place," she said.

"Who else knows about the anti-aging?" I asked.

"Only Zinty, Samuel, and now—you," Samantha said. "It's been secret all this time, but I knew that Zinty might get out of jail someday, and come looking for me."

"What about the other people?" I asked.

"I don't know about any other people, just my family."

"You age one year, for every ten?" Dominic said.

Disbelief was written all over his face.

"I was twenty-one when Buffalo City was blown up forty-five years ago," she said, "and the injections I received were for cancer research."

"Twenty-one? So, now you're . . . it's amazing," Dominic said. "You still look twenty-one."

"Who are these rich, powerful people, this group you talked about, and what are the hotels for?" I asked.

"People who want to control the world," she said. "They have the money, the power to do whatever they want, and the hotels are staging points."

"Staging points for what?" I asked.

"After guests check in they're monitored, then infused. It makes them a virtual zombie," she said. "They look normal, but are manipulated. The control centers are located at the Necker hotels. After infusion they're evaluated for skills or qualities that can benefit the project, then given commands." Samantha said.

"Commands?" I asked.

"Messages or instructions— anything that needs to be done," she said. "Everyone has a special talent."

"Does that include murder?" I asked.

"Anything," Samantha said. "People believe they are free, and doing what they want. They think being in the program gives them freedom, but they're really controlled by the project."

"Are any of the scientists who first worked on this project still involved or alive?" I asked.

"They were all killed by Zinty that night at the school," Samantha said, "except one."

"I can't believe what I'm hearing," I said. "What's the reason for the control? Why do it? For what purpose?"

"Originally, the program was designed to find

medicines to help people and cure illness, they were way ahead of their time," she said. "What they discovered was by accident, but once they understood what they had the project was taken over by someone else."

"So, Samuel Loyde isn't in charge anymore?" I asked.

"He never was in charge," she said, "he's an architect. He designed the hotels, managed the construction, and tried to protect me. Now, that he thinks I'm dead, maybe he'll get out all together, or worse, they'll infuse him, or— I don't know what to think anymore."

"What are some of the messages they send to the infused, and how are they sent?" I asked.

"They control life, property, everything," she said. "The instructions benefit the project. They've infused people who work in many areas," she said. "If anything needs to be done, a message is sent, and it's taken care of. The infused don't know what they're doing."

"When was the last time you spoke to Loyde?" I asked.

"I saw him the day you were at the Necker hotel when you jumped into the pool to get your wallet."

"You talked to him?" I asked. "What did he say?"

"He didn't say much, or anything unusual."

"Who's in control of the project now?" I asked.

"I don't know who's in control of the Shilo project now."

"Shilo!" I said. "At the hotel you wrote, S-h-i-l-o, on the mirror."

"Yes," she said.

"Why?" I asked.

"I wanted your help," she looked at me. "I hoped you would be curious enough to want to know more."

"What can I do?" I asked.

"I want you to help Samuel Loyde. He's changed," she said. "He wanted to build hotels, and help people, not control them." She looked down and softly said, "I hope he's okay."

"I think we're all going to need some help now," Dominic said. "It sounds like these Shilo guys are serious. They surely don't want anyone walking around talking about this." We all nodded in agreement.

"We can't go anywhere yet because Veronica's leg is still in bad shape," I said.

"I can walk, let's get out of here before—" Veronica said, but was interrupted by Dominic.

"Where can we go," he said, "and— what about that crazy old man, Zinty? He's still out for blood, and wants Samantha for anti-aging tests. He's not going to help us. For all we know he's working for Shilo again."

"I think I saw him here the other night by the door. A man was standing by the door looking into the room." I said. "I thought he resembled Nick Zinty. Maybe it was him."

"Oh—that's—just—great! Now he knows where we are," Dominic said, then waved his arms around while he paced the room.

"But he doesn't know that you and Samantha are alive. I might know someone that can help us," I said.

"Who's that?" Veronica asked.

"The painter," I said. "He might be able to give us a hand. We need a place to stay until we figure out what we're going to do. We have to come up with a plan, and he might have a place we can use."

"How do we contact him?" Veronica asked. "He's hard to find, isn't he?"

"I have his number, or—I can call the guy who runs the shop that sells his paintings. I think we should stay here for the night, take turns on watch, and in the morning we'll tell the doctor that Veronica wants to leave. We can get any medication she needs, then. How's your knee, Veronica?"

"It's swollen, but if I wear the brace I can walk."

"We can help you," Samantha said.

"Okay, we'll stay here tonight," I said. "We have to stay alert. Who wants to take the first watch?"

We all looked at each other in silence. "Okay," I said, "I'll take the first watch, then I'll wake you up, Dominic."

Dominic sat down in the chair next to the window and said, "I don't know if any of us will be able to sleep."

"Well, let's try," I said. "We've got to be fresh and sharp tomorrow. I'm going to take a walk and have a look around."

"Be careful, John," Veronica said.

"I'll be right back," I said then walked down the hall. What are we were going to do next? I thought.

I walked the quiet hallway watching the nurses who were sitting behind the counter speaking in whispers. I walked past them. "Morning," I said in a soft voice, and nodded, wondering, Are they infused? Are they controlled by Shilo?

"You're up early this morning," a nurse said. "Can't sleep?"

"No, I can't, too much excitement," I said, grinned and kept walking down the hallway, then stopped, turned and asked, "Is Veronica Wrigley's doctor coming in this morning?"

"Yes, he'll be in at about eight o'clock to do his rounds. Does she need anything," the nurse asked. "Is everything all right?"

"My friend, Veronica, would like to know when she can go home, that's all."

"She had knee surgery, didn't she?" The nurse said.

"Yes, that's right."

"Well, if there aren't any complications she can leave anytime."

"How about today, after the doctor sees her," I asked.

"If he thinks she's all right; it shouldn't be a problem."

"Great, I'll let her know," I said.

I went downstairs to look around, but it was quiet just some cleaning and medical staff. I walked over to an exit of the hospital and had a look outside. "It's getting light," I said to a guy mopping the floor.

"Yeah," the cleaning guy said. "Time for me to call it a day, or in my case, night, and go home."

I watched the sun come up as I called the painter. I dialed his number, but there was no answer.

In the room, Veronica and Dominic were sleeping, but Samantha was still awake, sitting comfortably in a chair reading her—BULLSHIT—book.

"Is that book any good, Samantha?" I asked.

"Yes," Samantha said. "Everyone can relate to it."

"That's right," I said, and laughed. "There's a lot of it around," then sat on the floor, leaned against the wall, and closed my eyes. A moment later I checked the time. It was 5:30 A.M., almost daybreak. The lights will be on soon, I thought, then we can start packing, and get out.

"Hey, Dominic, wake up," I whispered.

"Yeah—Yeah, I'm up," he mumbled; his eyes closed.

"I need to rest a few hours or won't be worth spit tomorrow. It's your turn to play watchdog," I said. "I don't think anything will happen, but just in case."

"Don't worry, I'll keep an eye out," Dominic said, then got up, and went to into the bathroom. A few minutes later he came out and asked, "Still awake?"

"Not for long," I said, and the last thing I remembered before falling asleep was seeing Dominic standing over Veronica's bed.

Chapter Thirty-three

Sunlight beamed through the windows striking the wall, and filling room. I slowly opened my eyes as it warmed my face. Aching and stiff in the chair by the window I stood, barely able to move my crooked and contorted frame. I stretched then glanced over at Veronica. She was asleep; her swollen leg elevated, resting on two pillows. On the table next to her bed was a tray of food that was recently put there, not a bite of it gone.

I faced the wall, put my hands flat against it level with my shoulders, pushed, and twisted left, then right. My spine cracked and popped. It was a habit I picked up in boot camp. During my back cracking ritual a nurse walked into the room and said, "Good morning," in a bright and cheerful way. "Sleep well?"

I looked at her, grinned and said, "No, not at all." "Is your back okay? I heard how it cracked," she said in a concerned tone, then checked the untouched tray of food next to Samantha's bed. "I've never seen anyone do that before. When I came into the room during my rounds you never woke. You were sleeping like a baby."

"It was horrible," I said, and turned left, then right, cracking the vertebrae in my back once again. "I didn't sleep much, but I don't feel tired. I remember seeing you come into the room." I watched the nurse check Veronica's pulse, and take her blood pressure. I stood next to her bed. Veronica was half asleep tossing and turning, trying to get comfortable.

"How are you? Feel hungry at all? This food looks pretty good. You should try eating something."

"Okay," she said, then sat up and moved the tray closer to the bed.

"Your temperature is fine; blood pressure's okay. I'll be back later after breakfast." She picked up her medical gear and walked out of the room.

"Try to eat something."

"Okay, I'll try," Veronica said.

"Here, let me give you a hand with the food." I picked up the plate and fed Veronica. She ate while watching Samantha asleep in the chair across from the bed.

"Samantha must really like that book," Veronica said. "She fell asleep reading it."

"Bullshit is like that," I said. "It lures you in slowly before you realize you've spent an enormous amount of time and money, wasting time and money. How's the food, good?"

"It's not bad," she said, and took another bite. "I feel my appetite coming back, could I have a little more?"

I held the spoon to her mouth, and said, "Here you go, open wide." I saw a smile appear on Veronica's face.

"That's good, here you go, eat up," I said.

"What about Samantha, maybe she'd like something to eat?" Veronica said.

"She's not making a sound, so let's not bother her, she needs rest. Open up," I said, and dished up the last of the food to Veronica.

"How's the knee feeling?" I asked. "Can you walk out of here today?"

"Well, I've got to go to the bathroom. Let's see if I can make it on my own."

"Okay, but I'll be right here just in case."

"My knee feels pretty good today," then she swung her leg across the bed and down to the floor. "It just feels a little swollen and tight."

"I'll try putting some weight on it." She put her feet on the floor, then stood. "Look, I can do it," she said as if she'd won a marathon, "and it doesn't hurt, too much. Okay, here I go." She took off walking slowly across the room, then closed the bathroom door with a sigh of relief. "I passed the first test."

"Let me know if you need a hand," I said and heard her cute staccato laugh as I walked over and checked the hallway. It looked like a busy morning. Doctors, nurses, and patients were moving around in the hospital, then Dominic came walking from the elevator, I waved.

"Hey, I brought you a cup of coffee," he said, and handed the cup to me.

"Just what I need," and took a sip. "Not bad, thanks, Dominic."

"The girls doing okay?"

"Samantha is still asleep, but Veronica is up and moving around," I said. "She just took her first trip to the to the little girls room all by herself, so we should be able to leave today."

"We need to talk to the doctor when he gets here."

"The nurse told me he's coming in around eight. We'll see what he has to say about Veronica leaving today, then get any medicine she needs and head out," I said. "And, I'll try calling the painter again in a little while."

"Do you think he'll be able to do anything for us?" Dominic asked.

"I hope so," I said, "there aren't many options. How about you?" I looked at him. "Have any ideas?"

"No, I can't think of anything," he said. "When are you going to call him?"

"I'll try again right now," I said, "but first, let's go back to the room, talk to the girls, and see how they're doing."

When we got back to the room, Veronica was on the bed doing leg exercises, and Samantha was sitting in the chair reading the *BULLSHIT* book.

"When the doctor gets here, let's ask about the procedure to be discharged," I said. "I'll try calling the painter again, and ask if he can put us up for a while."

"How about going to the police?" Dominic said.

"I don't know if that's a good idea," I said. "We can't be sure who to trust. I think we should find a place to stay, clear our heads, make a plan, then stick to it. It's ringing—Hello," I said.

"Hello, my friend," the painter said.

"What gave you the idea it was me?" I asked.

"I didn't know it was you. I always say that when I answer the phone. Who is this?" the painter asked.

"John Bird Ray, I bought one of your paintings. We met at the Mexican restaurant the other day, Charlie's, remember?"

"Oh, yes, hello," he said. "How's your girlfriend?"

"We're in trouble," I said. "Veronica's in the hospital. She had knee surgery."

"Oh," he said, surprised. "What happened?"

"It would just take too long to explain on the phone. Can we meet somewhere? We don't know each other that well, but I need your help."

"Sure," he said. "Where do want to meet?"

"What about Charlie's, the Mexican restaurant, or at the shop where you sell your paintings?"

"The shop is more private."

"Okay, this afternoon—the shop at two o'clock?"

"I'll see you there," he said and hung up.

"Well it's all set. We're meeting at two o'clock this afternoon at a shop that sells his paintings. I've been there, it's quiet, out of the way, and no one will pay any attention to us."

"When can we tell people we're not dead?" Dominic asked.

"I don't know, Dominic." If they find out that you're not dead, they may try to kill you."

"Do you know how weird that sounds," Dominic said. "They'll kill us—if they find out we're not dead."

"I think we should let everyone continue to think you're dead, and go through the motions as if you are," I said. "It's only for the time being; just until we get out of this mess, then you can be alive again."

"Don't you think people will know we're not dead" Dominic asked.

"The police didn't find any bodies at the accident, and you said the car was totally destroyed, so there's not much left to investigate. There's a lot of wildlife in the area, they'll think your remains were carried off by scavengers. How long was it before they found the car?"

"I don't know, but someone must have heard the explosion and called the police, it was huge. The woods started on fire," Dominic said in a high nasal, muscular tone while gesturing like an orchestra conductor.

"Well, whether you're dead or not, there's not much we can do about our circumstances," I said. "We have to figure it out—come up with a plan."

"I don't know," Dominic said, "I don't like it—don't like it at all."

Chapter Thirty-four

"*G*ood morning," the doctor said as he walked into the room.

"Hello," Veronica said. "Good morning."

"Morning," I said.

"How are you feeling this morning, Ms. Wrigley?"

"I feel a lot better, thank you."

"Oh, that's quite a change from yesterday. Let's take a look at your knee." He removed the tape, then squeezed the muscles around the joint, and tested her range of motion.

"There's some fluid, but as you walk more and more, your muscles will absorb it, and the swelling will go down. Continue using the ice cast. Do you have any questions?"

"Well, there is something."

"Certainly," Dr. Honda said.

"Can I leave today?" Veronica asked.

Doctor Honda took another look at Veronica's knee.

"Well, I advise against it, but if you want to go we can't keep you here. I think you're on the road to recovery."

"Can I get some pain medicine to take along?"

"Yes, I'll prescribe some medicine for the pain, and swelling," he said. "Are you in any pain now?"

"A little when I stand on it."

"It's the fluid in your knee, but you can leave anytime today, but make sure you wear the knee brace."

"That wonderful," Veronica said. "What do I have to do?"

"I'll tell the nurse in charge that you'll be leaving today, and they'll help you with the paperwork. You should come back for a check-up in a month. If everything looks good, and you're getting better, longer intervals at least for a year."

"Okay, I'll set up an appointment, thanks so much for everything, doctor."

"My pleasure, take care, bye."

We had just taken the first step to finding out what all of this was about. Step two was finding a place to stay. We would hopefully do that today after meeting the painter.

"Lets start packing everything up," I said. "Samantha, are you ready to go?"

"I'd like to take a shower if I could," Samantha said. "Do you think it's okay?"

"I don't see why not," Veronica said. "Anyone else want to take a shower?"

"A shower sounds good to me," Dominic said.

"Okay, we'll all take a shower before we leave. I'll go last," I said. "Where's your bag, Veronica?"

"In that closet," she said and pointed to the cabinet next to the bathroom.

I opened the closet, took out the bag, and everything else of hers. "Veronica, go take a shower," I said. "I'll pack it up for you." It's like we're on holiday, I thought.

"I'll help you walk," Samantha said.

Dominic walked to the bed. "I'll tag along."

I had to wait for everyone, so I took out my laptop. I thought, soon we'll be nomads and typed.

Nomads always travel, never staying put for any length of time. This is how I feel now, like the millions of people in the world who lead nomadic lifestyles. But, we were all nomads at one time, hunting, fishing, and gathering food. Learning about plants, which ones to eat and smoke. Adjusting to the climate; migrating with the seasons, free like the birds.

The song "Freebird" by Lynyrd Skynyrd rang in my head again. Change, life's all about change!

Being nomadic encouraged clans to grow in numbers and gain knowledge to improve life. One group knew how to make pottery, another how to fashion tools and weapons from bone and metal. This knowledge was passed on and traded for food or other goods. This fusion developed into large communities and made moving difficult, so towns and cities grew. This resulted in the decrease of the perpetual traveler.

Then a problem occurred in nomadic clans and tribes. Because of isolation they had no immunity from disease that cropped up in large crowded cities.

Simple viral organisms devastated entire nomadic clans. In the past nomads were self-reliant, but today those who live a quasi-nomadic lifestyle are the homeless. They live in the streets begging for sustenance. They come out of the darkness, searching for life, and selling their blood and bodies for food. Misplaced citizens who live short lives because of the harsh conditions of street life. Many are runaways or the dregs of society.

Actually, we're all nomads from the time we can walk. We have itchy feet, a desire for exploration, a wanting to discover our purpose in life. Older folk are jealous of the young. Jealous of their youth, curiosity, and determination. Open minds that wrap around all that surrounds them. We only experience youth once in our lives, then somehow get bogged down with knowledge and material desires that are always just out of reach. The older we become the more irritated we grow. We know the clock is ticking, and sooner or later it will stop.

I stopped typing and thought, Part of me is looking forward to this nomadic life. It's going to be dangerous and difficult, but the excitement is real, intense, and I feel alive.

The girls came back to the room. "That didn't take very long," I said.

"And now it's your turn," Veronica said. "No offense, but you're getting a little ripe."

"Okay, I'll take a shower," I said, and turned off my laptop. "Which way do I go? Where is the shower?"

"Go left out of the room, walk to the end of the hall, the shower's on the right. Here's a towel," Samantha said, and threw it at me, then laughed. "Don't get lost."

Samantha throwing the towel to me brought back the memory of the night we spent at the hotel together. I looked at her and grinned. "You were the one who got lost last time, not me." I put the towel under my arm. "I'll find it, but taking a shower in a hospital seems strange when you're not a patient." I grabbed my things. "I'll be right back," I said, then walked out of the room whistling the theme song from, *The Good, Bad, and Ugly.*

Some patients' rooms were open as I walked down the hall to the shower. I could see the recently repaired, stretching and exercising their bionic knees. Everyone was here for knee or hip surgery, orthopedic work of some kind. I noticed one guy sitting on the edge of his bed massaging his knee. There was a long red scar over the top of his knee cap. My guess was that he had a complete knee joint replacement. He walked into the hall, smiled, and looked happy just to be able to walk.

Smiling, I said, "Hi."

"Hello, visiting someone?" he asked.

"Yeah, my friend had knee surgery a few days ago."

"How's your friend doing?"

"She's doing great. We're leaving today. What about you? Leaving soon?"

"Oh, I think I'll be here a bit longer. Definitely a few more days, but I should be able to leave next week."

"You seem to be doing well," I said. "Walking and moving. Looks like you had a complete joint replacement?"

He joked. "Yes, it's the same as changing a flat tire these days."

"How long is it supposed last?" I asked. "Is there a warranty?"

He laughed. "I don't know if they call it a warranty, but they told me it should last from ten to fifteen years."

"Well, good luck to you," I said. We shook hands and I walked down the hall, then spotted the shower. I went in, cleaned up, and got out. It was refreshing. When I got back to the room everyone was waiting for me.

"All of the paperwork is finished," Samantha said. "Veronica's officially discharged."

"That was fast," I said. "Doesn't it usually take longer?"

Samantha just told them her name, and the paperwork was done in no time," Dominic said. "Now what?"

"Well, I guess it's time to meet the painter?" I said.

"How are we getting there?" My cab's a wreck. We need a vehicle."

"We'll rent something," I said. "Where's the closest rental place?"

"Wait!" Dominic said. "We don't have to go to a rental agency. I just thought of a guy I know who'll bring a van right here for us. I've got the number in my wallet. Just a second, I'll give him a call."

After a short phone conversation Dominic announced, "The van will be here in thirty minutes."

Chapter Thirty-five

"*L*et's get our stuff downstairs," I said.

We grabbed the bags, went down the service elevator, and out a back door of the hospital, then waited.

"You have your medicine, right, Veronica," I asked.

"Yes, I've got it."

"How's the leg?"

"It's okay, I'll be fine. The brace helps, don't worry."

"Here's the van," Dominic said. "Let me talk to this guy first, okay. I'll be right back."

Dominic went over to the driver of the van, then came back after ten minutes. "We're all set," he said. "I've got the keys, and we can keep it as long as we like. Let's load up."

The vehicle was a silver Cargo van with no windows on the sides, only in the rear door. After about fifteen minutes everything was loaded. It was a tight squeeze, but we managed to get ourselves, and everything in the van.

"Goodbye hospital," Dominic said, and drove away waving.

"I'm glad to get out of that place," Veronica said.

"I don't like hospitals either, and don't know who does, I said," except for insurance companies.

I sat in the back with Veronica, and Samantha was in the passenger seat next to Dominic.

"I was just writing about Nomads before we left the hospital," I said. "Now, that's what we are."

"Well, it's not quite the same as the Nomads from the old days," Dominic said. "We're in a van, and they were lucky to have a horse and wagon."

"That's not what I mean," I said. "I'm talking about how Nomads traveled from place to place to survive."

"Okay, right. Which way to the painter's place?" Dominic asked.

"It's not his place," I said. "It's the shop where he sells his paintings. Just stay on this road, and look for Huxley Street, then I'll know where I am." I scanned the streets for a landmark trying to remember which road the shop was on.

"Sure this is right?" Dominic asked.

"Yeah, I think so, just keep going."

After driving around for a while I said, "That place looks familiar," then I pointed, and said anxiously, "turn right up ahead, by that salon." Worried he'd miss the turn I barked, "Hurry, turn, that's the shop over there." I was amazed that I could actually locate this place again. "Find a place to park."

"How about right here?" he said, and pulled into a space across the street from the shop.

"This is good," I said. "I'll go in first, everyone wait here until I get back."

"Okay, but don't take too long," Dominic said.

"Hey, I'm coming right back," I replied, but then turned back to the van, and said, "The shop looks quiet." I walked across the street between the traffic, stood at the door, cupped my hands over my eyes and peered through the window. Nothing had changed much since the last time. When I opened the door the bells rang in the same quaint way as before. Hector was sitting behind the counter in a chair with his back to me. I walked over and said, "Hello, Hector," expecting him to turn around and greet me, but there was no response, so I repeated, "Hey, Hector, you okay?" in a loud voice—still no response.

I walked around behind the counter, and spun the chair around. When it stopped I looked at him and said, "Hector?" His face was pale and he wasn't moving. I hesitated, then wondered, Did he have a heart attack? I put my hand on his neck to feel for a pulse, but there was none. Great—another dead guy, I thought, and walked to the rear of the shop up the stairs that led to the second floor. I looked around, but there was no one in sight, not a sound. I went back down to the first floor, and looked for a message, or some clue from the painter.

I checked Hector's pockets, but found nothing. I walked out of the shop, and was about to close the door when the phone on the desk rang. I turned toward the ringing phone. I bet it's the painter. Should I answer it? I listened to it ring a few times, then slowly picked up the receiver. I raised it to my ear, and listened for a moment, then in a vague tone said, "Hello," but there was no reply, then repeated, "Hello—"

"It's me."

"Painter?" I said. "What's going on? Your friend, Hector is dead."

"I know, I know, I was just there! I saw him."

"Did he have a heart attack?"

"I'm not sure what happened."

"Was he sick? I didn't see any strange marks on him or anything unusual."

"I have no idea, but I don't think it was a heart attack. When I was walking to the shop I saw two guys marching out," the painter said. "I waited a while, then went in. Hector was sitting in the chair, his face was frozen like stone."

"Where are you now?" I asked.

"Sorry, I can't say; I don't trust the phone. What's on your mind?"

"Do you remember where we first met?" I said. "You know, where I bought the cat painting?"

"Yes, I do."

"Let's meet there," I said.

"Okay, I'll be there, bye."

I hung up the phone and walked back to the van. After I sat down, everyone looked at me with intense curiosity, as if I'd just come back from Mars, and wanted to know if life existed there. "We have got to leave right now." I said in a commanding voice.

Dominic looked at me, "What happened in there?"

"I don't know, but the guy who owns the shop is dead," I said.

"What!" Dominic said in a high nasal voice, then asked, "Are you sure?"

"Who's dead?" Veronica asked.

"Hector, the guy who owns the pawn shop." I said.

"What happened?" Samantha asked.

"You're asking the wrong guy. He looked fine sitting in his chair behind the counter; a smile on his face. I walked over next to him, then realized he was dead after I checked his pulse. The phone rang, and I picked it up, it was the painter. He told me he saw two guys walk out of the shop about thirty minutes ago."

"What now?" Dominic said.

"First, we get out of here, and make sure no one's following us," I said. "Can you do that, Dominic?"

"Yeah, I can do that," he said with a broad boyish grin. "Hold on!"

Dominic floored the van. "Everyone keep an eye out for anything suspicious," I said with a vigilant tension in my voice.

"Where are we going?" Dominic asked.

"We're meeting the painter downtown where I bought the painting," I said. "He thought someone was listening when we talked on the phone, so we just said we'd meet where I bought the cat painting."

"Just tell me which way to go," Dominic said as we drove through the maze of streets, turning left, then right.

"Anyone see anything unusual?" I asked.

"I can't tell," Veronica said, "I just see cars, and buildings."

"It doesn't look like anyone is following us," I said, "but let's drive around a little. Head downtown, let's be sure."

"Okay," Dominic said. "I'll skip around here, so if anyone's following they'll get twisted and tangled." We drove around in circles for about thirty minutes, then he parked the van.

I went on foot to meet the painter at the spot where I had bought the orange cat painting, but the place looked different because it wasn't crowded. I was checking the time, looking around, then felt a tap on my shoulder and turned. It was the painter.

"Hello," I said, "thanks for coming."

"Whatever I can do to help," he said. "Tell me, what is it we're involved in?"

"I'm not sure if we've been followed," I said while looking around a little paranoid. "We've got a van parked a few blocks away from here. I think we should go now. I can tell you more when we get somewhere quiet. Can you come with us?"

"Let's go to your van," the painter said.

"Sorry about your friend, Hector. I only met him once, but I liked him, he was friendly."

"Yes, he was. What is this all about?"

"There's the van," I said. "I'll introduce you to my friends."

Dominic rolled down the window and said, "We were wondering if anything happened. Is everything okay?"

"Yeah, fine," I said. "This is the painter."

"Hi," Dominic said with a friendly grin and handshake.

"Hello, again," he said to Veronica, kissed her hand, then took Samantha's hand.

"Hi, I'm Samantha."

"Hello, Senorita," he said, then kissed her hand, too. "How are you?"

"Okay, now that we all know each other, and are done greeting and kissing, let's get in the van," I said, "We don't think we were followed, but it doesn't hurt to be safe."

"Where are we going?" Dominic asked.

"I don't know." Then I looked at the painter. "We were hoping that you might have a place that we could use until we sort things out."

"I have a place," he said.

But was cut off by Dominic, "I think we have company," he said. "Look over there." He was pointing at a black SUV with tinted windows that was parked across the street. "Who do you think that is?"

"Don't know, but that black SUV looks familiar," I said, "Let's see what happens."

We sat frozen in the van and watched, our eyes filled with curiosity.

"Are you sure it's waiting for us," Dominic said.

"Yes, I'm sure," Samantha said. "That's my father walking across the street." We watched Samuel Loyde, encircled by a small entourage of barrel chested guys in black carrying a lot of artillery, stroll toward us in what looked like a defensive formation.

"I thought you were adopted?" I said.

"Yes, that's right, but he's still my father, and has taken care of me most of my life."

"Look at those guys with him," the painter said.

"Oh, yeah," I said. "They look pretty serious, and they're built like tanks."

"What should we say to him?" I asked.

"Nothing, just let him do the talking," she said in a voice that carried a sense of hope.

Loyde walked up to the driver's side window, and tapped on it with the gold ring on his finger. His intense gaze radiated through the glass, and he wasn't smiling. Dominic gave him a boyish grin, opened his window, and said, "Hello, nice day, isn't it?"

"Hi," Loyde said. "Samantha, you're a hard girl to keep track of. We thought you were gone after we heard about the car accident. Who are your friends?"

"This is Dominic, that's John, Veronica, and he's called the painter."

"Okay, I want you to follow my vehicle to Buffalo City. I know you need a place to stay, and I'll provide that, but you'll have to do something for me," he said.

"What's that?" I asked. "What do you want from us?"

"Join us," he said, "or at least, after we get there, hear me out. I have someone that I want you to meet."

"Who?" I asked.

"Someone who's been working with me, and just like you, had a problem with Zinty."

"Zinty's dead," I said.

Then, Veronica said, "I saw John shoot him."

"Yes, Nick Zinty is dead, but his father's alive and well. Peter Zinty knows all about you." Loyde's voice filled with gloom when he mentioned Peter Zinty's name.

"Come to Buffalo City, and listen to what I have to say. After you hear me out you can decide if you want to stay or leave. Keep in mind, if you don't follow me you may not have a tomorrow. You're pushing the envelope, and right on the edge."

Samuel returned to his SUV with his bodyguards, got in the back, pulled up next to us, rolled down the window, and said in a cool sophisticated manner, "Follow me." He looked at Samantha, then at all of us and urged. "I can help you. Follow me."

"What should I do?" Dominic asked.

I looked at Dominic and said, "Do we have a choice? Follow him."

Chapter Thirty-six

We felt a little uneasy as we followed Loyde's black SUV. We had no idea what was going to happen once we arrived at Buffalo City. I turned to Samantha. "Has Samuel had the bodyguards around a long time?"

"I'm not sure. He's hired more of them since Peter Zinty's release from prison," she said. "He doesn't go anywhere without them."

"I'm no weapons or security expert, but from my short stint in the service, it looks like Loyde's body guards are ex-military," I said. "They're well trained, and the weapons they have are heavy duty—those guys are for real!"

"I was thinking the same thing, and I'm a taxi driver," Dominic said.

"Did you see how they moved around the SUV when we met Loyde," Veronica said.

"They're pros," I said.

"They moved with the precision of a clock," the painter said, "as if they had rehearsed again and again."

"Not the kind of people I'd mess with," Dominic said.

Loyde mentioned meeting someone who survived the tragedy at the Buffalo City Architectural School, and a scheme to destroy Shilo. Loyde looked comfortable in his SUV, occasionally turning, and looking back at us. I thought about what he said—Zinty is after you. After us? Why? What a muddle? As we drove to the Buffalo City compound I watched Samantha, and remembered what she said about Shilo, and how Loyde wanted to put an end to it. This was going to be a huge task, and required more than our help. What am I doing here? I thought.

We followed Loyde's SUV up the twisting narrow valley road that cut through the forests and open fields. Eventually passing the dizzying rocky cliffs where Dominic and Samantha were forced into the iron barrier, and pushed off by the mysterious truck. Seeing the hairpin corner again made Samantha and Dominic sigh as we approached. The guardrail hadn't been repaired yet, and pieces of it were awkwardly piled off to the side of the road. A pile of modern art that looked similar to Picasso's metal sculpture in Daily Square.

"This is where it happened," Dominic said. "Remember, Samantha?"

"I can't look," she said.

Everyone, but Samantha looked out at the debris, then we continued up the winding road close behind Loyde's SUV. Finally, the house came into view.

"Look at that wall," I said.

"The place is surrounded by a sixteen-foot-high stone barrier," Dominic said looking at it in disbelief.

"It's more like a fortress than a house," the painter said. "Why does someone need such bulwark?"

Samantha looked at him, then said in a pleasant tone, "It's just home to us. Home sweet home."

It was uncanny how Loyde's place was similar to my story when I imagined and wrote about Samantha and Dominic on their drive up here. Huge columns in the middle of the entrance that supported a second floor balcony. Gigantic windows that reached from the second floor to the top of the third floor, and on either side of the main structure two octagonal towers encased in glass. Connected to them, two square sections that wrapped around to the back of the property. It was hard to tell how large the place actually was with all of the crazy angles and shapes.

We stopped at the front entrance of the house, and sat there waiting for someone to tell us what to do. Lined up all in a row was a number of huge potted trees. I happened to look up, and saw guards pacing the balcony and the roof. Then, more guards moved out from behind the trees, and into position around the vehicles. One of them, probably the leader, signaled for us to get out. Again, I had the feeling of being here before, but couldn't understand why? Perhaps I was still suffering some side effects from the laced tea. Samuel Loyde got out of his car, and waved for us to follow him to the house.

Before we entered the house the body-guards approached us. "We need to search you before letting you enter," the guard said. "Raise your hands."

"Just follow their orders," Loyde said. "They're trained to make sure we're safe. It's for our protection."

"Empty your pockets for me," the guard asked.

"What is this?" Dominic said. "I thought we were here to help. Why treat us like common criminals?"

Dominic took everything out of his pockets, then said, "I feel like I'm at the airport."

"You can go shopping at the airport," Veronica said.

"It's just a precaution," the guard said. "Please cooperate and we'll finish in no time."

They took our coats, checked in all of the pockets, inside our bags, then gave everything back to us.

"One more check, and we'll be done," the guard said. "Take off your shoes, please."

"Take off my shoes?" I questioned him, and looked at Loyde. "Is all of this necessary?"

"We've got to do it," Loyde said. "Why have security if we don't use it. We can't take any chances."

"Okay," I said, and took off my shoes, then handed them to the guard who waved an electronic device over the soles, and checked inside them.

"Here you are," he said, and handed them to me.

"Now, let's go inside," Loyde said, "and I'll introduce you to Dr. Melvade."

As we entered the foyer we were surrounded by vaulted windows. The splendor and spaciousness was magnificent, but not unexpected because Loyde was an architect. In front of us a circular stone staircase with ornate iron railings, and beautiful warm wood that twisted up three floors to an intricately designed glass dome over the foyer. The floor was covered with endless, exquisite marble. The space left of the staircase was home to a grand piano, and on the other side was an unusual opaque stone.

"What's that Mr. Loyde?" I asked as I pointed to the dark stone that sat under a soft glow of light from an oriel.

"Have you heard of the Rosetta Stone?"

"Yes, it's in the British museum, isn't it?" I said.

"Well, this is another piece similar to it," Loyde said. "No one knows it exists," then went on to explain about the stone, and the language carved on it.

"Formal language is thought to have come from an ancient culture, perhaps 3000 B.C., but it's possible a written language existed thousands of years before that—it's an unfinished puzzle that we're racing to piece together." We watched Loyde talk about his *secret stone*. We stood listening to him, captivated, his face glowing with angelic adoration as he gave us a cursory history of it.

"The Rosetta Stone displays two written languages, Egyptian and Greek in three scripts, hieroglyphic, demotic, and Greek. The stone is believed to have been carved around 200 B.C.," he said. Then rubbed his hand over the stone. "This one has a third, and is much older." He pointing out the different languages engraved on it. "It was found near a town called Rosetta, and the same stone was used to carve many things, statues, bowls, doorways, axes."

"How much does it weigh?" I asked.

"About 2000 pounds," Loyde said.

"How old is the stone?" I asked.

"How did you get it?" the painter asked?

"Sorry, I can't give you that information," he said, "but Rosetta is now a term for translation and decryption. In molecular biology the term *Rosetta* describes cell lines that contain genes of tRNA enabling translation of DNA."

"Shall we go to the library, now," Loyde said, and smiled. "Follow me, please."

Who's the man that you want us to meet?" I asked.

"He's a scientist," Loyde said. "Have you heard the term, Gene Expression?"

"No," I said. "What does it mean?"

"It's used to describe the process of a gene's coded information, and how it's translated into the structures that operate in a cell."

"Sorry, I don't follow you," I said.

"Statistical data is used to determine what genetic conditions and disorders exist in humans. Incidence, prevalence, mortality, lifetime are systematic terms used to interpret these conditions by taking into account a person's history."

"You mean a way to know when someone will get sick or die?" I asked.

"Something like that," he said.

We continued walking through the house entering a sunroom of lush green plants that covered the entire floor, a botanical garden encased with windows all around. My eyes scanned the room from the floor to the ceiling, and fixed on the trimmed yard and trees. The wrought iron gate hidden by a hedge, and off in the distance a small pond with a gurgling mermaid fountain.

We followed Samuel Loyde into the library, and were stunned by numerous bookshelves that lined the walls.

"The Carnegie library in my home town didn't have as many books as this place," I said.

The windows were divided into individual panes that lit the room with a warm ambient light. It reflected off the lion heads carved into the railing of the wooden staircase, and softly continued to the second tier of bookshelves. We walked through an open doorway that led to a smoking room with more bookshelves. On the left was a stone fireplace with a stuffed owl on the mantel; it's wings out ready for flight. A couple of solid blue armchairs sat beside an oak table with smoking paraphernalia, and the lingering aroma of tobacco followed us into the next room.

"Here we are," Loyde said. "Have a seat everyone."

I sunk into the black leather sofa in front of a hefty stone fireplace. Veronica and the painter on either side of me. Dominic and Samantha sat on the sofa opposite ours. Loyde stood in the middle waiting for us to get comfortable.

"Okay, let's see," Loyde said. "First, let me tell you about Dr. Melvade. He's one of the scientists who worked on the original Shilo project at the Buffalo City School. He was out of the lab the day Zinty went on his killing spree. He'll be joining us in few minutes. While we're waiting, would anyone care for something to drink?"

"Sure, why not," I said.

"Good, I'll have some drinks brought in."

He picked up a telephone, spoke to someone, then said, "The drinks will be here in a few minutes. I'll check on Dr. Melvade, make yourselves comfortable.

After a few minutes, a short, stout, ornamentally dressed man with slicked back dark hair arrived with an assortment of beverages. "Hello," he said, his voice distinctive. "I'll just put everything here on the table. If you need anything my name is Grain. Just pick up any phone and dial one." He smiled, then left quietly, carefully scanning the room, every detail under his eye.

Chapter Thirty-seven

Samuel Loyde came into the library with the man we were to meet. "Everyone, this is David Melvade."

"Hello," Melvade said as he walked around the room greeting us, and shaking hands. He was tall, thin, had a built-in smile that wouldn't quit. His unusually reddish tinted short crew-cut, was perhaps, to cover his gray hair.

Then Loyde said, "Doctor Melvade will give you some background on the Shilo project, and briefly touch on our plan and strategy. He's an old-hand when it comes to Shilo."

Melvade stood behind a round oak table in the room setting up something. We all noticed the burnished silver case, then he turned toward us and said, "Okay, let me give you a run down on how this all came about. Years ago, I was approached with a very lucrative offer by Peter Zinty. I was to work with other scientists on a project called, Shilo. And by now, I'm sure you've heard that name.

"Samantha told us a little about it," I said.

"Each one of us specialized in distinct areas of microbiology. Let me tell you their names and what kind of research they were doing." He continued this presentation in a step by step process to make sure we understood.

"Frank Miescher worked on infectious diseases, Lee Antonie researched the human immune system, John Mol was a DNA sequencing expert, and George Van Barrow worked on antiviral vaccines," then he pointed to himself, "I'm a weapons biologist. After I agreed, I was assigned here at the Buffalo City Architecture School. Peter Zinty told me the name Shilo was chosen because of some reference to the meeting place. Some special mythical place where all people would gather free from all disease—*bliss or nirvana* he called it.

He looked at us, raised his eyebrows, then asked, "Any questions, so far?"

Everyone was silent suggesting we didn't have any, so he continued as we sat quietly, and listened.

"This project was peddled as a program to study disease and immunity. Today, we call it gene therapy. A gene is inserted into a specific location; basically an abnormal gene is swapped for a normal gene."

"This is getting a little complex," I said.

"Sorry, in 1953, Watson and Crick discovered what we call, DNA. You've seen the double twisted helix structure composed of the basic elements of life," he asked.

We all nodded and replied, "Yes."

"Okay, all of life is stored in a DNA molecule. Proteins inform and communicate information to the organic cell using a unique messenger language."

He walked around the table and then continued.

"Imagine a language so complex, contains so much

information, that there's no practical way to print it. There are approximately thirty-five thousand genes in one DNA molecule arranged in three billion precise sequences."

"That's unbelievable," Dominic said.

"Yes, it is," the painter said. "Unfathomable."

"How do we become who we are? How do we know what we are? How do we learn? What is the ananc, or secret of life? Are we simple sequences of amino acids? Are these molecules the building blocks of life? Where did the sequence, structure, and composition of DNA originate? No one knows—"

"You mean even with all of this knowledge, no one knows anything about it?" Veronica asked.

"We know at the micro level there is continuous communication. Cells invisible to us communicate with the most sophisticated and complex language, still not completely understood by any means, or by anyone. This elaborate design, and keys to life, leaves many questions. How it works, who made the keys and locks, how to break it, and if we do—what happens next?"

"Why do we need to know all of this?" Dominic asked.

"It will give you some idea of what we did years ago, and what's happening now," Melvade said.

"What did you do years ago?" I asked.

"Okay," Melvade said, "I'll talk about that now. We explored how DNA duplicates so quickly and accurately. We ran experiments on informational capacity, how it facilitates protein interaction. We ran lines and lines of code." He picked up a glass from the table and took a drink of water.

Of course we sat quietly, nodding, somewhat lost, without much of an inkling of what he was talking about.

"DNA is the instructional book of life, and the self-replicating ability of DNA is one characteristic we worked on. We tried to determine how to design a communication mechanism that would function within a DNA molecule. DNA is like a snowflake slipping from one form to another, leaving only a memory behind. We must harvest the memory, and use it for communication.

"You harvest the memory," I said.

"During this research we discovered a blueprint for molecular communication. We created a data bank from the information that resulted in numerous script codes. The basic code for proteins looks like this," he said, and passed around some information, then held up a chart.

```
CACACACACACACACACACACACACACACACACAC
ACACACACACACACACACACACACACACACACACA
AAAAAAAAAAAAAAAAAAAAAAAAAAAAAAAAAAA
TATATATATATATATATATATATATATATATATAT
CACACACACACACACACACACACACACACACACAC
ACACACACACACACACACACACACACACACACACA
AAAAAAAAAAAAAAAAAAAAAAAAAAAAAAAAAAA
TATATATATATATATATATATATATATATATATAT
CACACACACACACACACACACACACACACACACAC
ACACACACACACACACACACACACACACACACACA
AAAAAAAAAAAAAAAAAAAAAAAAAAAAAAAAAAA
TATATATATATATATATATATATATATATATATAT
CACACACACACACACACACACACACACACACACAC
ACACACACACACACACACACACACACACACACACA
AAAAAAAAAAAAAAAAAAAAAAAAAAAAAAAAAAA
TATATATATATATATATATATATATATATATATAT
CACACACACACACACACACACACACACACACACAC
ACACACACACACACACACACACACACACACACACA
AAAAAAAAAAAAAAAAAAAAAAAAAAAAAAAAAAA
TATATATATATATATATATATATATATATATATAT
AAAAAAAAAAAAAAAAAAAAAAAAAAAAAAAAAAA
CACACACACACACACACACACACACACACACACAC
```

"Genes have specific base sequences of code that make proteins," he said, "called codeons."

Symbol	Name	Codeons
A	ALNINE	GCT, GCC, GCA, GCG
B	ASP or ASN	GAT, GAC, AAT, AAC
C	CYSTEINE	TGT, TGC
D	ASPARTIC	GAT, GAC
E	GLUTAMIC	GAA, GAG
F	PHENYLALANINE	TTT, TTC
G	GLYCINE	GGT, GGC, GGA, GGG
H	HISTIDINE	CAT, CAC
I	ISOLLEUCINE	ATT, ATA, ATA
J	LEU or ILE	
K	LYSINE	AAA, AAG
L	LEUCINE	TTG, TTA, CTT, CTC
M	METHIONINE	ATG
N	ASPARAGINE	AAT, AAC
O	PYRROLYSINE	
P	PROLINE	CCT, CCC, CCA, CCG
Q	GLUTAMINE	CAA, CAG
R	ARGININE	CGT, CGC, CGA, CGG
S	SERINE	TCT, TCC, TCA, TCG, AGT
T	THREONINE	ACT, ACC, ACA, ACG
U	SELENOCYSTEINE	
V	VALINE	GTT, GTC, GTA, GTC
W	TRYPTOPHAN	TGG
X	ANY AMINO ACID	
Y	TYROSINE	TAT, TAC
Z	GLU or GLN GLUTAMINE	GAA, GAC, CAA, CAG
*	STOP TERMINATOR TERMINATION CODEON	TAA, TAG, TGA

"DNA is complex, but the language used to send a message to a protein is unbelievably intricate. Code is contained in the reverse direction, on opposite strands, upside-down, right-side up, always twisting and turning."

Melvade paused for a moment, "Excuse me," he said, and took another drink of water which made me thirsty, and I licked my lips, then we all took a drink.

"The sequence can start at any point of the codeon, at any of the three letters in the code." He pointed to the chart again to show us.

"Also, DNA strands are anti-parallel, and cells in our bodies are always dividing. When a new cell divides, a copy of all sequencing is made, so there's a complete set of genetic instructions, and the blueprint to build a protein."

"So, with these instructions, and this blueprint, DNA can be manipulated," I asked.

"Yes, copying, replication, division, the messenger-RNA, then the transfer. We have genetic protein factories in our bodies. Life is similar between all life forms. If man could control genetic code what do you think would happen to man?" he asked.

What he was saying was interesting, but I didn't know what to make of it, and neither did anyone else.

Then the painter said, "So—DNA is like paint and canvas. The painter chooses the paint, then creates a picture of something he then brings to life."

"Yes, that's one way to put it, I guess," Melvade said. "Call it what you will, a painter, builder, a creator."

"Then, who is the painter in this molecular world?" the painter asked.

"We don't know? But, there are some people who would like to be the painter of life. We believe Zinty and some others want this authority," Melvade said, "and they'll use this power to control humans!"

I raised my hand and asked a question. "Who made the paint and the canvas?"

Then the painter added, "God?"

Melvade paused, then looked directly at us. "It's the mystery of mysteries. As far as we know manipulating DNA is like flipping a coin, random, but structured, or pre-arranged, and if man gets involved . . ." he didn't finish, but we all had an idea of what he was going to say.

It was quiet for a moment, then Melvade said, "Today we have genetically altered food. You probably have eaten it. It's the same genetic communication that does *code adding* in our device."

He took another drink of water. "During our research we used ideas from gene therapy. For example, to deliver the normal gene we need a vector, and a common vector is a virus," Melvade said.

"You're telling us that a virus is used," I said. "Isn't that dangerous?"

"Yes, but the virus is altered to carry normal DNA. There have been difficulties using this kind of vector. Some people have become ill—a few have died."

"What kind of virus is used?" Dominic asked.

"Usually, a retrovirus, HIV, or an adenovirus, one that causes infection, or herpes," he said.

"That sounds crazy," Veronica said.

"You have to understand that the vector gene has regular DNA information," Melvade said. "Of course, like I said, there have been problems."

"What kinds of problems?" I asked. "Do you mean like in the book, *The Island of Doctor Moreau* by H.G. Wells?"

"Ones that we wanted to avoid in the future," Melvade said. "We opted for a non-viral gene delivery system which has limited capacity, but we were able to compress the large amounts of DNA needed for our vector."

"What's a non-viral delivery system?" I asked.

"It's an artificial sphere made of Nano Carbon. Once infused, it's autonomous, and doesn't affect any workings of any chromosomes, or cause any mutations. Every human has twenty-three pairs of chromosomes. Twenty-two, numbered by size, are called autosomes. The last pair determines sex."

"This nano carbon just stays in the human body?" Dominic asked.

"Yes, the body's immune system won't attack Nano Carbon, and it has the capacity for fairly large amounts of genetic code. Through assessments we discovered a way to communicate with DNA molecules using these codes and this delivery system."

Melvade picked up a schematic that showed how DNA information was transmitted to a target.

"It's this easy," he said, and pointed to the chart, then asked, "You've heard of Morse Code, haven't you?"

We all nodded that we had.

"Then he added, "It's not used very much today, but this idea is in our work. Samuel Morse proved electric signals could be sent and received by wire. The pulses of dots and dashes he developed represent numbers and letters of the alphabet. Morse Code was the system of communication used by the world. You know what SOS means, right?"

"It's the signal for *help*," I said.

Melvade passed around a Morse Code chart. "We use Morse Code as a receptor for our transmissions."

A.- B-... C-.-. D-.. E. F.-. G--. H.... I.. J.--- K-.- L.-..
M-- N-. O--- P.--. Q--.- R .-. S... T- U..- V...- W.-- X-..-
Y-.-- Z--..
1.---- 2..--- 3...-- 4....- 5..... 6-.... 7--... 8---.. 9----. 0-----

"Alexander Graham Bell taught visible speech to students, trained teachers to use his sign language, and created a device to test hearing. Bell's interest in communication led him to the idea of continuous electrical waves of current to create sound waves. He transmitted musical tones, then his voice, through a device called the liquid transmitter. *'Mr. Watson, come here, I want you.'* was Bell's famous first telephone call, asking his assistant for *help*. Now we have communication at our fingertips."

"Nikola Tesla transmitted radio waves to a small boat on a lake. The crowd watched in disbelief—astonished, and newspapers reported that he used his mind to control it. Now, voices are transmitted across the ocean, digital transmission—finally thoughts and ideas will be transmitted by signals directly to others. Well—to some degree it's similar, only at a micro level." Melvade said, then passed a chart around that read.

[Information]>[Transmitter]>[Signal]>[Receiver]>[Destination]

= Control

"DNA is stored in organic molecules. Molecular identities expand as high as sixteen million. This is the language or map of the genetic code, and just like maps of the early world have changed, so will the maps of the genetic code. We map what we know, and learn as we go."

Melvade walked to the table in the middle of the library. On the top was the silver case. He continued talking. "The project head, Peter Zinty, saw some potential to use this discovery as a control device or weapon."

As Melvade spoke his hands caressed the case.

"How was he going to use it?" I asked.

"He wanted me to develop a delivery device that could be implanted into an individual."

We thought he would open the case and show us what was inside, but he just kept his hands on it while he spoke.

"Once Shilo operatives implant the mechanism into someone every aspect of their life, from how long they live, procreate, any illness they have, and how they die is kept in a secure data base.

"Records are kept of all the guests who stay at Necker Hotels. This data base is used to breed highly intelligent beings for more highly intelligent offspring to do the project's work. It's similar to the work that was done at Cold Springs Harbor.

"It's an ingenious plan," Melvade said. "Using the bubble device to send signals to guests, encourage sexual encounters. And with this data base follow the growth of the progeny, so the potential future thrall can contribute to the Shilo project."

Melvade never opened the case. He just walked back to the middle of the room and continued talking.

"Signals are launched from control points called CPs. Future plans are to incorporate the use of satellites to send transmissions directly to implants. It'll be as easy as making a telephone call. At the moment, a person must be at one of the Necker hotels to receive transmissions. All of the Necker hotels are CPs, and communication is delivered to the target from within any Necker hotel."

Melvade paused for a moment and was about to say something, but I asked a question first. "What's this device called," I asked.

"It's called—*The Bubble.*"

"Are you saying that if a person is given this bubble implant, they could be controlled to do anything?" I asked.

"How is it done?" Veronica asked.

"Anything," he said, "they're a walking antenna. It's a bit difficult to explain how it works in layman's terms, but just believe me—it does."

"Can it ever be removed?" Veronica asked.

"No, never," Melvade said. "Once implanted—it's for life as far as we know."

"Who's in charge of the project now?" I asked.

"We think his name is George Mulreck," Melvade said.

"I've met him," I said, and all heads in the room turned to me. "He's short, bald, and wears glasses, and has a sinister laugh."

"That's him, and he's deadly serious about his work. He's honed his craft working for government doing covert operations, and may still do some work for them, but we're not certain," Samuel said.

"What about Nick Zinty?" I asked.

"Zinty's son, Nick, was controlled by Peter Zinty after he was given the implant. We've heard, through Samuel, that Peter Zinty is working on the project again. Mulreck got him out of prison because Zinty convinced him that he could advance the Shilo project, and utilize the satellite capability."

"Is the government involved in the Shilo project?" I asked.

"Yes, we think so from time to time, but they have no idea what Mulreck and Zinty are capable of doing."

"What does Zinty want?" I asked.

"He wants to set up control centers around the world, and in time control millions, breeding them to become super human thralls. Mulreck and Peter Zinty work at the Necker CP here in Chicago. That's where they are developing the satellite capability that will launch signals directly to any implant at any location."

"They'll be able to send signals to anyone?" I asked.

"Yes," Melvade said.

"What can we do? Why are we important to this?" I asked.

"I've lost access to all of the Necker hotels, and underground facilities like the one you saw behind the waterfall," Loyde said. "Perhaps you can get in, again."

"That was a fluke," I said. "It won't work again."

"You got in once," Loyde said. "You can do it again."

Melvade stepped into the conversation. "Samuel has contributed a lot to the Shilo project, but like me wants to end it. He still has some influence, and invaluable information, but sooner or later they'll want to make sure he doesn't talk."

"Why not tell the media?" I said.

"Tell the media," Melvade said. "The media stay at the hotels. The Necker Hotel Corporation has contracts with all of the media. We have no idea how many people from the media are already implanted, and given orders via signals to do Shilo's bidding. Shilo controls the media."

"Is there any way an implanted person can be detected?" I asked.

"Yes, we have a way to detect a target, but it's difficult. It's not so obvious," Melvade said, and went on to explain how it could be done. "On the fingertips of an implant's left or right hand there's a raised line and dot pattern similar to Morse Code—a receptor is branded into the tips of the fingers. You have to get a look at the tip of someone's fingers to know if they've been implanted. The distinct marks can be used in various sequences."

"I've seen this before," I said. "When I was on the train a few days ago, a blind man, and a homeless guy, had those marks on their fingers."

"Are you sure?" Samuel asked.

"Yes," I said, "and Nick Zinty had them, too."

"How are the signals transmitted to the target?" the painter asked.

"The signals are beamed from transfer points located in the hotels," Melvade said. "You've seen electronic touch screen devices at hotels that provide information and help guests navigate, right?"

"We all nodded."

"The infused lay the branded hand on a TP, and the signals are sent through the receptors on the tips of their fingers. Perhaps soon the TP will be at ATMs, banks, airports, and even the supermarket."

Dominic broke out laughing, then said, "Is this for real? Can the receptors be put on toes, too?"

"Why do you find it so amusing?"

"Receptors on fingertips—now that's funny," Dominic said. "This whole thing is so weird."

Nodding he said, "I see," then with a hauntingly burning gaze added, "nevertheless, it's true."

"Does this bubble implant stay in one part of the body?" the painter asked.

"It bonds with DNA. The bubble is a delivery device, the mechanism is the information. It's microscopic and there's no way to remove it, but on my own I started doing research which demonstrated some interesting results."

"While the implanted bubble device cannot be removed, similar to treating disease, it became inert for a period of time. The mechanism Dr. Melvade experimented with neutralizes Shilo's transmissions," Samuel said.

"I don't know about anyone else," Dominic said, "but you've managed to scare the shit out me if this is true."

"Me too, Veronica said. "Stealing souls and turning people into zombies."

"I'll go along with being scared, nervous, worried, and scared shitless. I don't know what else to say," I said.

"Is there a plan?" the painter asked.

Dr. Melvade turned, looked at us silently a moment, his hands clasped held to his chest. I thought he was going to pray, then he brought his hands down and said, "We need your help."

"Us," we all said simultaneously. "What kind of help?"

"Let me be honest. We need people, but at the same time have to be very careful who we recruit."

"But we don't know what to do, or anything about DNA," Veronica said with a fearful tone in her voice.

"Samantha's explained how you helped her, we trust you, and hope that you'll join us," Samuel said. We'll train you. The leader of the penetration team is Antone Beatus. His background and knowledge of this kind of activity is invaluable. You'll meet him in a couple of days, if you decide to help us."

"Samuel designed the hotels, has layouts and blueprints that show all of the transfer points in every hotel, so we have a way to get into the hotels without being discovered."

"This sounds very complicated," Dominic said as he rolled his eyes.

"Once we're in the hotel, we'll the use the micro-device I've developed, to block Shilo's signals, commands and messages to the people who have been implanted. Shilo will continue sending signals to targets, everything will appear normal until we finish the job," Melvade said.

Samuel added, "Blocking the commands from Shilo should result in chaos, they'll lose control of the implants, and no longer be slaves to Shilo."

"Why do we have to go to every hotel?" I asked.

"Yes, good question. We go to the hotels because that's where most of the implants are. We won't have complete control unless we re-infuse as many implanted people as we can," Dr. Melvade said.

"Even if we go to all of the Necker Hotels, stopping Shilo will be a Herculean task," Loyde said.

"Why don't we just go to the homes of the infused people, and implant them with your device?" I asked.

"That may be the next step," Melvade said, "but at the moment we just don't know who they all are. We can implant more people at the hotels, so we're focusing there first."

"How many hotels are there, and where are they located?" I asked.

"There are 21 hotels at the moment, but they're planning to build more in the near future."

"21 hotels," I said as my jaw dropped open. "It's impossible. How can we go to 21 hotels, and what do we do once inside? And, what if we're caught?" I asked. "It all sounds crazy."

"What is your plan?" the painter asked.

"Yes, the plan," Melvade said. "We'll discuss all of the details of the plan later, if you decide to join us."

Everyone sat dumbfounded with blank, pale expressions on their faces. We watched Melvade as he spoke to Loyde.

"I wonder what they're talking about." I whispered to Veronica. Loyde left the room, then returned.

We sat quietly, waiting for Melvade to say something, then he turned toward us.

"It won't be difficult to transport the device because it's micro in size, and only takes a short time to complete the infusion. We'll show you how it's done. I think once you see the procedure you'll feel differently."

"How long will it take to go to every hotel?" I asked.

"A long time," Dominic said, in a flippant way.

"We don't know exactly," Melvade said.

"Here's the list," Loyde said, then passed around a slip of paper with the names of the cities. "Shilo has Necker Hotels in these cities."

New York, USA	Mexico City, Mexico
Los Angeles, USA	Madrid, SPAIN
San Francisco, USA	Mumbai, INDIA
Washington D.C., USA	Honolulu, HAWAII
Chicago, USA	Tokyo, JAPAN
Osaka, JAPAN	Berlin, GERMANY
Sydney, AUSTRALIA	London, UK
Moscow, RUSSIA	Hong Kong, CHINA
Vancouver, CANADA	Rome, ITALY
Montreal, CANADA	Paris, FRANCE
Johannesburg, SOUTH AFRICA	

I looked at the list and shook my head in disbelief. "You want us to go to all of these countries?" I said.

Loyde spoke again, "It's the only way," he said. "We don't know exactly how long it will take to finish, chances are we'll never be done, it's an on-going war." We looked at Loyde as he said, "You won't have to go to every hotel, we have others working in our group."

"Isn't this going to be expensive going to all of these countries?" Veronica asked.

"Yes, but we have the funds, financing the operation is not a problem. We'll plan the order of hotels, who will go where, and make it as systematic as possible. Will you do it?" Melvade asked.

"I don't know?" I said, then looked at Dominic, Samantha, the painter, and Veronica.

"Do you need all of us?" I asked.

"Yes, all of you," Loyde said. "The teams will consist of six members."

"Veronica just had major knee surgery," I said. "We don't know if she's up to it."

"I can do it—if you want me to," Veronica volunteered.

"Are you sure, Veronica," Dominic said.

"You won't be leaving on this operation until you're ready," Loyde said.

"Excuse me," Melvade interrupted. "I just want to say we'll go over everything carefully, rehearse the infusions, and back up plans, cover every possible detail."

"Mr. Loyde," the painter said. "What do you think?"

Samuel looked at us. "What do I think? What do I think about saving mankind from eternal servitude? I think you can walk away and forget everything we've spoken about," Loyde said. "It's fine by me," then he paused for a moment, "but we'll go through with this plan whether you help or not because it's got to be done."

"The Shilo project is out of control and these people must be stopped. You know what's waiting for you out there, remember the pawn shop, remember Hector," Melvade said. "It's up to you to decide."

We all looked at each other again and nodded in agreement that the cause was definitely legitimate. As I looked at everyone's face, thought, We're going to do it. I think we're going to do it.

Samuel stood, "We'll leave you to mull it over, then answer any questions you have," and before he left said, "I'll come back to show you to your rooms."

After Samuel, and Dr. Melvade, left the room we sat quietly, absorbing what we had just heard.

Chapter Thirty-eight

"**W**ell," I said, "we don't have to go through with this, we're not agents or police, just regular people, but it does sound fascinating."

"Training alone isn't enough?" Dominic said.

"What kind of training do we really need?" I asked. "All we have to do is infuse people with a micro-device."

Dominic looked at me, chuckled and said, "What the hell is a micro-device?"

"It's probably similar to giving someone an injection. Let's hear what we have to do tomorrow," I said. "If it's, too difficult, we'll just say no."

"That makes sense," Veronica said.

"What do you think, painter?" I asked.

"I think, if we say no, and this gets out of hand because we didn't pitch in, we'll never forgive ourselves. We have to go ahead and help if we can."

Loyde came back into the library. "I'll show you the rooms now. Have you decided whether to join us?"

"We're going to make up our minds after we know exactly what we have to do. If it's more than we can handle, then we'll have to back out," I said.

"Fair enough," Loyde said. "It's late so follow me, and I'll show you where you'll sleep."

As we climbed the circular staircase up to the third floor, I noticed more of the detail that went into building Loyde's palace and it was flawless. Maybe Loyde and Melvade know what they're doing, I thought.

"I have to say, Mr. Loyde, you have an amazing place here. I've never seen anything like it in my life. Did you work on it for a long time?"

"Design and construction took years."

"Everything's truly stunning," I said.

"It took a lot of effort to finish and get everything just right." Loyde said, and winked. "I worked with a number of architects who came up with some fantastic ideas, had input from students, and friends as well. We all express ourselves in different ways," he said. "Here are your rooms."

I stood at the top of the stairs looking down at the foyer, then down the long hall. "I feel like I'm in a hotel," I said. The rooms were next to each other on both sides all the way down the hallway.

"So, do I," Dominic said.

"Just choose any of them," Loyde said, "but let me show you something first."

We walked into a room; it was elaborate and luxurious. There was a bar, a TV as big as a picture window, and a huge bed sat in the middle of the room.

"This is extremely nice," Dominic said.

"Thanks," Loyde replied. "Here, let me show you

something in this closet. Every room is the same in a special way. He gestured for us to step into the closet. "Come in; here's room for all of us."

"This is a very big closet," Veronica said.

"Inside every closet is a hidden door, that leads down to the back of the house to a safe area, in case we have to leave quickly. We can use the boat at the dock, a car from the garage, or the helicopter. You can try it. First, let me show you how it works."

"You've got a helicopter?" I said with disbelief.

Loyde turned, and looked at me. "It's sometimes useful to have one," he said. "Grain's a pilot, and been with me for some time. He has talents other than cooking and serving drinks that occasionally come in handy."

Loyde walked to the back of the closet, placed his hand on the wall in a special position, and the wall opened.

"How do you know where to touch the wall?" the painter asked, then said, "Wait, I see it, the hand, there's a hand on the wall."

"Well, for everyone else look closely, and you'll see a 3-dimensional hand pattern on the wall. You have to focus on the two dots on the wall until they're one. Try it," Loyde said. "There are sensors embedded in the wall."

The painter focused on the two small dots until they came together. Slowly the hand image was there in plain sight, he put his hand on the wall over the 3-D hand image, and the secret door opened. "This is amazing, Mr. Loyde," then we walked through the opening, and down the narrow staircase.

"Incredible," Dominic said.

"I have door-activated hand prints everywhere in the house, and in the Necker hotels. I kept it off the design plans. I have them at other structures I've built, as well."

"Do you have maps of where they are?" I asked.

"Yes," Loyde said, "and you'll be using them to navigate around the hotels unnoticed if you decide to join us." He closed the closet door. "That's all for tonight, rest, and we'll talk more in the morning. Again, since the house has so many rooms you can each have your own. Just pick one and make yourself at home."

"A good night's sleep might be the best remedy to help make a clear decision tomorrow," I said. "Will you be all right, Veronica?"

"I'll be fine," she said. "I have ice for my knee, just need some sleep."

"I imagine you'll want to stay close, so why don't you use these rooms," Loyde said. "Grain can help you with anything, just use the intercom."

"See you in the morning," Dominic said.

"Good night all," the painter said, and went into his room singing, and humming a happy melody.

Samantha smiled, "Good night," and followed Loyde, then turned and said, "My room is downstairs."

"Good night, Samantha," I said and walked into my room. I fell on the bed looking up at the ceiling with the same feeling of familiarity that I had when we drove up to the house, but didn't know why. Then, I closed my eyes, and fell asleep dreaming of a painted 3-D hands, receptors on fingers, and my shadow.

Chapter Thirty-nine

I woke surprised and bewildered thinking, what a strange dream, then checked the time. It was three o'clock in the morning and quiet. I sat there on the bed a few minutes waking up, then went to the bathroom. Next, I grabbed a can of beer from the mini bar, and walked to the window to have a look outside. It was a pleasant night as I watched a boat tied to the dock slowly rock back and forth. I walked out on the balcony, looked up at the clear night, the stars gleaming, stirring, and reflecting off the lake as Pink Floyd's song, "Shine on You Crazy Diamond" floated through my mind. I thought about the dream I'd had for a moment, then went back into the room, and typed it.

    The Dream - I was carefully tramping
    through a thick mist on a murky evening,
    my footsteps crunching leaves and

branches as I stepped on the dark path in front of me. Along with hooting owls and twittering crickets, all the latent sounds of the night were in my mind and in my memory. Part of the night, and part of my dream.

I came upon an endless field of taxis. I looked down at my feet where I saw footprints. I followed them left, then right, between the cars, and occasionally straight.

I tried opening the doors, but they were locked. I continued following the footprints around and around until I realized I was going in circles. Then, just ahead, a car started, but didn't move. I approached slowly from behind. I glanced into the driver's window as a huge black dog leapt into the glass barking and biting at it voraciously. I jumped backwards and fell against the car behind me, where another dog flew into the window from inside that car.

Car after car started, the engines revved, and the dogs were barking in all of the cars. I scanned the parking lot, and saw more dogs crashing into the glass, howling and growling until the sound became thunderous. I closed my eyes, and put my hands over my ears to filter out the sound as it changed to a high pitched grinding squeal. A car door opened, a cat jumped out, then a man followed. He stood still a moment looking the area over, then marked me. He was tall, stocky, and had long black straight hair. He walked in my direction while holding out his hand for me to take. He stopped in front of me, and as I grabbed his hand I saw Morse Code implants on his fingertips. Then, I was immersed in color, covered in paint, paint from every work of art ever created. I was alive in the paint, then I was paint.

I started breathing hard, my heart thumping after thinking about the dream. I took one last gulp of beer, turned, and tossed the can into the trash basket on the other side of the room. "Time to call it a night," I said under my breath. "*Time*—it's what keeps everything from happening at once. Where did I read that?" I sat on the bed for a moment trying to relax and clear my mind, staring up at the ceiling of the bedroom looking at my hands and fingers, turning them, closing and opening them. I've heard musicians say, *It's like my fingers all have a brain; brainy end fingers.* I've heard similar accounts from others, and experts who study this phenomenon. They say the muscle remembers actions. Is all knowledge and information some how passed to others through DNA this way?

I stood, had just put my hand on the light switch, ready to turn it off, when I heard a soft knock on the door. Who's that? I thought. I walked over to the door, opened it, then smiled. "Veronica," I said surprised. "Are you okay?"

"I'm fine," she said. "What about you? Can't sleep?"

"No, I had the strangest dream." I looked at Veronica and was glad to see her, in fact, hoping she would come.

"A dream about what?" she asked.

"Are you thirsty?" I said, then opened the small fridge and took out another beer.

"No, just need the company," she said. "Tell me about the dream."

"Well, at the end of the dream," I said, "before I woke up, a man grabbed my hand, and I became part of a painting. Another part was about wild dogs barking in cars, and a cat. The dogs were jumping into the rolled up car windows trying to get out." I looked at Veronica and said, "Weird, huh?"

"I don't know. I've heard that being chased by barking dogs in a dream means that you may have trouble in the future. People dream about things they have, someone they've met—or know. Anything or anyone can be in a dream. I had a dream about us at the hospital."

"Oh, yeah," I said. "Tell me about it."

"How about if I show you," she said, and kissed me. Then took my hands, and put them around her waist. "Hold me."

We embraced in a robust clinch. I kissed her on the lips, face, and neck. Veronica sighed as I picked her up holding her tightly against my body, swirling, then I remembered her knee, and said, "Sorry, I should be careful."

"My knee is fine," she said. "Why don't we sit down?"

"Good idea." We slowly danced in the direction of the bed while caressing . . . eventually collapsing on it, still holding each other. "Tell me more about your dream, Veronica."

"Okay," she said as her eyes sparkled. "In my dream, I unbuttoned your shirt like this—and stroked your chest and shoulders like this." Her soft hand brushed my skin.

"Then we kissed," she whispered softly. Her breath

was sweet. Our bodies became tense. Energy pulsated through every muscle in my body blazing like a forest fire. I felt strong one moment, and powerless the next.

"In my dream we were together, holding each other," she said with a laboring moan. After a moment, I rested my head on her chest, and could feel her heart beating on my face. I felt alive.

"You held me in the dream, and I held you, skin on skin, love in love," she whispered in my ear.

I savored her with my lips, then moved my hands down, and around her waist. I kissed her on the neck, and lips again, while caressing her flowing body. She exhaled with another sigh as we rolled off the bed.

"Are you okay?" I asked with concern after we landed on the floor with a thump.

"Yes . . . Yes," Veronica said laughing "Yes!"

I pulled the blanket off the bed and over us while roaring in delight, panting, breathless as we kissed.

She whispered, "Hold me!" I did, and we fell asleep in each other's arms until the light from the morning sun warmed our bodies.

Chapter Forty

*S*oon after we woke—a short distinct knock echoed in the hallway, then we heard the ornamental man's distinct voice. "Mr. Ray—breakfast is being served. Mr. Ray—"

I sat up and said, "Okay—I'm up—I'm up—breakfast, okay, be right there," then looked at Veronica. "Hungry?" and kissed her. "I am, but not for food."

"Yes," she sighed, and caressed my face with her hand.

"Let's get cleaned up."

We walked into the bathroom together kissing, holding each other, "You're lovely, Veronica, like a dream," I said. We held on tightly breathing in each other's scent not wanting to let go.

"You go first."

"Okay," I said, and kissed her once more, then reluctantly went into the bathroom thinking only of her.

Ten minutes later I came out and said, "Your turn."

I was waiting patiently for Veronica, but wondering why it was taking her so long? "Are you ready?" I asked through the bathroom door, then walked over and stood looking out the window. In a raised voice I said once more, "Ready?" As I turned and looked toward the bathroom, she was standing there looking like a million bucks, with a gorgeous smile that made every thought in my mind stop. I was frozen dead in my tracks—thunderstruck.

"Okay," she said as she tossed and brushed her hair. "I'm ready, willing, able, and hungry."

She came close, caressed my cheek, and looked at me with her deep-brown-eyes. I'd wait for you forever, I thought, and kissed her, then we left the room and went downstairs.

On the way to eat breakfast we saw Dominic and the painter standing in the library being served coffee by the ornamental man. They stopped, motionless for a moment, looking at us, smiling, until I said, "Morning, Dominic." He waved, and the painter gave me a nod.

"The food is delicious, we'll wait for you in here."

I gave them the thumbs up. "We're going to check it out now," I said. "See you later, after we eat."

We followed our noses down the hall to the dining room. It was bright, full of light, with a spectacular view of the garden. Hanging from an ornate painted circle on the ceiling above the table was a mammoth chandelier. The circle was painted in a way that gave the impression of a falling sphere. A wainscot with built-in shelves went around the entire room. On one end, a gigantic stone fireplace with two large crystal stones resting on either side of the mantel. Between them, a hand carved wooden statue of *Atlas* holding the world on his shoulders. The room had three large glass doors that showed the way to the lake. In the middle was an intricately carved wooden table, and around it ten chairs covered in a brilliant floral pattern. On top of the table two glass-bird vases sat facing each other.

"This is a fantastic room," I said. "What do you think, Veronica?" I said.

"I love it," she said. "All of it!"

The same man who served drinks earlier brought in trays of fruit. "What would you desire for breakfast?" he asked.

Veronica smiled and asked curiously, "Can I have anything?"

"Whatever you would like," the ornamental man said with a hint of certainty in his voice.

"Well—let me see," she said and thought about what she wanted to eat.

While Veronica was thinking, I said, "I'll have a couple of poached eggs, toast, and a cup of coffee. What are you having, Veronica, he's waiting."

"Okay—I'll have a cheese and onion omelet, with toast and coffee, please."

"Will there be anything else?" he asked.

"No, that's all, thanks." Veronica said.

"Excuse me?" I said.

"Yes," he replied efficiently.

"I'm sorry, but I can't remember your name."

"It's Grain, sir," he said, and smiled. "I'll be back directly with your breakfast, sir."

I started thinking about how expression makes us feel, and changes how we perceive everything. This whole unreal setup, the huge house, breakfast, everything at our fingertips. I wanted to remember these feelings, so I could put it down on paper later, maybe use it in my book.

Mr. Grain came back with our coffee. "Here you are,

sir," he said, and placed the coffee in front of me. "And here you are, ma'am."

"Excuse me," I said. "Sorry to bother you, again."

"Yes," Mr. Grain said. "How can I help you, sir?"

"Could I have some paper and a pencil?"

"Certainly, I'll bring it straight away."

After he walked away I looked at Veronica. "He'll bring it straight away." We both laughed. It just sounded so formal.

We feasted like monarchs as we watched Mr. Grain, who took his work seriously, serve us. He enjoyed it, was kind, friendly, and treated us like royalty.

"Will there be anything else?" he asked.

"No, thank you," I said. "You've been great, and the food was delicious."

"Excuse me, sir. Mr. Loyde is waiting for you in the library," Mr. Grain said as he cleaned off the table. Do you remember the way?"

"Yes, I think we can find our way. Ready?"

"Sure," she said. "John, let's go out on the balcony."

"Okay," I said. I couldn't say no to her.

We walked though the glass doors into the most spectacular garden on the planet, a rival to *Eden*.

"It's beautiful!" Veronica said with a joyful tone, like a lyric from song.

"Sure is! Like a fairy tale," I said.

"Look at those trees, and the lake. Is it real? Let's go that way," she said and pointed to a trail that rambled from the mammoth house down to the lake.

"Maybe we are in a fairy tale?" I said, again.

Veronica grabbed my hand, and we strolled down to the lake on a path lined with twisted, tangled tree trunks surrounded by flowers of infinite color.

"Unbelievable and amazing! I don't know what else

to say. I've never seen anything like this. It's a painting come to life," I said, then thought about the painter, and how authentic his work looked, so real, and alive.

"Look at the ducks swimming," Veronica said, "and those fish jumping over there."

I turned in time to see them vanish into the soft velvet lake. As we made our way closer we stopped a moment, amazed at how it glazed over like a mirror.

"Look at those cameras on top of the wall," I said, then saw guards on the perimeter peering through binoculars. "I don't know whether to feel safe or worried."

"Samuel must have a good reason for having all of this security," Veronica said.

"Let's head back to the house. Loyde and Melvade are waiting for us." I turned for one last look at the wall that surrounded the Buffalo City School. "What are we getting ourselves into, Veronica?"

"Don't worry," Veronica said as she put her hand on my shoulder. "It'll all work out, John Bird Ray."

"Yeah, okay," I said with some dismay, then we turned from the stone hulk that surrounded the complex, and walked toward the house. Now, we had a view of the main house from the lake. The huge wide patio and flagstone steps spanned the length of the entire structure. I was amazed at how massive it really was. "It looks like a picture-postcard," I said, "and feels like we're strolling in the highest security park ever built."

We were jolted to reality when we heard Dominic shouting from the top of the patio, "Hey! Guys, come up here. Loyde and Melvade want to talk to us."

"Honeymoon's over, Veronica," I said.

Chapter Forty-one

We took our time getting back to the house enjoying every moment. "How's your knee, Veronica?"

"It feels okay. Some slight pain once in a while, but it's better. Walking is good exercise for it."

Melvade, Loyde, Samantha, Dominic, and the painter were waiting in the library. We saw them talking through the huge glass windows as we scaled the stone steps that rose up to the house like a mountain. We waved as we made our way to the patio, then through the multiple sets of French Doors that led to the library.

"Have a pleasant jaunt through the garden?" Loyde asked. His brilliant, steady eyes in control, then smiling, he added. "It looks as though your knee is getting much better, Veronica. You seem to be healing up nicely."

"Yes, hardly any pain at all," Veronica said as she gestured with her arm outstretched pointing at the lake and property. "You've got a wonderful place here, Mr. Loyde, and your garden is beautiful."

"Feel free to walk anywhere. Sorry about the security, but it's necessary," Loyde said, "for everyone's safety."

Melvade motioned with his arm and said, "Please, let's get comfortable." He stood in front of the fireplace waiting for us to sit down, then looked at us. "Have you decided whether or not to join us? We're hoping the answer is yes."

"It is—yes," I said. "We want to help, but run through, rehearse, and practice whatever it is we have to do. We need to know exactly what's going on, and make sure we can handle it. We want to know everything about Shilo."

"Great, that's brilliant," Melvade said, then turned around, picked up a silver metal case from the floor, put it on the table, and said, "In this case I have the device that you'll be infusing the guests with at the Necker Hotels."

He opened the case, but didn't take anything out, and just described it to us. "The device is invisible to the eye, and kept in a clear sphere made of a special durable material that's safe to hold in your hand. If dropped it won't break, but could be rendered useless because the information it contains may be scrambled. You'll carry it in a case like this which is distress proof."

He reached into the metal case, took out one of the tiny clear spheres, held it up to the light, and rolled it between his finger and thumb.

"Floating inside this clear ball is the device," Melvade said. "This minuscule clear ball looks empty, but there's a communication mechanism inside, and as I said before, it's called the bubble. You'll be inserting it into a ribbon injector."

"What's that?" I asked.

"It's the delivery apparatus," Melvade said. "It was

designed specifically for delivering the bubble."

"I'll show you on this diagram," Lovde said as he unfolded the blueprint, put it on the table, then pointed to the middle. "Right here," he said, "it's self-powered. The bubble is loaded into the ribbon injector, and one bubble is used to infuse one thrall." On the diagram it looked like a pen split into two sections.

"How is it done? Do we just point, and fire it like a gun?" I asked. "And, what's a thrall?

"A slave, he said. The ribbon has to be on the target's skin during the infusion," Melvade said. "It's just like pushing down the button on a pen." He picked up the ribbon injector, held it to his fingertip, clicked the button and said, "There, that's all there is to it, but the target must be asleep when it's done."

"Why?" I asked.

"The target needs to be in cream mode while the bubble's communication information attaches to the DNA strand."

"Okay?" I said, then asked, "What's dream mode?"

"It's REM sleep, somewhat like day dreaming," Melvade said. "The bubble is transmitted through the senses. The targets have a code embedded on their fingertips, and the ribbon has a variable head to match each point. This is how we'll infuse them with our bubble."

"Why do you call it a ribbon injector?" Veronica asked.

"The bubbles are held together with a microscopic like ribbon material," Melvade said.

"Can you tell us more about how we'll infuse the targets?" I asked.

"We'll go over that later," Melvade said. "It's not a complicated procedure, and we'll show you exactly what to do. We'll practice and rehearse, again and again."

"Can you tell us more about getting around the hotel,"

I asked. "Everything looks different on paper."

"Remember the waterfall?"

"Yes," I said.

"Behind the waterfall is an elevator that leads under the hotel to a control room," Loyde said, and pointed it out on the map. "You can get there from different places in the hotel using the 3-D doors that are located at various locations in the hotels."

"Do all of the hotels have the same layout?" I asked.

"Yes, all built with a similar blueprint," Loyde said.

"We'll discuss the passageways, and give you more information about the communications room later."

"What exactly is the bubble?" the painter asked.

"It's a bioreactor that discharges a DNA command," Melvade said. "It connects with the target's DNA, and communicates. Our DNA command will interfere with the signals from Shilo."

"I had total control when I designed the hotels, so the passageways are all here on this diagram," Loyde said, and pointed more of them out. "Here's one, and here's another one, they're everywhere."

"How will we practice and rehearse?" I asked.

"We have a mock-up here at Buffalo City," Loyde said.

"We'll show you exactly how to infuse the target, and go over different scenarios," Melvade said. "You'll have some dry runs. If you're willing we can start tomorrow."

"Okay, tomorrow," I said. "Is that good with everyone?" All gave nods of approval.

"Let's stop for today, then meet here tomorrow. I'll explain more about the infusion, and Samuel will explain the layout of the hotels, okay?"

We shook hands, then Samuel said, "Use the library, the garden, or the boat on the lake, and I have some very nice automobiles."

"Cars? I love cars," Dominic said.

"Collecting is a passion of mine," Samuel said. "I store them in the garage, so feel free to have a look."

Dominic looked like he was in heaven. "I've got to see them, Mr. Loyde," he said with his boyish grin.

"Sure, and drive them, too. There's a track we use for practicing evasive maneuvers on the grounds. Samantha can show you. Okay, Samantha?"

"Of course," she said.

"Feel like going for another walk in the garden. We could go for a boat ride?"

"Okay, John," Veronica said. "That would be fun. What about it, Mr. Loyde?"

"Sure, and if anyone has any questions or needs anything, just ask Grain. He's here to help you," Loyde said.

Loyde was quite the character, he had money, all the material possessions a person could want, but he was after something else, I could hear it in his voice, and feel it from him emotionally. Loyde and Melvade left the room, Samantha and Dominic went to the garage, I went out in the garden with Veronica.

"Let's walk through that wooden frame arch with the vine trained over the top," I said.

"That fragrance is wonderful, isn't it?" Veronica said as she looked up. "I could stand here forever."

"Yes, it's amazing," I said. "It looks like an endless tunnel of green. Think Dominic is enjoying himself in the garage playing with the cars."

"He loves cars," Veronica said. "Look at the fountain!"

"It's the mermaid fountain we saw when we walked through the sunroom when we first got here," I said. "Are mermaids good or bad luck?"

"I don't know, but let's make a wish," she said and threw a coin in the fountain. "Your turn, John, make a wish!"

I took out a coin, looked at Veronica, and tossed it into the fountain.

"I have something for you. I wrote a poem last night." I reached into my pocket and took out a piece of paper, "This is for you," I said, and handed it to her.

"You wrote this for me." She was surprised, then unfolded the paper. "Read it to me!"

Love is what I feel
Friendship
Is what we have
A hug, a kiss, a smile
When I think of you
Happy thoughts
Come my way!

"It's lovely," she said, then we kissed. I held her tightly never wanting to let go. I turned toward the house and saw Loyde and Melvade on the steps of the patio, they waved, then returned inside through glass doors.

"Soon we'll start the adventure of our lives," I whispered, "and wouldn't trade places with anyone."

"One—I hope never ends," she said.

I kissed her again as we held each other in a firm grip watching the sun slowly drop from the sky, and disappear behind the lake.

Chapter Forty-two

I stood at the window of my room over looking the grounds watching the warm peaceful morning sun reflect off the lake. I listened to birds chirp in song, and felt the quiet morning breeze lift the air sending ripples to the shore. I saw the path where we walked the day we arrived, and in the distance, the place where I had read her the poem. But, that was the past—and time has melted away.

Now was the day the action would begin, the last morning before the operation, and our last chance to back out. Turning from the window I saw my reflection in the mirror dressed in black quasi-military garb. All I needed to complete the transformation, from run-of-the-mill ordinary guy to soldier of fortune, was a weapon. But we weren't using standard weapons for this operation. This was going to be a bloodless maneuver, a new kind of war—a battle for minds, and a war for souls.

Our training was condensed, completed, and I hoped we were ready to leap into this formidable and incredible task. *No turning back now*, I thought. Loyde told us he chose the Chicago Necker Hotel to be first because all project decisions were made there. It held the targets data, and where Zinty and Mulreck controlled Shilo. Loyde never acknowledged it, but I felt he wanted Zinty and Mulreck removed, gone, terminated. Maybe, Beatus, the former special military expert knew something we didn't.

Arthur Beatus trained and pushed us from dawn to dusk, and we never had any down time. He taught and drilled us until we could do everything without thinking. From the first day we met, I thought he disliked us, or held a grudge because he always displayed the look of distaste on his face—a sour bitter look. Right at the beginning he was the tough old war-horse and wanted to prove it. The guy never let up, he was a machine. He didn't like talking about his various military escapades, but we could tell he was good at what he did, very, very good!

He wanted us in shape, and have the knowledge to overcome any situation that might arise. Every morning we lined up like trainees at boot camp while he checked our equipment. He always motivated when he spoke, got right in our faces, so we had to look up to six foot five inch frame. There was no formality about him, just training, organizing, and planning. He told us, *Use—and do what you need, to get the job done.* Surprise was his advice, and he always did. I believe he was about fifty, in great physical shape, chiseled like a marble statue, a Michelangelo, and a vast martial arts background—the guy was made of iron.

Today he wanted to give us some last minute instruction, wish us well, or have something like a graduation ceremony. We gathered in the library, the same room where we first heard about Shilo project from Samuel

Loyde and Melvade. I sat on the same sofa in the same spot, and like before, Grain brought in drinks. Beatus walked in, razor sharp, ready to pour d sand up the ass of anyone who looked at him the wrong way. Beatus and Grain were buddies, always talking, making jokes, and laughing when they had their bullshit sessions. I never asked how they met, perhaps through Loyde, back in the day during their warrior jaunts.

"Does anyone have any questions?" Beatus asked in a clear, raised voice.

"Yes, I do," Dominic said, "When will we know the bubble infusions are blocking Shilo's signals?"

"Dr. Melvade," Beatus said. "I think that question is for you."

"We should know soon after it's done," Melvade said. "We'll be monitoring the transmissions from control, which will be wherever Grain is. Some infused may act strangely, or be confused after receiving a Shilo transmission followed by our blocker message."

"What do you mean by acting strangely?" I asked.

"We don't know exactly," Melvade said, "This is the first time we've done this, so a target might shout or scream, arbitrarily wander aimlessly like they have dementia, perhaps have a sense of freedom."

Then Samuel stepped into the conversation. "We have got to infuse as many people as possible. We've got one night, and one night only," he said, "some of the infused will pass the word once they're Shilo free."

"You mean word of mouth?" I asked.

"Yes," Melvade said, "exactly, word of mouth. It'll spread like a virus; they'll all want to be free."

Beatus walked over to the table and pointed to the layout of the Necker hotel, then in his rough, gravely voice said, "As we planned, we'll enter through the 3-D door in the rear of the hotel near the loading area right here. Follow the passages, then split up on the top floors. On the way down hit as many rooms as possible infusing as many people as we can. There's a Shilo conference this weekend, so the hotel should be completely occupied."

"What time will we go in?" Dominic asked.

"We'll enter the Necker at 2400—" Beatus said. "After everyone's in position, wait for the signal, then move!"

"What's the signal?" I asked.

"How about using *Shilo* as the signal?" Beatus said. "Grain, will be in the observation vehicle monitoring us. When we're in position and ready, he'll give the signal, and we'll go. If there's a problem, he can assist and support us."

"John and Veronica will go in first," Beatus said, "then I'll follow with the painter. Samantha and Dominic will follow Grain into the parking area, then enter here after parking the SUV." Beatus pointed to a 3-D-door in the parking area. "At 0600, we'll meet, and exit from the same 3-D door."

"Remember the targets have to be unconscious before infusion," Melvade said. "First, put them under with the knock-out dart, then infuse them."

"These darts can be fired up to fifteen feet," Beatus said, "and they take effect immediately."

"Each target should take five minutes to infuse," Loyde said. "If we move quickly, roughly twenty targets an hour between the teams, about one-hundred eighty for the night, if we're lucky two-hundred."

"Remember, at 0600 we rendezvous at the same 3-D door where Samantha and Dominic went in, then leave together," Beatus said. "Grain will be there to pick us up. Dominic, Samantha, John, and Veronica will take the SUV.

Be there or . . ." he didn't finish, but we knew.

"And then, we'll have ourselves a nice early morning drive back to Buffalo City," Grain said.

"Most of the guests will check in for the three-day Shilo event, so we'll have that time to monitor the targets from Buffalo City," Melvade said, "and have an idea of how well the bubble blocker is working."

"After we finish, we'll appraise the operation, make changes or modifications, then head for the next Necker hotel." Beatus said.

"What if we run into trouble?" Dominic asked.

"We talked about that in training, didn't we?" Beatus said. "We're working together as a team now, and we help each other. If a problem arises use what we trained for," then added, "we can't rehearse every scenario. Work with what you have."

"Does anyone have any questions?" Loyde asked.

The room was quiet, like an empty church, no sound bouncing off the walls or reverberating through the air.

Beatus walked between the sofas and said, "Okay, we'll meet in the garage, pack our gear, and take care of any last minute preparations."

"How much time do we have?" I asked.

"Meet in the garage at 1700, that's one hour before we leave," Beatus said. "One hour to double check everything before we head out."

We all stood. "Good luck tonight," Loyde said and shook my hand.

"We'll do our best," I said. "That's all we can do."

"That's all I can ask," Loyde said.

Then Samantha stood, quiet for a moment and said, "I have something to tell all of you before we leave, something important."

She paused, took a few deep breaths, choked up, unwilling to say what was on her mind. "I haven't spoken about this because I was waiting for the right time. I think that time is now."

Our eyes locked on Samantha wondering what she about to say. We all new about the testing on her family, and because of her longevity from the DNA research would live many years after we were gone.

"I'm sorry for keeping this from all of you, but it was necessary for everyone's safety."

"What is it, Samantha?" Dominic asked.

"It concerns everyone, but above all, Veronica and Dominic," she said. "This operation could be called off after I tell you this information."

"Samantha!" Loyde demanded, and tried to stop her from speaking.

"You know who I am Samuel, but everyone here believes I'm your daughter," Samantha said as she cried. "I have to tell them."

"What is it, Samantha?" I asked. "Who are you?"

With her faced flushed said. "I'm Peter Zinty's wife. Peter Zinty is my husband." The scorn she had for Zinty emerged from her voice. "I left him after he talked me into doing a trial test for the longevity study." Samantha sat, then sulked with her head in her hands.

Abruptly Dominic said, "What!" with astonishment chiseled on his face. "You're Zinty's wife?"

"And—what you told us about your father volunteering because he needed money was all just a lie."

"I made it up," she said. "I had to tell you something."

"Then, that means—Nick Zinty was your son!" I said. She cleared her throat. "Yes, he was my son."

"I—killed your son?" I felt gloom looming, and rising beneath me, a deathly haunting gloom. After a long pause I sat on the sofa next to Samantha. "Why didn't you say anything until now? Why—now?"

"Samuel wanted me to remain silent," her voice wobbly. "He said it was to protect me from Peter Zinty."

"You mean," I paused then slowly said, "Peter Zinty doesn't know . . . about you?"

"No, he doesn't," Samuel said. "And—he doesn't know that Dominic and Veronica are my children."

Samuel Loyde's words were hypnotic. We all had vacant looks on our faces. We all were frozen in time, just staring at each other through a hazy fog of what was just said—stunned, and couldn't believe our ears.

Dominic's eyes turned toward Samuel, then to Veronica. She was focused squarely on Samuel trying to see if there was a resemblance, then swallowed as she approached him a rill of tears fell as they embraced each other. Veronica looked toward Dominic to coax him over.

Dominic stood, walked over and said, "It's a little hard for me to call you dad. How about if I just stick to Samuel for the time being?"

"That's fine, Dominic, that's fine," Samuel said. "We're together again, a family again."

"What about our mother?" Veronica asked.

"She died in the fire trying to save you," Samuel said. "It was a long time ago, but I'll never forget." Samuel's face changed from soft and gentle, to hard and determined. "I'll never forget Peter Zinty."

"How did we get out of the school after the explosion and fire?" Veronica asked.

"It was Samantha who saved you," Samuel said. "I was away. She took both of you to a friend to buy some time, until we figured out what to do."

"I don't remember anything—absolutely nothing." How old were we?" Dominic asked.

"You were both two," Samuel said. "I watched you grow, but couldn't hold, or speak to you."

"So, our grandparents, the people who raised us, the Wrigleys were your friends?" Veronica asked.

"They had no idea who you were," Samuel said. "They were an older couple looking for children to adopt. Since Zinty believed you were killed in the fire, I thought it best for your safety to continue with the charade."

Veronica and Dominic walked and stood next to Samantha. "We can never repay you for what you did, Samantha," Veronica said.

"Thank you, Samantha," Dominic said. "I still can't get over how young you look." He leaned downed and kissed her.

"If I could have a moment—and your attention," Beatus said. "The family reunion is nice, but we've still got the operation to consider."

"Could anyone have painted a better story than this," the painter said. "It twists and turns."

"Yeah," I said, "it does that."

"Okay," Beatus said. "It's time to get ready. Everyone do what you have to, then meet downstairs in the garage."

Grain and Beatus were in the garage when we arrived, "Do you need any help?" I asked as I looked into the back of the black van and saw that they had already loaded three silver aluminum cases, and three black cases, some computer and communication equipment.

"No, we're done," Beatus said.

I looked at Grain, and asked. "Are the bubble implants in the silver cases?"

"Yes, sir, they are."

"What's in the black cases?" Dominic asked.

"Those would be the darts, and ribbons, sir."

"Grain, please stop calling me, sir," Dominic said.

"Sorry, what shall I call you?"

"You don't have to be so formal. Call me, Dominic."

"Okay, Dominic, here's your weapon."

"I thought—we weren't carrying any weapons on this job."

"Change of plan," Beatus said.

"Samuel wants us to have a backup in case we're caught with our pants down," Grain said. "He wants everyone to carry a weapon, just in case."

"What if we have to use it?" Veronica said.

"Don't worry, Veronica, we'll all watch each others backs," Samantha said.

"I want to check everyone one last time before we load up," Beatus said. "Let's line up in front of the garage door." We all stood in formation while he checked us over. "Does anyone have any questions before we leave?"

No one said anything, we just smiled at each other, nodded, then got into the vehicles and started on our five-hour journey to Chicago. Dominic drove the SUV out first, the van followed with Grain at the wheel. Samantha sat next to Dominic, and I was next to Veronica in the back seat of the SUV, the painter and Beatus were in the van. I could hear the tires compress and grind the gravel as we rolled through the compound down the long driveway. I turned back for one last look, then the house dropped from sight leaving the narrow driveway converging on the knoll.

Once we get to Chicago our tranquil surroundings will be replaced with cold-hard-lifeless concrete and steel. I closed my eyes for a moment and recalled the strange incident after drinking the tea, and shooting Zinty. I replayed it over in my mind, and could smell gun powder.

I opened my eyes after Veronica shook me. I turned and looked at her, my hand ready to pull out my weapon.

"Are you okay, John," she asked. "You looked like you were in another world."

"For a moment, I was in another world," I said, took a deep breath, and released the grip on my firearm.

"Did you have a dream?"

"Something like that—" I muttered, then smiled at Veronica. As I held her hand a Beatle's song, "I Want To Hold Your Hand" popped into my head.

"Loyde has a great place here hidden away in the woods, doesn't he?" Dominic said. "It could be a resort."

"Yeah, that's for sure," I said as I watched the headlights flicker through the leaves of the trees when the gate opened. We drove through not losing a beat, not slowing down, then it closed. As we headed down the narrow valley country road I saw a sign that read **XX**—it's all so familiar, I thought.

"Look at that moon," Veronica said.

I watched the orange ball of light fall behind the ridge. "Wish I had a camera," I said.

"It's beautiful," Veronica said, then kissed me.

I saw Dominic eyeing me in the rear view mirror. "Now, let's not have any of that," he said, "remember, we've got a job to do."

"Keep your eyes on the road, driver," I said.

Dominic turned to Samantha. "Just out of curiosity," he said. "How long did you take care of us after the fire?"

"Not long," Samantha said. "I took you from Buffalo City, and found a safe place until Samuel got back. I contacted him a few weeks later, we met, and when I told him that you were alive, he cried."

"When did you take us to the Wrigleys?" Veronica asked.

"Samuel thought it best to hide you for a while until it was safe," Samantha said. "Peter Zinty was locked in jail, but only a short time. He had connections and got out. Samuel didn't want to take any chances, so you stayed with the Wrigleys."

"I don't remember any of this," Veronica said.

"How did Zinty get out of prison?" Dominic asked.

"Mulreck got him out, then Peter used our son, Nick, for research. Samuel knew if Peter had found out that you were alive, he would have killed you both."

"Why did you marry him, Samantha?" Dominic asked.

"He wasn't always, so ruthless," Samantha said. "After he was put in charge of the laboratory at Buffalo City the power went to his head. He wanted to live forever, and control the world, he went mad."

Samantha's face grew heavy, and she was about to break into tears, so I gave Dominic a stop asking-her-questions stare, then pointed, "Look!" I said, "over there—a falling star—right over there."

Then, Veronica looked out the window and started singing in a soft whisper, *"Twinkle, twinkle, little star, How I wonder what you are, Up above the world so high, like a diamond in the sky. Twinkle, twinkle, little star, How I wonder what you are!"*

"They're heavenly ornaments," I said. "Decoration for dreamers," then whispered, "I wonder what's out there?"

Chapter Forty-three

"**W**e're getting closer," I said, then turned to see the bright lights of the city glow, reflect off the passing cars, and radiated into the night sky. The hum of heavy traffic cut the air, penetrated our vehicle, and vibrated through my body, then this living breathing animal of concrete and steel inhaled, and swallowed us. I checked the time, 2300 and closing in on our target—the Necker Hotel. Off in the distance I saw a train slither between towers of steel and hulks of stone, then shrink and disappear into brilliant mesmerizing neon color. Damn, this place is big!

Dominic gave us a quick glance, and pointed to his ear. "Beatus wants us to listen in."

"What?" I said coming out of another hypnotic trance. "What did you say?"

"Turn-on-your-communicators," Dominic repeated. Grain rigged a communication device that allowed us to talk with each other, and was using it to talk with Dominic on the drive from Buffalo City to Chicago. Dominic was talking more and more to Grain, and Beatus.

I clipped on the small ear piece and miniature microphone. "Okay," I said. "I'm hot, testing one-two-three. Is anyone out there?"

"Yes, I hear you loud and clear," then Grain asked, "Can you read me?"

We all replied, "Yes," at the same time.

"Okay, I've got a green light for everyone," Grain said. "Go ahead, Beatus."

"Listen up," Beatus said. "We'll be at the Necker in about twenty minutes. Keep the communicators on all of the time from now on."

"What if the battery goes dead?" Dominic asked.

"The batteries are good for more than twenty-four hours," Grain said.

"We'll drive to the rear of the hotel near the loading area," Beatus said. "After we stop, we'll secure the area and unload."

"How long will that take," I asked.

"Five minutes—no longer," Beatus said. "We move without interruption, and unload the van fast—just like we drilled. Grain will proceed to the parking area and set up the monitoring equipment. Dominic will follow him in the SUV. We'll enter through the 3-D door at the service area in back of the hotel, follow the passages, and meet up on the roof. John, you go with Veronica, I'll follow with the painter. Any questions?"

"No questions," we all said.

Samantha looked out the window and pointed. "That's it! The Necker Hotel."

"Take the next right, Dominic," Grain said.

"Okay, got it, next right."

We turned, then slowly drove down a blanch alley behind the Necker Hotel.

"Park in front of that big door near the loading dock, Dominic," Grain said.

"Okay, got it."

"Let's move," Beatus said. "We've only got a few minutes."

We jumped out of the SUV. "Go—Go—Go," Beatus commanded. "Take the cases over there."

"Okay, let's find that 3-D door," the painter said.

"It's here," I said. "Over here." I put my hand on the hand image and watched it open.

"Let's get these cases inside," Beatus said, then waved to Grain, and gave him a thumbs up, as he drove to the parking area followed by Dominic.

"That's everything, close the door," Beatus said.

"It's so dark in here," I said, "I can't see a thing."

"Turn on your night vision goggles," Beatus said. "We should be able to take them off when we reach the next floor. Loyde installed luminous optical fiber when he built these passageways. Let's go!"

We followed Beatus carrying the cases of equipment. I had two, the painter had two, Beatus had two, and Veronica carried a small bag with the rest of the gear. We inched our way up to the roof. "If all goes well, Dominic and Samantha will be there waiting," I said.

"How long do you think it'll take to get to the roof," Veronica asked as we marched through the narrow passage.

"My guess is—thirty minutes," I said breathing heavily.

Beatus kept moving, never slowing, never taking a break, prodding us like a cattle dog nipping at our heels.

"We're here," Beatus said. He opened a door above his head inviting the smell of the city. We left the gear and crawled through the square cut-out exit, climbed onto the roof, and paused, captivated by the stunning vista of the city. Dominic and Samantha arrived after a few minutes.

"Any problems getting here?" Beatus asked.

"Smooth sailing all the way," Dominic said.

"Okay, everyone," Beatus said, "you know what to do—go! We all meet down at the loading area at 0600. Watches synchronized? Good luck!"

We took the knock-out darts, the bubbles, ribbon injectors, and slid them into the sewn in bandoliers of our uniforms. I put in the last one in, looked at Veronica, "Ready?" she nodded. "Let's go," I said, and we headed into one of the hidden passageways that led to a guest's room with the Pink Floyd song, "Welcome To The Machine" pounding in my head.

"What's that?" Peter Zinty said grabbing at his earpiece. "That signal?" Then, with a grimace commanding a prompt response roared, "Where-is-it-coming-from?"

"From the roof," a jittery security guard said.

"The roof?" Zinty said. "Why? What's on the roof?"

"There seems to be some movement up there," the guard watching the security monitor said.

Zinty was in the control room under the hotel. He was always in the control room monitoring guests; always on the lookout for the next gifted Shilo comrade.

"Do we have any cameras on the roof?" Zinty barked.

"Yes, sir, but they're not picking anything up."

"Let's get some people up there right away," then Zinty added in a suspicious tone. "I'm going to the roof."

"Do you want help?" the security guard asked.

"Yes, have a small squad of security men meet me in the lobby right away. Call them now!"Zinty checked his revolver, then holstered it. He had a sense of something going on, but couldn't explain it; he had to see with his own eyes.

"I want people on the monitors, and more surveillance in the hotel, especially the roof," he commanded.

Zinty was an old evil wizard barking orders at everyone in the room, an out of control power hungry mad-man, just like his pal, Mulreck.

"Yes, sir," the security guard complied.

"Let's see what's going on upstairs," Zinty said to a guard in the control room. "Come with me," then together they went to the lobby to meet the security force.

"Ready, Veronica?" I asked, and she nodded. "Grain said there are three people staying in this room."

"Being here in the dark reminds me of the night at the Pomona Travel Agency," Veronica said.

"Oh—don't say that," I said. "Don't say that, it's something I never want to repeat, once was enough for me."

"For me, too," Veronica said.

"Let's open the door."

"Okay," Veronica replied.

The door easily opened, and it was quiet in the guest's hotel room, not a sound.

"Everyone's asleep," I whispered, then looked at Veronica, "I'm going in the room." After slowly taking out my knock-out dart gun, I paused, then quickly aimed and fired knock-out darts into two people on one bed, and a dart into the person in the next bed. I stood silent a moment, then motioned for Veronica to come into the room.

"Okay, Veronica, get the ribbon ready?"

"Okay," she said. "It's loaded."

"Ready?"

"Yes," she said. "I'm ready."

I took the hand of the man, and turned it palm up. Veronica held the ribbon with the bubble to each finger tip. There was a slight beeping sound when the infusion was complete.

"Okay, let's do the woman next," I said.

We finished the infusion, went back into the tunnel, and on to the next room.

"How are things going," Grain said in my receiver.

"We're good here," I replied.

"How's everything on your end?" I asked.

"Good," Grain said. "I see on the monitor the guest you just infused is free."

"You can see that already," I asked.

"Yes, I can," Grain said. "Keep going, and head to the next target."

"Let's go into the next room, Grain said the people we just infused are free. The bubble blocker is working."

"I'm right behind you, John Bird."

I stopped in my tracks. It was exactly what she said at the Pomona Travel Agency before it blew up. I turned to Veronica and said, "Remember what happened last time you called me that."

"I'm not superstitious," Veronica said, "but—okay, I won't say it again. I wonder how everyone else is doing?"

"They're okay," I said as we went through the 3-D door into the closet, "let's go." I moved a suitcase, and some clothes hanging down out of the way, then opened the door. It was peaceful in the room as I peered through the opening, and saw two people sleeping on a king size bed in the center of the room. I turned to Veronica, and whispered, "It looks clear; I guess it's show time. Let's go free some people!" I held my breath, aimed, and fired the sleeper darts, hitting the targets. "Get the ribbon ready, Veronica," I said as we hurried into the room. "Got it ready, Veronica?"

"Okay—it's ready," she said. "Hold up his hand." Veronica froze. "He doesn't have receptors on his fingers." Her voice was filled with tension. "There's nothing here!"

"What!" I said. "Let me see." She was right, then I looked at his other hand, nothing. What's going on?"

"What do we do now?" Veronica asked with a flutter.

"I don't know? I said. "Let me get Grain on the radio. You there Grain? Beatus-Dominic-Samantha—anybody?"

"I hear you," he said. "Just get out of that room, now!"

"What's going on Grain?" I asked in a troubled tone, then looked at Veronica, and shrugged.

Grain's excited voice was muffled, then there was some static on the line, so I adjusted my ear-piece to get a signal, and heard, "Get out!" then a moment later, Grain's breathless voice whispered, "Do you hear me? Get . . . out . . . now." Then—nothing.

"Where are we supposed to go?" Veronica said.

"There's no signal, it's gone."

Veronica took a deep breath, and said, "I think we're on our own."

"We're screwed! Shit!" I said frustrated, clenching my fists. "I think we've lost Grain," then looked at Veronica's pale face glowing in the ambient light of the hotel room.

"Let's get out of here, Veronica!" I said in an anxious and commanding voice.

We grabbed our gear, and moved quickly at a good clip through the passage way.

"Where are we going, John?"

"I don't know just out," I said. "How about to the roof? Hopefully, Beatus and the painter will be there."

"But—" she said quivering, "but what if they're not!"

"Think positive, Veronica, they'll be there."

We continued through the narrow passageway. "Okay, let me open the door and check if the roof is clear." I turned and looked at Veronica. "If anything goes wrong, run," I said. "Run—understand—just run," then kissed her, and opened the door that led to the roof. I saw the stars glimmer above, heard the sounds of the city rise on the wind, and felt it caress my face.

"It's okay," I said, "come on up."

I grabbed Veronica's hand to help her to the roof. "We made it," I said. Veronica's frightened eyes open wide as she gave me a something-is-wrong-look, then pushed me to the side. I fell to the ground as a gun blast echoed. Veronica flew back from the force, and landed flat on her back. I knelt next to her, and touch her soft face.

"Veronica!" I shouted, "Veronica!"

She looked at me. "Looks like I stumbled this time, John Bird Ray, but remember, cats have nine lives."

She coughed and struggled to take in air, her breathing quickened, blood trickled from her lips.

"Veronica," I said, "I love you!"

"Part of the ocean and part of the sky," she said, then closed her eyes, she was gone, now a memory.

From the side, in the dim shadowy light, I saw a silhouette walking toward me, the shadow moved slowly, then a face emerged. It was an old face, but a familiar face. Like his son, Nick, we were going to battle, but this time it was different, Veronica was gone and my rage swelled. I felt strength, I'd never had, course through my body, and I had no fear. He walked closer, lifting his weapon, aiming it directly at me.

"Now, I'm going to finish this!" he said in the same gruff voice as his son.

"So, you're Nick Zinty's father," I said stalling for time,

thinking, *How am I getting out of this? Maybe, I'll wake up and find out this is all a dream.*

My mind raced as he came toward me, then I stood. He stopped about ten paces from me, the distance of a dual.

"My son wanted to help you."

"Your son was an asshole," I said, probably not the right choice of words. "What did you do with Samantha?"

"My son," he said forlorn. "My son is dead, and that's what you're going to be—dead! Like everyone else."

I stood next to Veronica who was lying in a pool of blood. I looked at her and whispered, "I'd change places with you if I could."

Then I looked at Peter Zinty. "You've caused nothing but grief for everyone. What kind of person are you? How can you kill innocent people?"

"She was living on borrowed time," Zinty said. "It just caught up with her."

He slowly stepped closer, the weapon still pointed at me spewing on about his son, and Veronica. Now, I clearly saw his face, it was filled with revenge, and I despised him. I wanted to rip out his heart and feed it to the buzzards. I cleared my throat and spat on the ground. "That's what you are Zinty," I said. "A slimy slug, time for you to crawl back under the rock where you came from."

"Don't move Peter," Samantha said. She had come through the door behind Zinty. "Put down the rifle or I'll shoot—I mean it!"

Zinty turned. "You're going to kill me?" he said in a comical way. "You should thank me for giving you the gift of eternal life."

"Eternal hell is more like it, Peter."

"If you don't put down the weapon, I'll blow you to kingdom come," Samantha declared. "Put it down—now,

Peter," she screamed. "Now!" then raised her weapon, and held it tightly against her shoulder with Zinty in the crosshairs.

"You'll be sorry for this," Zinty said. "I could have helped you. You killed our son."

"No, Peter, you killed him. Infused him with the bubble, brainwashed him to hate, to hate me, to hate everyone. You made him your slave."

"Talk is over," Zinty said. Two resounding blasts rang out, the triggers pulled simultaneously—they both fell. Samantha lay motionless on the ground. Peter Zinty stood, wobbly, looking up to the sky holding his bloody hands high above his head, laughing, then screamed, "No one can stop me. No one!"

He turned sharply like a soldier doing close quarter drill, looked at me, then at the weapon on the deck. I charged, hitting, and knocking him down. He stood again. What's this guy made of? I thought. Did he perform some, DNA, experiment on himself? He's invincible? I forced myself up.

Zinty pointed at me with his old bony finger, and said with an evil growl, "You're next, John Bird Ray."

I fumbled with a sleeper dart, loaded and fired. It struck him in the throat. He pulled it out, looked at it, laughed, then fell to the ground spastic—fighting the effects. This is my last chance, I thought. I grabbed him by the collar and beat his ugly face silly until my fists were covered in blood, Veronica's, mine, and his. Then, I picked him up, flung him over my shoulder in a firemen's carry, and staggered to the edge of the building.

"To the bottom of hell is where you're going, Zinty," I said. Still formidable, he pounded my back with his fists, grunting and squirming, trying to get free. "Have any last words?" I asked. "Didn't think so!" I let go—and with a hollow wail he melted into the darkness below.

"The nightmare's over," I thought. Energy pulsated through me as I fell, collapsing on my back, my vision blurred. I looked up to the stars, then over at Veronica, and closed my eyes.

Chapter Forty-four

*L*ooking through my squinted eyes I saw and heard my cell phone ring. The alarm was always set for six-thirty A.M. I reached over to the table next to the bed and turned it off. It rang again, then stopped by itself. I sat up, stretched, and looked around the room bewildered. I rubbed my eyes, and face. Where am I? What happened to everyone, and how did I get here?

I was back at the bed and breakfast. My suitcase was on the floor in the middle of the room half unpacked, clothes on the floor, on the chair, and on a small table near the window. Dust particles floated through the amber rays that criss-crossed the room in the modest sunlight that splashed through the cracks of the curtain.

There were people talking outside my bedroom door, then the sound of a car engine revving, and squealing tires, made me look toward the window just as a bird landed on the railing of the balcony. I watched it vanish into the sky. Is that what happened to everyone? They've vanished into the sky. I heard footsteps in the hallway and turned toward the door. Someone must be leaving? I sat on the bed motionless; my eyes closed a moment, and opened them when I had the energy.

The last thing I remember is throwing Peter Zinty off the roof of the Necker Hotel. How did I get back here? I looked around the room again confused. Why am I here, and not at Loyde's place? Was I brought here while I was asleep? Was there a new plan that I hadn't been told about? I sat there on the bed opening and closing my eyes, wondering if the room would change—it didn't.

Now, wide awake, and feeling more puzzled, I looked for my laptop. "That's it!" I muttered and dragged myself to the table near the window overlooking the street. I looked out shading my eyes to block the sunlight, then opened and turned on my laptop. I scanned over the part about Samantha reading the bullshit book on the train, shooting Zinty, the painter, Samuel Loyde, Veronica, her brother, Dominic, going to Samuel Lee Loyde's house, and the plan to dismantle the Shilo project. It was all there, the whole story typed on my computer and in my memory, as if it really happened, and not just a story.

I tried to make sense of it; running it over in my mind. I looked up at the wall behind me and saw the orange cat painting hanging next to the door in the space where Tracy had been staring when I checked in. "My painting," I said charged with excitement; staggered over, took it off the wall, looked at it carefully, then at the faded outline. Tracy was looking at this spot when I checked in. It was the painting I had bought there was no doubt. I held it close, trying to read the signature, but couldn't. I put the painting on the bed, stared at it, and looked around the room again.

Why am I here? And, where is everyone else?

I was in a state of confusion and needed to wake up. I dragged myself to into shower, and thought, *I'll clean up and figure this out later.* In the shower images of being with Veronica at Buffalo City, the breakfast, walking through the garden and her reading my poem hit me. She was beautiful. How could it all be a dream . . . a story? How . . . . can she . . . not be real?

After the shower I went over to the sink, brushed my teeth, combed my hair, and looked at myself in the mirror. "Are you real?" I whispered, then touched my reflection in the glass, it just felt like glass. I touched my face, pinched my cheek. Was it all a dream?

I packed my things and was ready to check out; about to close the door to my room when I looked at the cat painting on the bed. Should I take it? It's mine, I bought it! I hesitated a moment, then picked it up and put it in my bag. I took one last look at the room before closing the door.

"Good morning," I said to Tracy who was sitting on the sofa knitting. "Nice day, isn't it?"

"Yes, it is," she said.

"Are you checking out today?"

"Yes, I am," I said.

"I've got your bill right here," she said and picked it up off the table and handed it to me.

"Thanks. The bill looks fine," I said, but had a strange feeling, and thought I had checked out once before. "Here's my credit card," I said. What's happening? I looked around the room, then smiled at Tracy.

"Tracy, did you see me leave my room last night, or notice anyone with me since I've been here?"

She echoed, "I don't know, I don't know," then said,

"Don't you remember, I told you, I lock the door at twelve, so you wouldn't have been able to get back in if you were out late. Have a rough time last night?

"You have no idea!" I said. No idea what I've been through, I thought. Maybe I did turn into a pumpkin.

"I could ask some of the other guests if it's important," she said.

"That's okay," I said, "never mind," and left perplexed.

The next bed and breakfast was near Lincoln Park, so I headed in the direction of the train station on foot. As I walked I thought about the Shilo project. How Melvade and Loyde wanted to stop it, about Dominic ,and how we met after the Pomona Travel Agency blew up.

I got to Daley Square where the Picasso stood. I walked around the unusual sculpture. What is this thing? I thought. It's the second time I've seen it, and still have no idea what it is. How does a person imagine such an object?

On the ground was a pamphlet; its pages being turned by the wind. I picked it up and read about Picasso.

Picasso, born,1881, died, 1973. During that period he created art, and changed his style throughout his life. He once said, "I think of death all of the time. She's the only woman who never leaves me, and art is the only lie that tells the truth."

That's the key! Change, change, and nothing ever stays the same. Art, dreams, life, death, memories; Picasso's style was a reflection of a reflection. Upside down and inverted; a real life dream. Woman and death—I thought, that must have pressed him to live every day of his life like it was his last. Women—can't live with'em, can't live without'em. I've heard the expression, *Live everyday, like it's your last*, but how many people actually do. Picasso was definitely a genius who created the legend of one charming, confusing, provoking, and intimidating man, and no one's come close. He expressed his art from many perspectives, put a slant and trademark on his work, and left footprints everywhere. His work is from a part of life only he could see.

I took out the cat painting. What is it with this painting? Is it a part of life only the painter can imagine? I thought of Veronica's poem about Van Gogh who had so much passion that it drove him crazy. He was able to put it on canvas for all to see, but in the end it consumed him.

Shakespeare is still being quoted today. His stories of expression are extreme examples of our emotions ripping us to pieces, and we love every word.

Socrates, Michelangelo, Alexander the Great, Da Vinci, Mozart, Beethoven, Newton, Einstein, Edison, Tesla, Bell, Poe, and others, along with all of the artists, pirates and gangsters, used their expression to live every moment of this vast well of time we call eternity. There are many ways and forms of expression, I thought. Live every day like it's the last? I wasn't sure, but, I could live every day—and dream! And what's the difference? Sometimes I don't know what's real? What's fantasy or— who's in control? Then I walked over to the Field Museum and saw an advertisement for an exhibition of cat mummies from Egypt. The picture in the ad looked similar to my cat painting. I opened the brochure and read about cats, and how there were admired by the Egyptians.

Egyptians—believed in cat goddesses who represented fertility, and the moon. As protectors of cats, for them, it was a crime to kill one; the punishment—death.

Cats kept out the vermin, and were admired for their hunting skills, cleanliness, beauty, and instinct for mothering.

The Egyptians embraced cats, loved them, put statues of gold cats everywhere—after death; they were mummified.

Some hated cats; seen as evil, and they were killed. With a depleted cat population, millions of people died from the plague. When the cat population increased; the plague disappeared.

Are cats some intrinsic link in the chain of life? Are they the guardians of mystery? Thinking about all of this cat and black plague history was so familiar. Had I thought or read about this before. I picked up another brochure with a picture of a human mummy. I noticed that the arms were crossed like an X. People are always buried with their arms crossed like an X, I thought. Why is the X the symbol for so many things, a signature, the Roman numeral ten, the unknown, even our chromosomes are shaped like an X. Some ancient mysterious groups used the X symbol for transformation rituals, or to trigger some kind of message. **XX** was on the road-sign to Loyde's house, I thought.

After the exhibition I went to a small restaurant for lunch. I was sitting there waiting for my food, then took out the cat painting. It seemed different, and I couldn't exactly grasp why, but it looked like the cat had stepped out of the painting, then gone back in, or like it had been repainted. If I could find Samantha's or Veronica's telephone number I'd know it happened. I rummaged through my bag, but couldn't find any phone numbers.

Thinking about numbers again in this puzzling state reminded me of something I had read about the M-Theory, or String-Theory. According to this fundamental theory of everything, dimensions in super-gravity are coupled together in thin layers of membranes or strings that are held under tension. Have I somehow wandered in and out of altered dimensions of super-gravity. Maybe it's not minds I'm reading, but memories. I tried to think back to what triggered all of this in the first place. It started after getting into the taxi, going to the bed and breakfast, then buying the cat painting, or after drinking the laced tea. Who are the people in this story? Is there a plot to control the human race? Is it possible to desire a thing so much that it transpires? Can events in dimensions be manipulated? That would be the ultimate expression, to make your life whatever you think it to be. They say cats have nine lives. Is it like getting three wishes from a genie? If I had three wishes . . . now I was spooked, leaving my mind racing, lost, thinking about the Shilo project, and everything else that had transpired. I decided to head for the next bed & breakfast, and get some rest. I hopped on the train, stayed on until Lincoln Park, then walked to the street. I waited a minute at the corner, then an old taxi pulled over. I gave a piece of paper with the address to the driver. "Can you take me to this place?"

He looked at the paper. "*Orwell Drive*," he mumbled. "Sure, no problem, want to put your—bag in the trunk?"

"Okay," I said, then thought, this is all so familiar.

After arriving at Orwell Drive, I got out, and stood there out in front looking at the house. I took out the picture that I'd downloaded from the web site. It looked exactly like the picture. This place is so familiar, I thought, then walked to the door, and rang the buzzer.

"Yes, can I help you?" a woman's voice said over the intercom.

That voice sounds familiar, I thought. "Hi, I have a reservation," I said into the intercom.

"Okay—come on in," the voice on the speaker said, then the door unlocked.

I walked into the foyer, "Hello," I said in raised tone. "Hello, anybody, here?"

"Hello! Anybody, here?"

"I'm in here," a woman's voice echoed in the hall. "In the kitchen. Just walk down the hall."

I made my way into the kitchen. As I walked down the hallway a cat ran around and through my legs brushing against me purring. There was a woman in an apron standing at the counter with her back to me preparing some food. When she turned I was speechless. I knew her! It was Veronica. I stepped closer, "Hello," I said, in a lonesome voice, and smiled. "I have a reservation. My name is John Bird Ray."

"Nice to see you, again, John Bird Ray."

She extended her hand. I held it, and didn't let go.

"Veronica?" I said stunned. "You know me?"

"We've met many times, John."

"What do you mean, many times?" I asked.

"It's always the same," she said. "You never remember."

"I remember that you were killed," I said.

"So were you, John Bird Ray, long ago," she said. "The story starts the same every time, and we have many names."

"Is it real?" I asked. "The Necker Hotels, and the Shilo project? Are you real, Veronica?"

"I'm real, John Bird Ray, and this moment is real," she said. "It's what you hoped for? To create, express your dreams, and have them come true." She held out her hand. "Here you are."

"What's this?" I asked.

"It's the registration form, fill it out, and you can start writing your book, and live the next adventure."

I looked at the form she handed me, and printed at the top was, **The Necker House**.

"I'll show you the room, follow me—"

Chapter Forty-five

*I*t all begins over and over again, with memories floating in space and time. Memories of who we were, who we are, and what we dream. And as time goes by we look at our reflection in the mirror, reach out, and touch the person we see and ask—Who are you, and who am I?

Far in the fog laden countryside, where clammy pale air looms broad, hollow cries echo through the surrounding forest then drift and fade. A timeless silence hangs heavy when a ghostly moon emerges, then disappears behind shadowless clouds. Without warning a massive explosion shakes the night air mounting into an unyielding fire engulfing the Buffalo City Architectural School. The roaring fire billows like a star in super nova, and the night sky turns into a huge orange blush pulsating heart. The local police telephones ring constantly, and endlessly. Emergency crews arrive at the Buffalo City School to nothing but smoldering ash and ruins. A comprehensive investigation, and autopsy, reveals that the victims were burned alive. The evidence leads to the caretaker, Zinty! A story of memories that never die, and dreams that never end!

John Bird Ray hands a folded piece of paper to a taxi driver. "Can you take me to this place?"

The driver opens it, and looks at the address for a moment, then at his new passenger. "Hop in my friend!"

.-- .... .- -

-.. ---

-.-- --- ..-

.-- .- -. -

- ---

-... .

?

johnbirdray@hotmail.com

John Siwicki

Books by John Siwicki

Poetry

Inflexation
Fences
The Poetry of Food and Drink
Warbles
Are You Casablanca

Novels

ExPRESSION
AWAKE ASLEEP DREAMING DEAD